PREJUDICES
THIRD SERIES

PREJUDICES
THIRD SERIES

By H. L. MENCKEN

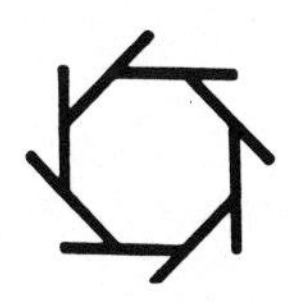

OCTAGON BOOKS

A DIVISION OF FARRAR, STRAUS AND GIROUX

New York 1977

Reprinted 1977
by special arrangement with Alfred A. Knopf, Inc.

OCTAGON BOOKS
A DIVISION OF FARRAR, STRAUS & GIROUX, INC.
19 Union Square West
New York, N.Y. 10003

Library of Congress Cataloging in Publication Data

Mencken, Henry Louis, 1880-1956.
Prejudices, third series.

Reprint of the ed. published by Knopf, New York.
Includes index.
I. Title.

PS3525.E43P83 1977 818'.5'209 76-54784
ISBN 0-374-95580-8

Manufactured by Braun-Brumfield, Inc.
Ann Arbor, Michigan
Printed in the United States of America

CONTENTS

CONTENTS

PREJUDICES
THIRD SERIES

PREJUDICES: THIRD SERIES

I. ON BEING AN AMERICAN

I

APPARENTLY there are those who begin to find it disagreeable—nay, impossible. Their anguish fills the Liberal weeklies, and every ship that puts out from New York carries a groaning cargo of them, bound for Paris, London, Munich, Rome and way points—anywhere to escape the great curses and atrocities that make life intolerable for them at home. Let me say at once that I find little to cavil at in their basic complaints. In more than one direction, indeed, I probably go a great deal further than even the Young Intellectuals. It is, for example, one of my firmest and most sacred beliefs, reached after an inquiry extending over a score of years and supported by incessant prayer and meditation, that the government of the United States, in both its legislative arm and its executive arm, is ignorant, incompetent, corrupt, and disgusting—and from this judgment I except no more than twenty living lawmakers and no more than twenty executioners of their laws. It is a belief no less piously cherished that the administration of justice in the Republic is stupid, dishonest, and against all reason and equity—and from this judgment I except no more than thirty judges, including two upon the bench of the Supreme Court of the United States. It is another that the foreign policy of the United States—its habitual manner of dealing with other nations, whether friend or foe—is hypocritical, disingenuous, knavish, and dishonorable—and from this judgment I consent to no exceptions whatever, either recent or long past. And it is my fourth (and, to avoid too depressing a bill, final) conviction that the American people, taking one with another, constitute the most timorous, sniveling, poltroonish, ignominious mob of serfs and goose-steppers ever gathered under one flag in Christendom since the end of the Middle Ages, and that they grow more timorous, more sniveling, more poltroonish, more ignominious every day.

So far I go with the fugitive Young Intellectuals—and into the Bad Lands beyond. Such, in brief, are the cardinal articles of my political faith, held passionately since my admission to citizenship and now growing stronger and stronger as I gradually disintegrate into my component carbon, oxygen, hydrogen, phosphorus, calcium, sodium, nitrogen and iron. This is what I believe and preach, *in nomine Domini*,

Amen. Yet I remain on the dock, wrapped in the flag, when the Young Intellectuals set sail. Yet here I stand, unshaken and undespairing, a loyal and devoted Americano, even a chauvinist, paying taxes without complaint, obeying all laws that are physiologically obeyable, accepting all the searching duties and responsibilities of citizenship unprotestingly, investing the sparse usufructs of my miserable toil in the obligations of the nation, avoiding all commerce with men sworn to overthrow the government, contributing my mite toward the glory of the national arts and sciences, enriching and embellishing the native language, spurning all lures (and even all invitations) to get out and stay out—here am I, a bachelor of easy means, forty-two years old, unhampered by debts or issue, able to go wherever I please and to stay as long as I please—here am I, contentedly and even smugly basking beneath the Stars and Stripes, a better citizen, I daresay, and certainly a less murmurous and exigent one, than thousands who put the Hon. Warren Gamaliel Harding beside Friedrich Barbarossa and Charlemagne, and hold the Supreme Court to be directly inspired by the Holy Spirit, and belong ardently to every Rotary Club, Ku Klux Klan, and Anti-Saloon League, and choke with emotion when the band plays "The Star-Spangled Banner," and believe with the faith of little children that one of Our Boys, taken at random, could dispose in a fair fight of ten Englishmen, twenty Germans, thirty Frogs, forty Wops, fifty Japs, or a hundred Bolsheviki.

Well, then, why am I still here? Why am I so complacent (perhaps even to the point of offensiveness), so free from bile, so little fretting and indignant, so curiously happy? Why did I answer only with a few academic "Hear, Hears" when Henry James, Ezra Pound, Harold Stearns and the *emigrés* of Greenwich Village issued their successive calls to the corn-fed *intelligentsia* to flee the shambles, escape to fairer lands, throw off the curse forever? The answer, of course, is to be sought in the nature of happiness, which tempts to metaphysics. But let me keep upon the ground. To me, at least (and I can only follow my own nose) happiness presents itself in an aspect that is tripartite. To be happy (reducing the thing to its elementals) I must be:

a. Well-fed, unhounded by sordid cares, at ease in Zion.
b. Full of a comfortable feeling of superiority to the masses of my fellow-men.
c. Delicately and unceasingly amused according to my taste.

It is my contention that, if this definition be accepted, there is no country on the face of the earth wherein a man roughly constituted as I am—a man of my general weaknesses, vanities, appetites, prejudices, and aversions—can be so happy, or even one-half so happy, as he can be in these free and independent states. Going further, I lay down the proposition that it is a sheer physical impossibility for such a man to live in These States and *not* be happy—that it is as impossible to him as it would be to a schoolboy to weep over the burning down of his school-house. If he says that he isn't happy here, then he either lies or is insane. Here the business of getting a living, particularly since the war brought the loot of all Europe to the national strong-box, is enormously easier than it is in any other Christian land—so easy, in fact, that an educated and fore-handed man who fails at it must actually make deliberate efforts to that end. Here the general average of intelligence, of knowledge, of competence, of integrity, of self-respect, of honor is so low that any man who knows his trade, does not fear ghosts, has read fifty good books, and practices the common decencies stands out as brilliantly as a wart on a bald head, and is thrown willy-nilly into a meager and exclusive aristocracy. And here, more than anywhere else that I know of or have heard of, the daily panorama of human existence, of private and communal folly—the unending procession of governmental extortions and chicaneries, of commercial brigandages and throat-slittings, of theological buffooneries, of æsthetic ribaldries, of legal swindles and harlotries, of miscellaneous rogueries, villainies, imbecilities, grotesqueries, and extravagances—is so inordinately gross and preposterous, so perfectly brought up to the highest conceivable amperage, so steadily enriched with an almost fabulous daring and originality, that only the man who was born with a petrified diaphragm can fail to laugh himself to sleep every night, and to awake every morning with all the eager, unflagging expectation of a Sunday-school superintendent touring the Paris peep-shows.

A certain sough of rhetoric may be here. Perhaps I yield to words as a chautauqua lecturer yields to them, belaboring and fermenting the hinds with his Message from the New Jerusalem. But fundamentally I am quite as sincere as he is. For example, in the matter of attaining to ease in Zion, of getting a fair share of the national swag, now piled so mountainously high. It seems to me, sunk in my Egyptian night, that the man who fails to do this in the United States to-day is a man who is somehow stupid—maybe not on the surface, but certainly deep down. Either he is one who cripples himself unduly, say by setting up a family before he can care for it, or by making a bad bargain for the sale of his wares, or by concerning himself too much about the affairs of other men; or he is one who endeavors fatuously to sell something that no normal American wants. Whenever I hear a professor of philosophy complain that his wife has eloped with some moving-picture actor or bootlegger who can at least feed and clothe her, my natural sympathy for the man is greatly corrupted by contempt for his lack of sense. Would it be regarded as sane and laudable for a man to travel the Soudan trying to sell fountain-pens, or Greenland offering to teach double-entry bookkeeping or counterpoint? Coming closer, would the judicious pity or laugh at a man who opened a shop for the sale of incunabula in Little Rock, Ark., or who demanded a living in McKeesport, Pa., on the ground that he could read Sumerian? In precisely the same way it seems to me to be nonsensical for a man to offer generally some commodity that only a few rare and dubious Americans want, and then weep and beat his breast because he is not patronized. One seeking to make a living in a country must pay due regard to the needs and tastes of that country. Here in the United States we have no jobs for grand dukes, and none for *Wirkliche Geheimräte,* and none for palace eunuchs, and none for masters of the buck-hounds, and none (any more) for brewery *Todsaufer*—and very few for oboe-players, metaphysicians, astrophysicists, assyriologists, water-colorists, stylites and epic poets. There was a time when the *Todsaufer* served a public need and got an adequate reward, but it is no more. There may come a time when the composer of string quartettes is paid as much as a railway conductor, but it is not yet. Then why practice such trades—that is, as trades? The man of independent means may venture into them prudently; when he does so, he is seldom molested; it may even be argued that he performs a public service by adopting them. But the man who has a living to make is simply silly if he goes into them; he is like a soldier going over the top with a coffin strapped to his back. Let him abandon such puerile vanities, and take to the uplift instead, as, indeed, thousands of other victims of the industrial system have already done. Let him bear in mind that, whatever its neglect of the humanities and their monks, the Republic has never got half enough bond salesmen, quack doctors, ward leaders, phrenologists, Methodist evangelists, circus clowns, magicians, soldiers, farmers, popular song writers, moonshine distillers, forgers of gin labels, mine guards, detectives, spies, snoopers, and *agents provocateurs*. The rules are set by Omnipotence; the discreet man observes them. Observing them, he is safe beneath the starry bed-tick, in fair weather or foul. The *boobus Americanus* is a bird that knows no closed season—and if he won't come down to Texas oil stock, or one-night cancer cures, or building lots in Swampshurst, he will always come down to Inspiration and Optimism, whether political, theological, pedagogical, literary, or economic.

The doctrine that it is *infra digitatem* for an educated man to take a hand in the snaring of this goose is one in which I see nothing convincing. It is a doctrine chiefly voiced, I believe, by those who have tried the business and failed. They take refuge behind the childish notion that there is something honorable about poverty *per se*—the Greenwich Village complex. This is nonsense. Poverty may be an unescapable misfortune, but that no more makes it honorable than a cocked eye is made honorable by the same cause. Do I advocate, then, the ceaseless, senseless hogging of money? I do not. All I advocate—and praise as virtuous—is the hogging of enough to provide security and ease. Despite all the romantic superstitions to the contrary, the artist cannot do his best work when he is oppressed by unsatisfied wants. Nor can the philosopher. Nor can the man of science. The best and clearest thinking of the world is done and the finest art is produced, not by men who are hungry, ragged and harassed, but by men who are well-fed, warm and easy in mind. It is the artist's first duty to his art to achieve that tranquility for himself. Shakespeare tried to achieve it; so did Beethoven, Wagner, Brahms, Ibsen and Balzac. Goethe, Schopenhauer, Schumann and Mendelssohn were born to it. Joseph Conrad, Richard Strauss and Anatole France have got it for themselves in our own day. In the older countries, where competence is far more general and competition is thus more sharp, the thing is often cruelly difficult, and sometimes almost impossible. But in the United States it is absurdly easy, given ordinary luck. Any man with a superior air, the intelligence of a stockbroker, and the resolution of a hat-check girl—in brief, any man who believes in himself enough, and with sufficient cause, to be called a journeyman—can cadge enough money, in this glorious commonwealth of morons, to make life soft for him.

And if a lining for the purse is thus facilely obtainable, given a reasonable prudence and resourcefulness, then balm for the ego is just as unlaboriously got, given ordinary dignity and decency. Simply to exist, indeed, on the plane of a civilized man is to attain, in the Republic, to a distinction that should be enough for all save the most vain; it is even likely to be too much, as the frequent challenges of the Ku Klux Klan, the American Legion, the Anti-Saloon League, and other such vigilance committees of the majority testify. Here is a country in which all political thought and activity are concentrated upon the scramble for jobs—in which the normal politician, whether he be a President or a village road supervisor, is willing to renounce any principle, however precious to him, and to adopt any lunacy, however offensive to him, in order to keep his place at the trough. Go into politics, then, without seeking or wanting office, and at once you are as conspicuous as a red-haired blackamoor—in fact, a great deal more conspicuous, for red-haired blackamoors have been seen, but who has ever seen or heard of an American politician, Democrat or Republican, Socialist or Liberal, Whig or Tory, who did not itch for a job? Again, here is a country in which it is an axiom that a business man shall be a member of a Chamber of Commerce, an admirer of Charles M. Schwab, a reader of the *Saturday Evening Post,* a golfer—in brief, a vegetable. Spend your hours of escape from *Geschäft* reading Remy de Gourmont or practicing the violoncello, and the local Sunday newspaper will infallibly find you out and hymn the marvel—nay, your banker will summon you to discuss your notes, and your rivals will spread the report (probably truthful) that you were pro-German during the war. Yet again, here is a land in which women rule and men are slaves. Train your women to get your slippers for you, and your ill fame will match Galileo's or Darwin's. Once more, here is the Paradise of back-slappers, of democrats, of mixers, of go-getters. Maintain ordinary reserve, and you will arrest instant attention —and have your hand kissed by multitudes who, despite democracy, have all the inferior man's unquenchable desire to grovel and admire.

Nowhere else in the world is superiority more easily attained or more eagerly admitted. The chief business of the nation, as a nation, is the setting up of heroes, mainly bogus. It admired the literary style of the late Woodrow; it respects the theological passion of Bryan; it venerates J. Pierpont Morgan; it takes Congress seriously; it would be unutterably shocked by the proposition (with proof) that a majority of its judges are ignoramuses, and that a respectable minority of them are scoundrels. The manufacture of artificial *Durchlauchten, k.k. Hoheiten* and even gods goes on feverishly and incessantly; the will to worship never flags. Ten iron-molders meet in the back-room of a near-beer saloon, organize a lodge of the Noble and Mystic Order of American Rosicrucians, and elect a wheelwright Supreme Worthy Whimwham; a month later they send a notice to the local newspaper that they have been greatly honored by an official visit from that Whimwham, and that they plan to give him a jeweled fob for his watch-chain. The chief national heroes—Lincoln, Lee, and so on—cannot remain mere men. The mysticism of the mediæval peasantry gets into the communal view of them, and they begin to sprout haloes and wings. As I say, no intrinsic merit—at least, none commensurate with the mob estimate—is needed to come to such august dignities. Everything American is a bit amateurish and childish, even the national gods. The most conspicuous and respected American in nearly every field of endeavor, saving only the purely commercial (I exclude even the financial) is a man who would attract little attention in any other country. The leading American critic of literature, after twenty years of diligent exposition of his ideas, has yet to make it clear what he is in favor of, and why. The queen of the *haut monde,* in almost every American city, is a woman who regards Lord Reading as an aristocrat and her superior, and whose grandfather slept in his underclothes. The leading American musical director, if he went to Leipzig, would be put to polishing trombones and copying drum parts. The chief living American military man—the national heir to Frederick, Marlborough, Wellington, Washington and Prince Eugene—is a member of the Elks, and proud of it. The leading American philosopher (now dead, with no successor known to the average pedagogue) spent a lifetime erecting an epistemological defense for the national æsthetic maxim: "I don't know nothing about music, but I know what I like." The most eminent statesman the United States has produced since Lincoln was fooled by Arthur James Balfour, and miscalculated his public support by more than 5,000,000 votes. And the current Chief Magistrate of the nation—its defiant substitute for czar and kaiser—is a small-town printer who, when he wishes to enjoy himself in the Executive Mansion, invites in a homeopathic doctor, a Seventh Day Adventist evangelist, and a couple of moving-picture actresses.

2

All of which may be boiled down to this: that the United States is essentially a commonwealth of third-rate men—that distinction is easy here because the general level of culture, of information, of taste and judgment, of ordinary competence is so low. No sane man, employing an American plumber to repair a leaky drain, would expect him to do it at the first trial, and in precisely the same way no sane man, observing an American Secretary of State in negotiation with Englishmen and Japs, would expect him to come off better than second best. Third-rate men, of course, exist in all countries, but it is only here that they are in full control of the state, and with it of all the national standards. The land was peopled, not by the hardy adventurers of legend, but simply by incompetents who could not get on at home, and the lavishness of nature that they found here, the vast ease with which they could get livings, confirmed and augmented their native incompetence. No American colonist, even in the worst days of the Indian wars, ever had to face such hardships as ground down the peasants of Central Europe during the Hundred Years War, nor even such hardships as oppressed the English lower classes during the century before the Reform Bill of 1832. In most of the colonies, indeed, he seldom saw any Indians at all: the one thing that made life difficult for him was his congenital dunderheadedness. The winning of the West, so rhetorically celebrated in American romance, cost the lives of fewer men than the single battle of Tannenberg, and the victory was much easier and surer. The immigrants who have come in since those early days have been, if anything, of even lower grade than their forerunners. The old notion that the United States is peopled by the offspring of brave, idealistic and liberty loving minorities, who revolted against injustice, bigotry and mediævalism at home—this notion is fast succumbing to the alarmed study that has been given of late to the immigration of recent years. The truth is that the majority of non-Anglo-Saxon immigrants since the Revolution, like the majority of Anglo-Saxon immigrants before the Revolution, have been, not the superior men of their native lands, but the botched and unfit: Irishmen starving to death in Ireland, Germans unable to weather the *Sturm und Drang* of the post-Napoleonic reorganization, Italians weed-grown on exhausted soil, Scandinavians run to all bone and no brain, Jews too incompetent to swindle even the barbarous peasants of Russia, Poland and Roumania. Here and there among the immigrants, of course, there may be a bravo, or even a superman—*e. g.*, the ancestors of Volstead, Ponzi, Jack Dempsey, Schwab, Daugherty, Debs, Pershing—but the average newcomer is, and always has been simply a poor fish.

Nor is there much soundness in the common assumption, so beloved of professional idealists and wind-machines, that the people of America constitute "the youngest of the great peoples." The phrase turns up endlessly; the average newspaper editorial writer would be hamstrung if the Postoffice suddenly interdicted it, as it interdicted "the right to rebel" during the war. What gives it a certain specious plausibility is the fact that the American Republic, compared to a few other existing governments, is relatively young. But the American Republic is not necessarily identical with the American people; they might overturn it to-morrow and set up a monarchy, and still remain the same people. The truth is that, as a distinct nation, they go back fully three hundred years, and that even their government is older than that of most other nations, *e. g.*, France, Italy, Germany, Russia. Moreover, it is absurd to say that there is anything properly describable as youthfulness in the American outlook. It is not that of young men, but that of old men. All the characteristics of senescence are in it: a great distrust of ideas, an habitual timorousness, a harsh fidelity to a few fixed beliefs, a touch of mysticism. The average American is a prude and a Methodist under his skin, and the fact is never more evident than when he is trying to disprove it. His vices are not those of a healthy boy, but those of an ancient paralytic escaped from the *Greisenheim.* If you would penetrate to the causes thereof, simply go down to Ellis Island and look at the next shipload of immigrants. You will not find the spring of youth in their step; you will find the shuffling of exhausted men. From such exhausted men the American stock has sprung. It was easier for them to survive here than it was where they came from, but that ease, though it made them feel stronger, did not actually strengthen them. It left them what they were when they came: weary peasants, eager only for the comfortable security of a pig in a sty. Out of that eagerness has issued many of the noblest manifestations of American *Kultur*: the national hatred of war, the pervasive suspicion of the aims and intents of all other nations, the short way with heretics and disturbers of the peace, the unshakable belief in devils, the implacable hostility to every novel idea and point of view.

All these ways of thinking are the marks of the peasant—more, of the peasant long ground into the mud of his wallow, and determined at last to stay there—the peasant who has definitely renounced any lewd desire he may have ever had to gape at the stars. The habits of mind of this dull, sempiternal *fellah*—the oldest man in Christendom—are, with a few modifications, the habits of mind of the American people. The peasant has a great practical cunning, but he is unable to see any further than the next farm. He likes money and knows how to amass property, but his cultural development is but little above that of the domestic animals. He is intensely and cocksurely moral, but his morality and his self-interest are crudely identical. He is emotional and easy to scare, but his imagination cannot grasp an abstraction. He is a violent nationalist and patriot, but he admires rogues in office and always beats the tax-collector if he can. He has immovable opinions about all the great affairs of state, but nine-tenths of them are sheer imbecilities. He is violently jealous of what he conceives to be his rights, but brutally disregardful of the other fellow's. He is religious, but his religion is wholly devoid of beauty and dignity. This man, whether city or country bred, is the normal Americano—the 100 per cent. Methodist, Odd Fellow, Ku Kluxer, and Know Nothing. He exists in all countries, but here alone he rules—here alone his anthropoid fears and rages are accepted gravely as logical ideas, and dissent from them is punished as a sort of public offense. Around every one of his principal delusions—of the sacredness of democracy, of the feasibility of sumptuary law, of the incurable sinfulness of all other peoples, of the menace of ideas, of the corruption lying in all the arts—there is thrown a barrier of taboos, and woe to the anarchist who seeks to break it down!

The multiplication of such taboos is obviously not characteristic of a culture that is moving from a lower plane to a higher—that is, of a culture still in the full glow of its youth. It is a sign, rather, of a culture that is slipping downhill—one that is reverting to the most primitive standards and ways of thought. The taboo, indeed, is the trade-mark of the savage, and wherever it exists it is a relentless and effective enemy of civilized enlightenment. The savage is the most meticulously moral of men; there is scarcely an act of his daily life that is not conditioned by unyielding prohibitions and obligations, most of them logically unintelligible. The mob-man, a savage set amid civilization, cherishes a code of the same draconian kind. He believes firmly that right and wrong are immovable things—that they have an actual and unchangeable existence, and that any challenge of them, by word or act, is a crime against society. And with the concept of wrongness, of course, he always confuses the concept of mere differentness—to him the two are indistinguishable. Anything strange is to be combatted; it is of the

Devil. The mob-man cannot grasp ideas in their native nakedness. They must be dramatized and personalized for him, and provided with either white wings or forked tails. All discussion of them, to interest him, must take the form of a pursuit and scotching of demons. He cannot think of a heresy without thinking of a heretic to be caught, condemned, and burned.

The Fathers of the Republic, I am convinced, had a great deal more prevision than even their most romantic worshipers give them credit for. They not only sought to create a governmental machine that would be safe from attack without; they also sought to create one that would be safe from attack within. They invented very ingenious devices for holding the mob in check, for protecting the national polity against its transient and illogical rages, for securing the determination of all the larger matters of state to a concealed but none the less real aristocracy. Nothing could have been further from the intent of Washington, Hamilton and even Jefferson than that the official doctrines of the nation, in the year 1922, should be identical with the nonsense heard in the chautauqua, from the evangelical pulpit, and on the stump. But Jackson and his merry men broke through the barbed wires thus so carefully strung, and ever since 1825 *vox populi* has been the true voice of the nation. To-day there is no longer any question of statesmanship, in any real sense, in our politics. The only way to success in American public life lies in flattering and kowtowing to the mob. A candidate for office, even the highest, must either adopt its current manias *en bloc*, or convince it hypocritically that he has done so, while cherishing reservations *in petto*. The result is that only two sorts of men stand any chance whatever of getting into actual control of affairs—first, glorified mob-men who genuinely believe what the mob believes, and secondly, shrewd fellows who are willing to make any sacrifice of conviction and self-respect in order to hold their jobs. One finds perfect examples of the first class in Jackson and Bryan. One finds hundreds of specimens of the second among the politicians who got themselves so affectingly converted to Prohibition, and who voted and blubbered for it with flasks in their pockets. Even on the highest planes our politics seems to be incurable mountebankish. The same Senators who raised such raucous alarms against the League of Nations voted for the Disarmament Treaty—a far more obvious surrender to English hegemony. And the same Senators who pleaded for the League on the ground that its failure would break the heart of the world were eloquently against the treaty. The few men who maintained a consistent course in both cases, voting either for or against both League and treaty, were denounced by the newspapers as deliberate marplots, and found their constituents rising against them. To such an extent had the public become accustomed to buncombe that simple honesty was incomprehensible to it, and hence abhorrent!

As I have pointed out in a previous work, this dominance of mob ways of thinking, this pollution of the whole intellectual life of the country by the prejudices and emotions of the rabble, goes unchallenged because the old landed aristocracy of the colonial era has been engulfed and almost obliterated by the rise of the industrial system, and no new aristocracy has arisen to take its place, and discharge its highly necessary functions. An upper class, of course, exists, and of late it has tended to increase in power, but it is culturally almost indistinguishable from the mob: it lacks absolutely anything even remotely resembling an aristocratic point of view. One searches in vain for any sign of the true *Junker* spirit in the Vanderbilts, Astors, Morgans, Garys, and other such earls and dukes of the plutocracy; their culture, like their aspiration, remains that of the pawnshop. One searches in vain, too for the aloof air of the don in the official *intelligentsia* of the American universities; they are timorous and orthodox, and constitute a reptile Congregatio de Propaganda Fide to match Bismarck's *Reptilienpresse.*

Everywhere else on earth, despite the rise of democracy, an organized minority of aristocrats survives from a more spacious day, and if its personnel has degenerated and its legal powers have decayed it has at least maintained some vestige of its old independence of spirit, and jealously guarded its old right to be heard without risk of penalty. Even in England, where the peerage has been debauched to the level of a political baptismal fount for Jewish money-lenders and Wesleyan soap-boilers, there is sanctuary for the old order in the two ancient universities, and a lingering respect for it in the peasantry. But in the United States it was paralyzed by Jackson and got its death blow from Grant, and since then no successor to it has been evolved. Thus there is no organized force to oppose the irrational vagaries of the mob. The legislative and executive arms of the government yield to them without resistance; the judicial arm has begun to yield almost as supinely, particularly when they take the form of witch-hunts; outside the official circle there is no opposition that is even dependably articulate. The worst excesses go almost without challenge. Discussion, when it is heard at all, is feeble and superficial, and girt about by the taboos that I have mentioned. The clatter about the so-called Ku Klux Klan, two or three years ago, was typical. The astounding program of this organization was discussed in the newspapers for months on end, and a committee of Congress sat in solemn state to investigate it, and yet not a single newspaper or Congressman, so far as I am aware, so much as mentioned the most patent and important fact about it, to wit, that the Ku Klux was, to all intents and purposes, simply the secular arm of the Methodist Church, and that its methods were no more than physical projections of the familiar extravagances of the Anti-Saloon League. The intimate relations between church and Klan, amounting almost to identity, must have been plain to every intelligent American, and yet the taboo upon the realistic consideration of ecclesiastical matters was sufficient to make every public soothsayer disregard it completely.

I often wonder, indeed, if there would be any intellectual life at all in the United States if it were not for the steady importation in bulk of ideas from abroad, and particularly, in late years, from England. What would become of the average American scholar if he could not borrow wholesale from English scholars? How could an inquisitive youth get beneath the surface of our politics if it were not for such anatomists as Bryce? Who would show our statesmen the dotted lines for their signatures if there were no Balfours and Lloyd-Georges? How could our young professors formulate æsthetic judgments, especially in the field of letters, if it were not for such gifted English mentors as Robertson Nicoll, Squire and Clutton-Brock? By what process, finally, would the true style of a visiting card be determined, and the *höflich* manner of eating artichokes, if there were no reports from Mayfair? On certain levels this naïve subservience must needs irritate every self-respecting American, and even dismay him. When he recalls the amazing feats of the English war propagandists between 1914 and 1917—and their even more amazing confessions of method since—he is apt to ask himself quite gravely if he belongs to a free nation or to a crown colony. The thing was done openly, shamelessly contemptuously, cynically, and yet it was a gigantic success. The office of the American Secretary of State, from the end of Bryan's grotesque incumbency to the end of the Wilson administration, was little more than an antechamber of the British Foreign Office. Dr. Wilson himself, in the conduct of his policy, differed only legally from such colonial premiers as Hughes and Smuts. Even after the United States got into the war it was more swagger for a Young American blood to wear the British uniform than the American uniform. No American ever seriously questions an Englishman or Englishwoman of official or even merely fashionable position at home. Lord Birkenhead was accepted as a gentleman everywhere in the United States; Mrs. Asquith's almost unbelievable imbecilities were heard with hushed fascination; even Lady Astor, an American married to an expatriate German-American turned English viscount, was greeted with solemn effusiveness. During the latter part of 1917, when New York swarmed with British military missions, I observed in *Town Topics* a polite protest against a very significant habit of certain of their gallant members: that of going to dances wearing spurs, and so macerating the frocks and heels of the fawning fair. The protest, it appears, was not voiced by the hosts and hostesses of these singular officers: they would have welcomed their guests in trench boots. It was left to a dubious weekly, and it was made very gingerly.

The spectacle, as I say, has a way of irking the American touched by nationalistic weakness. Ever since the day of Lowell—even since the day of Cooper and Irving—there have been denunciations of it. But however unpleasant it may be, there is no denying that a chain of logical causes lies behind it, and that they are not to be disposed of by objecting to them. The average American of the Anglo-Saxon majority, in truth, is simply a second-rate Englishman, and so it is no wonder that he is spontaneously servile, despite all his democratic denial of superiorities, to what he conceives to be first-rate Englishmen. He corresponds, roughly, to an English Nonconformist of the better-fed variety, and he shows all the familiar characters of the breed. He is truculent and cocksure, and yet he knows how to take off his hat when a bishop of the Establishment passes. He is hot against the dukes, and yet the notice of a concrete duke is a singing in his heart. It seems to me that this inferior Anglo-Saxon is losing his old dominance in the United States—that is, biologically But he will keep his cultural primacy for a long, long while, in spite of the overwhelming inrush of men of other races, if only because those newcomers are even more clearly inferior than he is. Nine-tenths of the Italians, for example, who have come to these shores in late years have brought no more of the essential culture of Italy with them than so many horned cattle would have brought. If they become civilized at all, settling here, it is the civilization of the Anglo-Saxon majority that they acquire, which is to say, the civilization of the English second table. So with the Germans, the Scandinavians, and even the Jews and Irish. The Germans, taking one with another, are on the cultural level of green-grocers. I have come into contact with a great many of them since 1914, some of them of considerable wealth and even of fashionable pretensions. In the whole lot I can think of but a score or two who could name offhand the principal works of Thomas Mann, Otto Julius Bierbaum, Ludwig Thoma or Hugo von Hofmannsthal. They know much more about Mutt and Jeff than they know about Goethe. The Scandinavians are even worse. The majority of them are mere clods, and they are sucked into the Knights of Pythias, the chautauqua and the Methodist Church almost as soon as they land; it is by no means a mere accident that the national Prohibition Enforcement Act bears the name of a man theoretically of the blood of Gustavus Vasa, Svend of the Forked Beard, and Eric the Red. The Irish in the United States are scarcely touched by the revival of Irish culture, despite their melodramatic concern with Irish politics. During the war they supplied diligent and dependable agents to the Anglo-Saxon White Terror, and at all times they are very susceptible to political and social bribery. As for the Jews, they change their names to Burton, Thompson and Cecil in order to qualify as true Americans, and when they are accepted and rewarded in the national coin they renounce Moses altogether and get themselves baptized in St. Bartholomew's Church.

Whenever ideas enter the United States from without they come by way of England. What the London *Times* says to-day, about Ukranian politics, the revolt in India, a change of ministry in Italy, the character of the King of Norway, the oil situation in Mesopotamia, will be said week after next by the *Times* of New York, and a month or two later by all the other American newspapers. The extent of this control of American opinion by English news mongers is but little appreciated in the United States, even by professional journalists. Fully four-fifths of all the foreign news that comes to the American newspapers comes through London, and most of the rest is supplied either by Englishmen or by Jews (often American-born) who maintain close relations with the English. During the years 1914-1917 so many English agents got into Germany in the guise of American correspondents—sometimes with the full knowledge of their Anglomaniac American employers—that the Germans, just before the United States entered the war, were considering barring American correspondents from their country altogether. I was in Copenhagen and Basel in 1917, and found both towns—each an important source of war news—full of Jews representing American journals as a side-line to more delicate and confidential work for the English department of press propaganda. Even to-day a very considerable proportion of the American correspondents in Europe are strongly under English influences, and in the Far East the proportion is probably still larger. But these men seldom handle really important news. All that is handled from London, and by trustworthy Britons. Such of it as is not cabled directly to the

American newspapers and press associations is later clipped from English newspapers, and printed as bogus letters or cablegrams.

The American papers accept such very dubious stuff, not chiefly because they are hopelessly stupid or Anglomaniac, but because they find it impossible to engage competent American correspondents. If the native journalists who discuss our domestic politics avoid the fundamentals timorously, then those who venture to discuss foreign politics are scarcely aware of the fundamentals at all. We have simply developed no class of experts in such matters. No man comparable, say to Dr. Dillon, Wickham Steed, Count zu Reventlow or Wilfrid Scawen Blunt exists in the United States. When, in the Summer of 1920, the editors of the Baltimore *Sun* undertook plans to cover the approaching Disarmament Conference at Washington in a comprehensive and intelligent manner, they were forced, willy-nilly, into employing Englishmen to do the work. Such men as Brailsford and Bywater, writing from London, three thousand miles away, were actually better able to interpret the work of the conference than American correspondents on the spot, few of whom were capable of anything beyond the most trivial gossip. During the whole period of the conference not a professional Washington correspondent—the flower of American political journalism—wrote a single article upon the proceedings that got further than their surface aspects. Before the end of the sessions this enforced dependence upon English opinion had an unexpected and significant result. Facing the English and the Japs in an unyielding alliance, the French turned to the American delegation for assistance. The issue specifically before the conference was one on which American self-interest was obviously identical with French self-interest. Nevertheless, the English had such firm grip upon the machinery of news distribution that they were able, in less than a week, to turn American public opinion against the French, and even to set up an active Francophobia. No American, not even any of the American delegates, was able to cope with their propaganda. They not only dominated the conference and pushed through a set of treaties that were extravagantly favorable to England; they even established the doctrine that all opposition to those treaties was immoral!

When Continental ideas, whether in politics, in metaphysics or in the fine arts, penetrate to the United States they nearly always travel by way of England. Emerson did not read Goethe; he read Carlyle. The American people, from the end of 1914 to the end of 1918, did not read first-handed statements of the German case; they read English interpretations of those statements. In London is the clearing house and transformer station. There the latest notions from the mainland are sifted out, carefully diluted with English water, and put into neat packages for the Yankee trade. The English not only get a chance to ameliorate or embellish; they also determine very largely what ideas Americans are to hear of at all. Whatever fails to interest them, or is in any way obnoxious to them, is not likely to cross the ocean. This explains why it is that most literate Americans are so densely ignorant of many Continentals who have been celebrated at home for years, for example, Huysmans, Hartleben, Vaihinger, Merezhkovsky, Keyserling, Snoilsky, Mauthner, Altenberg, Heidenstam, Alfred Kerr. It also explains why they so grossly overestimate various third-raters, laughed at at home, for example, Brieux. These fellows simply happen to interest the English *intelligentsia*, and are thus palmed off upon the gaping colonists of Yankeedom. In the case of Brieux the hocus-pocus was achieved by one man, George Bernard Shaw, a Scotch blue-nose disguised as an Irish patriot and English soothsayer. Shaw, at bottom, has the ideas of a Presbyterian elder, and so the moral frenzy of Brieux enchanted him. Whereupon he retired to his chamber, wrote a flaming Brieuxiad for the American trade, and founded the late vogue of the French Dr. Sylvanus Stall on this side of the ocean.

This wholesale import and export business in Continental fancies is of no little benefit, of course, to the generality of Americans. If it did not exist they would probably never hear of many of the salient Continentals at all, for the obvious incompetence of most of the native and resident introducers of intellectual ambassadors makes them suspicious even of those who, like Boyd and Nathan, are thoroughly competent. To this day there is no American translation of the plays of Ibsen; we use the William Archer Scotch-English translations, most of them atrociously bad, but still better than nothing. So with the works of Nietzsche, Anatole France, Georg Brandes, Turgeniev, Dostoyevsky, Tolstoi, and other moderns after their kind. I can think of but one important exception: the work of Gerhart Hauptmann, done into English by and under the supervision of Ludwig Lewisohn. But even here Lewisohn used a number of English translations of single plays: the English were still ahead of him, though they stopped half way. He is, in any case, a very extraordinary American, and the Department of Justice kept an eye on him during the war. The average American professor is far too dull a fellow to undertake so difficult an enterprise. Even when he sports a German Ph.D. one usually finds on examination that all he knows about modern German literature is that a *Mass* of Hofbräu in Munich used to cost 27 *Pfennig* downstairs and 32 *Pfennig* upstairs. The German universities were formerly very tolerant of foreigners. Many an American, in preparation for professing at Harvard, spent a couple of years roaming from one to the other of them without picking up enough German to read the *Berliner Tageblatt.* Such frauds swarm in all our lesser universities, and many of them, during the war, became eminent authorities upon the crimes of Nietzsche and the errors of Treitschke.

3

In rainy weather, when my old wounds ache and the four humors do battle in my spleen, I often find myself speculating sourly as to the future of the Republic. Native opinion, of course, is to the effect that it will be secure and glorious; the superstition that progress must always be upward and onward will not down; in virulence and popularity it matches the superstition that money can accomplish anything. But this view is not shared by most reflective foreigners, as any one may find out by looking into such a book as Ferdinand Kürnberger's "Der Amerikamüde," Sholom Asch's "America," Ernest von Wolzogen's "Ein Dichter in Dollarica," W. L. George's "Hail, Columbia!", Annalise Schmidt's "Der Amerikanische Mensch" or Sienkiewicz's "After Bread," or by hearkening unto the confidences, if obtainable, of such returned immigrants as Georges Clemenceau, Knut Hamsun, George Santayana, Clemens von Pirquet, John Masefield and Maxim Gorky, and, via the ouija board, Antonin Dvořák, Frank Wedekind and Edwin Klebs. The American Republic, as nations go, has led a safe and easy life, with no serious enemies to menace it, either within or without, and no grim struggle with want. Getting a living here has always been easier than anywhere else in Christendom; getting a secure foothold has been possible to whole classes of men who would have remained submerged in Europe, as the character of our plutocracy, and no less of our *intelligentsia* so brilliantly shows. The American people have never had to face such titanic assults as those suffered by the people of Holland, Poland and half a dozen other little countries; they have not lived with a ring of powerful and unconscionable enemies about them, as the Germans have lived since the Middle Ages; they have not been torn by class wars, as the French, the Spaniards and the Russians have been torn; they have not thrown their strength into far-flung and exhausting colonial enterprises, like the English. All their foreign wars have been fought with foes either too weak to resist them or too heavily engaged elsewhere to make more than a half-hearted attempt. The combats with Mexico and Spain were not wars; they were simply lynchings.

Even the Civil War, compared to the larger European conflicts since the invention of gunpowder, was trivial in its character and transient in its effects. The population of the United States, when it began, was about 31,500,000—say 10 per cent. under the population of France in 1914. But after four years of struggle, the number of men killed in action or dead of wounds, in the two armies, came but 200,000—probably little more than a sixth of the total losses of France between 1914 and 1918. Nor was there any very extensive destruction of property. In all save a small area in the North there was none at all, and even in the South only a few towns of any importance were destroyed. The average Northerner passed through the four years scarcely aware, save by report, that a war was going on. In the South the breath of Mars blew more hotly, but even there large numbers of men escaped service, and the general hardship everywhere fell a great deal short of the hardships suffered by the Belgians, the French of the North, the Germans of East Prussia, and the Serbians and Rumanians in the World War. The agonies of the South have been much exaggerated in popular romance; they were probably more severe during Reconstruction, when they were chiefly psychical, than they were during the actual war. Certainly General Robert E. Lee was in a favorable position to estimate the military achievement of the Confederacy. Well,

Lee was of the opinion that his army was very badly supported by the civil population, and that its final disaster was largely due to that ineffective support.

Coming down to the time of the World War, one finds precious few signs that the American people, facing an antagonist of equal strength and with both hands free, could be relied upon to give a creditable account of themselves. The American share in that great struggle, in fact, was marked by poltroonery almost as conspicuously as it was marked by knavery. Let us consider briefly what the nation did. For a few months it viewed the struggle idly and unintelligently, as a yokel might stare at a sword-swallower at a county fair. Then, seeing a chance to profit, it undertook with sudden alacrity the ghoulish office of *Kriegslieferant*. One of the contestants being debarred, by the chances of war, from buying, it devoted its whole energies, for two years, to purveying to the other. Meanwhile, it made every effort to aid its customer by lending him the cloak of its neutrality—that is, by demanding all the privileges of a neutral and yet carrying on a stupendous wholesale effort to promote the war. On the official side, this neutrality was fraudulent from the start, as the revelations of Mr. Tumulty have since demonstrated; popularly it became more and more fraudulent as the debts of the customer contestant piled up, and it became more and more apparent—a fact diligently made known by his partisans—that they would be worthless if he failed to win. Then, in the end, covert aid was transformed into overt aid. And under what gallant conditions! In brief, there stood a nation of 65,000,000 people, which, without effective allies, had just closed two and a half years of homeric conflict by completely defeating an enemy state of 135,000,000 and two lesser ones of more than 10,000,000 together, and now stood at bay before a combination of at least 140,000,000. Upon this battle-scarred and war-weary foe the Republic of 100,000,000 freemen now flung itself, so lifting the odds to 4 to 1. And after a year and a half more of struggle it emerged triumphant—a knightly victor surely!

There is no need to rehearse the astounding and unprecedented swinishness that accompanied this glorious business—the colossal waste of public money, the savage persecution of all opponents and critics of the war, the open bribery of labor, the half-insane reviling of the enemy, the manufacture of false news, the knavish robbery of enemy civilians, the incessant spy hunts, the floating of public loans by a process of blackmail, the degradation of the Red Cross to partisan uses, the complete abandonment of all decency, decorum and self-respect. The facts must be remembered with shame by every civilized American; lest they be forgotten by the generations of the future I am even now engaged with collaborators upon an exhaustive record of them, in twenty volumes folio. More important to the present purpose are two things that are apt to be overlooked, the first of which is the capital fact that the war was "sold" to the American people, as the phrase has it, not by appealing to their courage, but by appealing to their cowardice—in brief, by adopting the assumption that they were not warlike at all, and certainly not gallant and chivalrous, but merely craven and fearful. The first selling point of the proponents of American participation was the contention that the Germans, with gigantic wars still raging on both fronts, were preparing to invade the United States, burn down all the towns, murder all the men, and carry off all the women—that their victory would bring staggering and irresistible reprisals for the American violation of the duties of a neutral. The second selling point was that the entrance of the United States would end the war almost instantly—that the Germans would be so overwhelmingly outnumbered, in men and guns, that it would be impossible for them to make any effective defense—above all, that it would be impossible for them to inflict any serious damage upon their new foes. Neither argument, it must be plain, showed the slightest belief in the warlike skill and courage of the American people. Both were grounded upon the frank theory that the only way to make the mob fight was to scare it half to death, and then show it a way to fight without risk, to stab a helpless antagonist in the back. And both were mellowed and reënforced by the hint that such a noble assault, beside being safe, would also be extremely profitable—that it would convert very dubious debts into very good debts, and dispose forever of a diligent and dangerous competitor for trade, especially in Latin America. All the idealist nonsense emitted by Dr. Wilson and company was simply icing on the cake. Most of it was abandoned as soon as the bullets began to fly, and the rest consisted simply of meaningless words—the idiotic babbling of a Presbyterian evangelist turned prophet and seer.

The other thing that needs to be remembered is the permanent effect of so dishonest and cowardly a business upon the national character, already far too much inclined toward easy ventures and long odds. Somewhere in his diaries Wilfrid Scawen Blunt speaks of the marked debasement that showed itself in the English spirit after the brutal robbery and assassination of the South African Republics. The heroes that the mob followed after Mafeking Day were far inferior to the heroes that it had followed in the days before the war. The English gentleman began to disappear from public life, and in his place appeared a rabble-rousing bounder obviously almost identical with the American professional politician—the Lloyd-George, Chamberlain, F. E. Smith, Isaacs-Reading, Churchill, Bottomley, Northcliffe type. Worse, old ideals went with old heroes. Personal freedom and strict legality, says Blunt, vanished from the English tables of the law, and there was a shift of the social and political center of gravity to a lower plane. Precisely the same effect is now visible in the United States. The overwhelming majority of conscripts went into the army unwillingly, and once there they were debauched by the twin forces of the official propaganda that I have mentioned and a harsh, unintelligent discipline. The first made them almost incapable of soldierly thought and conduct; the second converted them into cringing goose-steppers. The consequences display themselves in the amazing activities of the American Legion, and in the rise of such correlative organizations as the Ku Klux Klan. It is impossible to fit any reasonable concept of the soldierly into the familiar proceedings of the Legion. Its members conduct themselves like a gang of Methodist vice-crusaders on the loose, or a Southern lynching party. They are forever discovering preposterous burglars under the national bed, and they advance to the attack, not gallantly and at fair odds, but cravenly and in overwhelming force. Some of their enterprises, to be set forth at length in the record I have mentioned, have been of almost unbelievable baseness—the mobbing of harmless Socialists, the prohibition of concerts by musicians of enemy nationality, the mutilation of cows designed for shipment abroad to feed starving children, the roughing of women, service as strike-breakers, the persecution of helpless foreigners, regardless of nationality.

During the last few months of the war, when stories of the tyrannical ill-usage of conscripts began to filter back to the United States, it was predicted that they would demand the punishment of the guilty when they got home, and that if it was not promptly forthcoming they would take it into their own hands. It was predicted, too, that they would array themselves against the excesses of Palmer, Burleson and company, and insist upon a restoration of that democratic freedom for which they had theoretically fought. But they actually did none of these things. So far as I know, not a single martinet of a lieutenant or captain has been manhandled by his late victims; the most they have done has been to appeal to Congress for revenge and damages. Nor have they thrown their influence against the mediæval despotism which grew up at home during the war; on the contrary, they have supported it actively, and if it has lessened since 1919 the change has been wrought without their aid and in spite of their opposition. In sum, they show all the stigmata of inferior men whose natural inferiority has been made worse by oppression. Their chief organization is dominated by shrewd ex-officers who operate it to their own ends—politicians in search of jobs, Chamber of Commerce witch-hunters, and other such vermin. It seems to be wholly devoid of patriotism, courage, or sense. Nothing quite resembling it existed in the country before the war, not even in the South. There is nothing like it anywhere else on earth. It is a typical product of two years of heroic effort to arouse and capitalize the worst instincts of the mob, and it symbolizes very dramatically the ill effects of that effort upon the general American character.

Would men so degraded in gallantry and honor, so completely purged of all the military virtues, so submerged in baseness of spirit—would such pitiful caricatures of soldiers offer the necessary resistance to a public enemy who was equal, or perhaps superior in men and resources, and who came on with confidence, daring and resolution—say England supported by Germany as *Kriegslieferant* and with her inevitable swarms of Continental allies, or Japan with the Asiatic hordes behind her? Against the best opinion of the chatauquas, of Congress and of the patriotic press I presume to doubt it. It seems to me quite certain, indeed, that an American army fairly representing the American people, if it ever meets another army of anything remotely resembling like strength, will be defeated, and that defeat will be indistinguishable from rout. I believe that, at any odds less than two to one, even the exhausted German army of 1918 would have defeated it, and in this view, I think, I am joined by many men whose military judgment is far better than mine—particularly by many French officers. The changes in the American character since the Civil War, due partly to the wearing out of the old Anglo-Saxon stock, inferior to begin with, and partly to the infusion of the worst elements of other stocks, have surely not made for the fostering of the military virtues. The old cool head is gone, and the old dogged way with difficulties. The typical American of to-day has lost all the love of liberty that his forefathers had, and all their distrust of emotion, and pride in self-reliance. He is led no longer by Davy Crocketts; he is led by cheer leaders, press agents, word-mongers, uplifters. I do not believe that such a faint-hearted and inflammatory fellow, shoved into a war demanding every resource of courage, ingenuity and pertinacity, would give a good account of himself. He is fit for lynching-bees and heretic-hunts, but he is not fit for tight corners and desperate odds.

Nevertheless, his docility and pusillanimity may be overestimated, and sometimes I think that they *are* overestimated by his present masters. They assume that there is absolutely no limit to his capacity for being put on and knocked about—that he will submit to any invasion of his freedom and dignity, however outrageous, so long as it is depicted in melodious terms. He permitted the late war to be "sold" to him by the methods of the grind-shop auctioneer. He submitted to conscription without any of the resistance shown by his brother democrats of Canada and Australia. He got no further than academic protests against the brutal usage he had to face in the army. He came home and found Prohibition foisted on him, and contented himself with a few feeble objurgations. He is a pliant slave of capitalism, and ever ready to help it put down fellow-slaves who venture to revolt. But this very weakness, this very credulity and poverty of spirit, on some easily conceivable to-morrow, may convert him into a rebel of a peculiarly insane kind, and so beset the Republic from within with difficulties quite as formidable as those which threaten to afflict it from without. What Mr. James N. Wood calls the corsair of democracy —that is, the professional mob-master, the merchant of delusions, the pumper-up of popular fears and rages—is still content to work for capitalism, and capitalism knows how to reward him to his taste. He is the eloquent statesman, the patriotic editor, the fount of inspiration, the prancing milch-cow of optimism. He becomes public leader, Governor, Senator, President. He is Billy Sunday, Cyrus K. Curtis, Dr. Frank Crane, Charles E. Hughes, Taft, Wilson, Cal Coolidge, General Wood, Harding. His, perhaps, is the best of trades under democracy—but it has its temptations! Let us try to picture a master corsair, thoroughly adept at pulling the mob nose, who suddenly bethought himself of that Pepin the Short who found himself mayor of the palace and made himself King of the Franks. There were lightnings along that horizon in the days of Roosevelt; there were thunder growls when Bryan emerged from the Nebraska steppes. On some great day of fate, as yet unrevealed by the gods, such a professor of the central democratic science may throw off his employers and set up a business for himself. When that day comes there will be plenty of excuse for black type on the front pages of the newspapers.

I incline to think that military disaster will give him his inspiration and his opportunity—that he will take the form, so dear to democracies, of a man on horseback. The chances are bad to-day simply because the mob is relatively comfortable—because capitalism has been able to give it relative ease and plenty of food in return for its docility. Genuine poverty is very rare in the United States, and actual hardship is almost unknown. There are times when the proletariat is short of phonograph records, silk shirts and movie tickets, but there are very few times when it is short of nourishment. Even during the most severe business depression, with hundreds of thousands out of work, most of these apparent sufferers, if they are willing, are able to get livings outside their trades. The cities may be choked with idle men, but the country is nearly always short of labor. And if all other resources fail, there are always public agencies to feed the hungry: capitalism is careful to keep them from despair. No American knows what it means to live as millions of Europeans lived during the war and have lived, in some places, since: with the loaves of the baker reduced to half size and no meat at all in the meatshop. But the time may come and it may not be far off. A national military disaster would disorganize all industry in the United States, already sufficiently wasteful and chaotic, and introduce the American people, for the first time in their history, to genuine want—and capital would be unable to relieve them. The day of such disaster will bring the savior foreordained. The slaves will follow him, their eyes fixed ecstatically upon the newest New Jerusalem. Men bred to respond automatically to shibboleths will respond to this worst and most insane one. Bolshevism, said General Foch, is a disease of defeated nations.

But do not misunderstand me: I predict no revolution in the grand manner, no melodramatic collapse of capitalism, no repetition of what has gone on in

Russia. The American proletarian is not brave and romantic enough for that; to do him simple justice, he is not silly enough. Capitalism, in the long run, will win in the United States, if only for the reason that every American hopes to be a capitalist before he dies. Its roots go down to the deepest, darkest levels of the national soil; in all its characters, and particularly in its antipathy to the dreams of man, it is thoroughly American. To-day it seems to be immovably secure, given continued peace and plenty, and not all the demagogues in the land, consecrating themselves desperately to the one holy purpose, could shake it. Only a cataclysm will ever do that. But is a cataclysm conceivable? Isn't the United States the richest nation ever heard of in history, and isn't it a fact that modern wars are won by money? It is not a fact. Wars are won to-day, as in Napoleon's day, by the largest battalions, and the largest battalions, in the next great struggle, may not be on the side of the Republic. The usurious profits it wrung from the last war are as tempting as negotiable securities hung on the wash-line, as pre-Prohibition Scotch stored in open cellars. Its knavish ways with friends and foes alike have left it only foes. It is plunging ill-equipped into a competition for a living in the world that will be to the death. And the late Disarmament Conference left it almost ham-strung. Before the conference it had the Pacific in its grip, and with the Pacific in its grip it might have parleyed for a fair half of the Atlantic. But when the Japs and the English had finished their operations upon the Feather Duster, Popinjay Lodge, Master-Mind Root, Vacuum Underwood, young Teddy Roosevelt and the rest of their so-willing dupes there was apparent a baleful change. The Republic is extremely insecure to-day on both fronts, and it will be more insecure to-morrow. And it has no friends.

However, as I say, I do not fear for capitalism. It will weather the storm, and no doubt it will be the stronger for it afterward. The inferior man hates it, but there is too much envy mixed with his hatred, in the land of the theoretically free, for him to want to destroy it utterly, or even to wound it incurably. He struggles against it now, but always wistfully, always with a sneaking respect. On the day of Armageddon he may attempt a more violent onslaught. But in the long run he will be beaten. In the long run the corsairs will sell him out, and hand him over to his enemy. Perhaps—who knows?—the combat may raise that enemy to genuine strength and dignity. Out of it may come the superman.

4

All the while I have been forgetting the third of my reasons for remaining so faithful a citizen of the Federation, despite all the lascivious inducements from expatriates to follow them beyond the seas, and all the surly suggestions from patriots that I succumb. It is the reason which grows out of my mediæval but unashamed taste for the bizarre and indelicate, my congenital weakness for comedy of the grosser varieties. The United States, to my eye, is incomparably the greatest show on earth. It is a show which avoids diligently all the kinds of clowning which tire me most quickly—for example, royal ceremonials, the tedious hocus-pocus of *haut politique*, the taking of politics seriously—and lays chief stress upon the kinds which delight me unceasingly—for example, the ribald combats of demagogues, the exquisitely ingenious operations of master rogues, the pursuit of witches and heretics, the desperate struggles of inferior men to claw their way into Heaven. We have clowns in constant practice among us who are as far above the clowns of any other great state as a Jack Dempsey is above a paralytic—and not a few dozen or score of them, but whole droves and herds. Human enterprises which, in all other Christian countries, are resigned despairingly to an incurable dullness—things that seem devoid of exhilarating amusement by their very nature—are here lifted to such vast heights of buffoonery that contemplating them strains the midriff almost to breaking. I cite an example: the worship of God. Everywhere else on earth it is carried on in a solemn and dispiriting manner; in England, of course, the bishops are obscene, but the average man seldom gets a fair chance to laugh at them and enjoy them. Now come home. Here we not only have bishops who are enormously more obscene than even the most gifted of the English bishops; we have also a huge force of lesser specialists in ecclesiastical mountebankery—tin-horn Loyolas, Savonarolas and Xaviers of a hundred fantastic rites, each performing untiringly and each full of a grotesque and illimitable whimsicality. Every American town, however small, has one of its own: a holy clerk with so fine a talent for introducing the arts of jazz into the salvation of the damned that his performance takes on all the gaudiness of a four-ring circus, and the bald announcement that he will raid Hell on such and such a night is enough to empty all the town blind-pigs and bordellos and pack his sanctuary to the doors. And to aid him and inspire him there are traveling experts to whom he stands in the relation of a wart to the Matterhorn—stupendous masters of theological imbecility, contrivers of doctrines utterly preposterous, heirs to the Joseph Smith, Mother Eddy and John Alexander Dowie tradition—Bryan, Sunday, and their like. These are the eminences of the American Sacred College. I delight in them. Their proceedings make me a happier American.

Turn, now, to politics. Consider, for example, a campaign for the Presidency. Would it be possible to imagine anything more uproariously idiotic—a deafening, nerve-wracking battle to the death between Tweedledum and Tweedledee, Harlequin and Sganarelle, Gobbo and Dr. Cook—the unspeakable, with fearful snorts, gradually swallowing the inconceivable? I defy any one to match it elsewhere on this earth. In other lands, at worst, there are at least intelligible issues, coherent ideas, salient personalities. Somebody says something, and somebody replies. But what did Harding say in 1920, and what did Cox reply? Who was Harding, anyhow, and who was Cox? Here, having perfected democracy, we lift the whole combat to symbolism, to transcendentalism, to metaphysics. Here we load a pair of palpably tin cannon with blank cartridges charged with talcum powder, and so let fly. Here one may howl over the show without any uneasy reminder that it is serious, and that some one may be hurt. I hold that this elevation of politics to the plane of undiluted comedy is peculiarly American, that nowhere else on this disreputable ball has the art of the sham-battle been developed to such fineness. Two experiences are in point. During the Harding-Cox combat of bladders an article of mine, dealing with some of its more melodramatic phases, was translated into German and reprinted by a Berlin paper. At the head of it the editor was careful to insert a preface explaining to his readers, but recently delivered to democracy, that such contests were not taken seriously by intelligent Americans, and warning them solemnly against getting into sweats over politics. At about the same time I had dinner with an Englishman. From cocktails to bromo seltzer he bewailed the political lassitude of the English populace—its growing indifference to the whole partisan harliquinade. Here were two typical foreign attitudes: the Germans were in danger of making politics too harsh and implacable, and the English were in danger of forgetting politics altogether. Both attitudes, it must be plain, make for bad shows. Observing a German campaign, one is uncomfortably harassed and stirred up; observing an English campaign (at least in times of peace), one falls asleep. In the United States the thing is done better. Here politics is purged of all menace, all sinister quality, all genuine significance, and stuffed with such gorgeous humors, such inordinate farce that one comes to the end of a campaign with one's ribs loose, and ready for "King Lear," or a hanging, or a course of medical journals.

But feeling better for the laugh. *Ridi si sapis,* said Martial. Mirth is necessary to wisdom, to comfort, above all, to happiness. Well, here is the land of mirth, as Germany is the land of metaphysics and France is the land of fornication. Here the buffoonery never stops. What could be more delightful than the endless struggle of the Puritan to make the joy of the minority unlawful and impossible? The effort is itself a greater joy to one standing on the side-lines that any or all of the carnal joys that it combats. Always, when I contemplate an uplifter at his hopeless business, I recall a scene in an old-time burlesque show, witnessed for hire in my days as a dramatic critic. A chorus girl executed a fall upon the stage, and Rudolph Krausemeyer, the Swiss comedian, rushed to her aid. As he stooped painfully to succor her, Irving Rabinovitz, the Zionist comedian, fetched him a fearful clout across the cofferdam with a slap-stick. So the uplifter, the soul-saver, the Americanizer, striving to make the Republic fit for Y. M. C. A. secretaries. He is the eternal American, ever moved by the best of intentions, ever running *a la* Krausemeyer to the rescue of virtue, and ever getting his pantaloons fanned by the Devil. I am naturally sinful, and such spectacles caress me. If the slap-stick were a sash-weight the show would be cruel, and I'd probably complain to the *Polizei*. As it is, I know that the uplifter is not really hurt, but simply shocked. The blow, in fact, does him good, for it helps to get him into Heaven, as exegetes prove from Matthew v, 11: *Heureux serez-vous, lorsqu'on vous outragera, qu'on vous persécutera*, and so on. As for me, it makes me a more contented man, and hence a better citizen. One man prefers the Republic because it pays better wages than Bulgaria. Another because it has laws to keep him sober and his daughter chaste. Another because the Woolworth Building is higher than the cathedral at Chartres. Another because, living here, he can read the New York *Evening Journal*. Another because there is a warrant out for him somewhere else. Me, I like it because it amuses me to my taste. I never get tired of the show. It is worth every cent it costs.

That cost, it seems to me is very moderate. Taxes in the United States are not actually high. I figure, for example, that my private share of the expense of maintaining the Hon. Mr. Harding in the White House this year will work out to less than 80 cents. Try to think of better sport for the money: in New York it has been estimated that it costs $8 to get comfortably tight, and $17.50, on an average, to pinch a girl's arm. The United States Senate will cost me perhaps $11 for the year, but against that expense set the subscription price of the *Congressional Record*, about $15, which, as a journalist, I receive for nothing. For $4 less than nothing I am thus entertained as Solomon never was by his hooch dancers. Col. George Brinton McClellan Harvey costs me but 25 cents a year; I get Nicholas Murray Butler free. Finally, there is young Teddy Roosevelt, the naval expert. Teddy costs me, as I work it out, about 11 cents a year, or less than a cent a month. More, he entertains me doubly for the money, first as naval expert, and secondly as a walking *attentat* upon democracy, a devastating proof that there is nothing, after all, in that superstition. We Americans subscribe to the doctrine of human equality—and the Rooseveltii reduce it to an absurdity as brilliantly as the sons of Veit Bach. Where is your equal opportunity now? Here in this Eden of clowns, with the highest rewards of clowning theoretically open to every poor boy—here in the very citadel of democracy we found and cherish a clown *dynasty!*

II. HUNEKER: A MEMORY

THERE was a stimulating aliveness about him always, an air of living eagerly and a bit recklessly, a sort of defiant resiliency. In his very frame and form something provocative showed itself—an insolent singularity, obvious to even the most careless glance. That Caligulan profile of his was more than simply unusual in a free republic, consecrated to good works; to a respectable American, encountering it in the lobby of the Metropolitan or in the smoke-room of a *Doppelschraubenschnellpostdampfer*, it must have suggested inevitably the dark enterprises and illicit metaphysics of a Heliogabalus. More, there was always something rakish and defiant about his hat—it was too white, or it curled in the wrong way, or a feather peeped from the band—, and a hint of antinomianism in his cravat. Yet more, he ran to exotic tastes in eating and drinking, preferring occult goulashes and risi-bisis to honest American steaks, and great floods of Pilsner to the harsh beverages of God-fearing men. Finally, there was his talk, that cataract of sublime trivialities: gossip lifted to the plane of the gods, the unmentionable bedizened with an astounding importance, and even profundity.

In his early days, when he performed the tonal and carnal prodigies that he liked to talk of afterward, I was at nurse, and too young to have any traffic with him. When I encountered him at last he was in the high flush of the middle years, and had already become a tradition in the little world that critics inhabit. We sat down to luncheon at one o'clock; I think it must have been at Lüchow's, his favorite refuge and rostrum to the end. At six, when I had to go, the waiter was hauling in his tenth (or was it twentieth?) *Seidel* of Pilsner, and he was bringing to a close *prestissimo* the most amazing monologue that these ears (up to that time) had ever funnelled into this consciousness. What a stew, indeed! Berlioz and the question of the clang-tint of the viola, the psychopathological causes of the suicide of Tschaikowsky, why Nietzsche had to leave Sils Maria between days in 1887, the echoes of Flaubert in Joseph Conrad (then but newly dawned), the precise topography of the warts of Liszt, George Bernard Shaw's heroic but vain struggles to throw off Presbyterianism, how Frau Cosima saved Wagner from the libidinous Swedish baroness, what to drink when playing Chopin, what Cézanne thought of his disciples, the defects in the structure of "Sister Carrie," Anton Seidl and the musical union, the complex love affairs of Gounod, the early days of David Belasco, the varying talents and idiosyncrasies of Lillian Russell's earlier husbands, whether a girl educated at Vassar could ever really learn to love, the exact composition of chicken paprika, the correct tempo of the Vienna waltz, the style of William Dean Howells, what George Moore said about German bathrooms, the true inwardness of the affair between D'Annunzio and Duse, the origin of the theory that all oboe players are crazy, why Löwenbräu survived exportation better than Hofbräu, Ibsen's loathing of Norwegians, the best remedy for Rhine wine *Katzenjammer*, how to play Brahms, the degeneration of the Bal Bullier, the sheer physical impossibility of getting Dvořák drunk, the genuine last words of Walt Whitman. . . .

I left in a sort of fever, and it was a couple of days later before I began to sort out my impressions, and formulate a coherent image. Was the man allusive in his books—so allusive that popular report credited him with the actual manufacture of authorities? Then he was ten times as allusive in his discourse—a veritable geyser of unfamiliar names, shocking epigrams in strange tongues, unearthly philosophies out of the backwaters of Scandinavia, Transylvania, Bulgaria, the Basque country, the Ukraine. And did he, in his criticism, pass facilely from the author to the man, and from the man to his wife, and to the wives of his friends? Then at the *Biertisch* he began long beyond the point where the last honest wife gives up the ghost, and so, full tilt, ran into such complexities of adultery that a plain sinner could scarcely follow him. I try to give you, ineptly and grotesquely, some notion of the talk of the man, but I must fail inevitably. It was, in brief, chaos, and chaos cannot be described. But it was chaos made to gleam and corruscate with every device of the seven arts—chaos drenched in all the colors imaginable, chaos scored for an orchestra which made the great band of Berlioz seem like a fife and drum corps. One night a few months before the war, I sat in the Paris Opera House listening to the first performance of Richard Strauss's "Josef's Legend," with Strauss himself conducting. On the stage there was a riot of hues that swung the eyes 'round and 'round in a crazy mazurka; in the orchestra there were such volleys and explosions of tone that the ears (I fall into a Hunekeran trope) began to go pale and clammy with surgical shock. Suddenly, above all the uproar, a piccolo launched into a new and saucy tune—in an unrelated key! . . . Instantly and quite naturally, I thought of the incomparable James. When he gave a show at Lüchow's he never forgot that anarchistic passage for the piccolo.

I observe a tendency since his death to estimate him in terms of the content of his books. Even Frank

Harris, who certainly should know better, goes there for the facts about him. Nothing could do him worse injustice. In those books, of course, there is a great deal of perfectly sound stuff; the wonder is, in truth, that so much of it holds up so well to-day—for example, the essays on Strauss, on Brahms and on Nietzsche, and the whole volume on Chopin. But the real Huneker never got himself formally between covers, if one forgets "Old Fogy" and parts of "Painted Veils." The volumes of his regular canon are made up, in the main, of articles written for the more intellectual magazines and newspapers of their era, and they are full of a conscious striving to qualify for respectable company. Huneker, always curiously modest, never got over the notion that it was a singular honor for a man such as he—a mere diurnal scribbler, innocent of academic robes—to be published by so austere a publisher as Scribner. More than once, anchored at the beer-table, we discussed the matter at length, I always arguing that all the honor was enjoyed by Scribner. But Huneker, I believe in all sincerity, would not have it so, any more than he would have it that he was a better music critic than his two colleagues, the pedantic Krehbiel and the nonsensical Finck. This illogical modesty, of course, had its limits; it made him cautious about expressing himself, but it seldom led him into downright assumptions of false personality. Nowhere in all his books will you find him doing the things that every right-thinking Anglo-Saxon critic is supposed to do—the Middleton Murry, Paul Elmer More, Clutton-Brock sort of puerility—solemn essays on Coleridge and Addison, abysmal discussions of the relative merits of Schumann and Mendelssohn, horrible treatises upon the relations of Goethe to the Romantic Movement, dull scratchings in a hundred such exhausted and sterile fields. Such enterprises were not for Huneker; he kept himself out of that black coat. But I am convinced that he always had his own raiment pressed carefully before he left Lüchow's for the temple of Athene—and maybe changed cravats, and put on a boiled shirt, and took the feather out of his hat. The simon-pure Huneker, the Huneker who was the true essence and prime motor of the more courtly Huneker—remained behind. This real Huneker survives in conversations that still haunt the rafters of the beer-halls of two continents, and in a vast mass of newspaper impromptus, thrown off too hastily to be reduced to complete decorum, and in two books that stand outside the official canon, and yet contain the man himself as not even "Iconoclasts" or the Chopin book contains him, to wit, the "Old Fogy" aforesaid and the "Painted Veils" of his last year. Both were published, so to speak, out of the back door—the former by a music publisher in Philadelphia and the latter in a small and expensive edition for the admittedly damned. There is a chapter in "Painted Veils" that is Huneker to every last hitch of the shoulders and twinkle of the eye—the chapter in which the hero soliloquizes on art, life, immortality, and women—especially women. And there are half a dozen chapters in "Old Fogy"—superficially buffoonery, but how penetrating! how gorgeously flavored! how learned!—that come completely up to the same high specification. If I had to choose one Huneker book and give up all the others, I'd choose "Old Fogy" instantly. In it Huneker is utterly himself. In it the last trace of the pedagogue vanishes. Art is no longer, even by implication, a device for improving the mind. It is wholly a magnificent adventure.

That notion of it is what Huneker brought into American criticism, and it is for that bringing that he will be remembered. No other critic of his generation had a tenth of his influence. Almost single-handed he overthrew the æsthetic theory that had flourished in the United States since the death of Poe, and set up an utterly contrary æsthetic theory in its place. If the younger men of to-day have emancipated themselves from the Puritan æsthetic, if the schoolmaster is now palpably on the defensive, and no longer the unchallenged assassin of the fine arts that he once was, if he has already begun to compromise somewhat absurdly with new and sounder ideas, and even to lift his voice in artificial hosannahs, then Huneker certainly deserves all the credit for the change. What he brought back from Paris was precisely the thing that was most suspected in the America of those days: the capacity for gusto. Huneker had that capacity in a degree unmatched by any other critic. When his soul went adventuring among masterpieces it did not go in Sunday broadcloth; it went with vine leaves in its hair. The rest of the appraisers and criers-up—even Howells, with all his humor—could never quite rid themselves of the professorial manner. When they praised it was always with some hint of ethical, or, at all events, of cultural purpose; when they condemned that purpose was even plainer. The arts, to them, constituted a sort of school for the psyche; their aim was to discipline and mellow the spirit. But to Huneker their one aim was always to make the spirit glad—to set it, in Nietzsche's phrase, to dancing with arms and legs. He had absolutely no feeling for extra-æsthetic valuations. If a work of art that stood before him was honest, if it was original, if it was beautiful and thoroughly alive, then he was for it to his last corpuscle. What if it violated all the accepted canons? Then let the accepted canons go hang! What if it lacked all purpose to improve and lift up? Then so much the better! What if it shocked all right-feeling men, and made them blush and tremble? Then damn all men of right feeling forevermore.

With this ethical atheism, so strange in the United States and so abhorrent to most Americans, there went something that was probably also part of the loot of Paris: an insatiable curiosity about the artist as man. This curiosity was responsible for two of Huneker's salient characters: his habit of mixing even the most serious criticism with cynical and often scandalous gossip, and his pervasive foreignness. I believe that it is almost literally true to say that he could never quite make up his mind about a new symphony until he had seen the composer's mistress, or at all events a good photograph of her. He thought of Wagner, not alone in terms of melody and harmony, but also in terms of the Tribschen idyl and the Bayreuth tragicomedy. Go through his books and you will see how often he was fascinated by mere eccentricity of personality. I doubt that even Huysmans, had he been a respectable French Huguenot, would have interested him; certainly his enthusiasm for Verlaine, Villiers de l'Isle Adam and other such fantastic fish was centered upon the men quite as much as upon the artists. His foreignness, so often urged against him by defenders of the national tradition, was grounded largely on the fact that such eccentric personalities were rare in the Republic—rare, and well watched by the *Polizei*. When one bobbed up, he was alert at once—even though the newcomer was only a Roosevelt. The rest of the American people he dismissed as a horde of slaves, goose-steppers, cads, Methodists; he could not imagine one of them becoming a first-rate artist, save by a miracle. Even the American executant was under his suspicion, for he knew very well that playing the fiddle was a great deal more than scraping four strings of copper and catgut with a switch from a horse's tail. What he asked himself was how a man could play Bach decently, and then, after playing, go from the hall to a soda-fountain, or a political meeting, or a lecture at the Harvard Club. Overseas there was a better air for artists, and overseas Huneker looked for them.

These fundamental theories of his, of course, had their defects. They were a bit too simple, and often very much too hospitable. Huneker, clinging to them, certainly did his share of whooping for the sort of revolutionist who is here to-day and gone tomorrow; he was fugleman, in his time, for more than one cause that was lost almost as soon as it was stated. More, his prejudices made him somewhat anæsthetic, at times, to the new men who were not brilliant in color but respectably drab, and who tried to do their work within the law. Particularly in his later years, when the old gusto began to die out and all that remained of it was habit, he was apt to go chasing after strange birds and so miss seeing the elephants go by. I could put together a very pretty list of frauds that he praised. I could concoct another list of genuine *arrivés* that he overlooked. But all that is merely saying that there were human limits to him; the professors, on their side, have sinned far worse, and in both directions. Looking back over the whole of his work, one must needs be amazed by the general soundness of his judgments. He discerned, in the main, what was good and he described it in terms that were seldom bettered afterward. His successive heroes, always under fire when he first championed them, almost invariably moved to secure ground and became solid men, challenged by no one save fools—Ibsen, Nietzsche, Brahms, Strauss, Cézanne, Stirner, Synge, the Russian composers, the Russian novelists. He did for this Western world what Georg Brandes was doing for Continental Europe—sorting out the new comers with sharp eyes, and giving mighty lifts to those who deserved it. Brandes did it in terms of the old academic bombast; he was never more the professor than when he was arguing for some hobgoblin of the professors. But Huneker did it with verve and grace; he made it, not schoolmastering, but a glorious deliverance from schoolmastering. As I say, his influence was enormous. The fine arts, at his touch, shed all their Anglo-American lugubriousness, and became provocative and joyous. The spirit of senility got out of them and the spirit of youth got into them. His criticism, for all its French basis, was thoroughly American—vastly more American, in fact, than the New England ponderosity that it displaced. Though he was an Easterner and a cockney of the cockneys, he picked up some of the Western spaciousness that showed itself in Mark Twain. And all the young men followed him.

A good many of them, I daresay, followed him so ardently that they got a good distance ahead of him, and often, perhaps, embarrassed him by taking his name in vain. For all his enterprise and iconoclasm, indeed, there was not much of the Berserker in him, and his floutings of the national æsthetic tradition seldom took the form of forthright challenges. Here the strange modesty that I have mentioned always stayed him as a like weakness stayed Mark Twain. He could never quite rid himself of the feeling that he was no more than an amateur among the gaudy doctors who roared in the reviews, and that it would be unseemly for him to forget their authority. I have a notion that this feeling was born in the days when he stood almost alone, with the whole faculty grouped in a pained circle around him. He was then too miserable a worm to be noticed at all. Later on, gaining importance, he was lectured somewhat severely for his violation of decorum; in England even Max Beerbohm made an idiotic assault upon him. It was the Germans and the French, in fact, who first praised him intelligently—and these friends were too far away to help a timorous man in a row at home. This sensation of isolation and littleness, I suppose, explains his fidelity to the newspapers, and the otherwise inexplicable joy that he always took in his forgotten work for the *Musical Courier,* in his day a very dubious journal. In such waters he felt at ease. There he could disport without thought of the dignity of publishers and the eagle eyes of campus reviewers. Some of the connections that he formed were full of an ironical inappropriateness. His discomforts in his *Puck* days showed themselves in the feebleness of his work; when he served the *Times* he was as well placed as a Cabell at a colored ball. Perhaps the *Sun,* in the years before it was munseyized, offered him the best berth that he ever had, save it were his old one on *Mlle. New York.* But whatever the flag, he served it loyally, and got a lot of fun out of the business. He liked the pressure of newspaper work; he liked the associations that it involved, the gabble in the press-room of the Opera House, the exchanges of news and gossip; above all, he liked the relative ease of the intellectual harness. In a newspaper article he could say whatever happened to pop into his mind, and if it looked thin the next day, then there was, after all, no harm done. But when he sat down to write a book—or rather to compile it, for all of his volumes were reworked magazine (and sometimes newspaper) articles—he became self-conscious, and so knew uneasiness. The tightness of his style, its one salient defect, was probably the result of this weakness. The corrected clippings that constituted most of his manuscripts are so be-laden with revisions and rerevisions that they are almost indecipherable.

Thus the growth of Huneker's celebrity in his later years filled him with wonder, and never quite convinced him. He was certainly wholly free from any desire to gather disciples about him and found a school. There was, of course, some pride of authorship in him, and he liked to know that his books were read and admired; in particular, he was pleased by their translation into German and Czech. But it seemed to me that he shrank from the bellicosity that so often got into praise of them—that he disliked being set up as the opponent and superior of the professors whom he always vaguely respected and the rival newspaper critics whose friendship he esteemed far above their professional admiration, or even respect. I could never draw him into a discussion of these rivals, save perhaps a discussion of their historic feats at beer-guzzling. He wrote vastly better than any of them and knew far more about the arts than most of them, and he was undoubtedly aware of it in his heart, but it embarrassed him to hear this superiority put into plain terms. His intense gregariousness probably accounted for part of this reluctance to pit himself against them; he could not imagine a world without a great deal of easy comradeship in it, and much casual slapping of backs. But under it all was the chronic underestimation of himself that I have discussed—his fear that he had spread himself over too many arts, and that his equipment was thus defective in every one of them. "Steeplejack" is full of this apologetic timidity. In its very title, as he explains it, there is a confession of inferiority that is almost maudlin: "Life has been the Barmecide's feast to me," and so on. In the book itself he constantly takes refuge in triviality from the harsh challenges of critical parties, and as constantly avoids facts that would shock the Philistines. One might reasonably assume, reading it from end to end, that his early days in Paris were spent in the fashion of a Y. M. C. A. secretary. A few drinking bouts, of course, and a love affair in the manner of Dubuque, Iowa—but where are the wenches?

More than once, indeed, the book sinks to downright equivocation—for example, in the Roosevelt episodes. Certainly no one who knew Huneker in life will ever argue seriously that he was deceived by the Roosevelt buncombe, or that his view of life was at all comparable to that of the great demagogue. He stood, in fact, at the opposite pole. He saw the world, not as a moral show, but as a sort of glorified Follies. He was absolutely devoid of that obsession with the problem of conduct which was Roosevelt's main virtue in the eyes of a stupid and superstitious people. More, he was wholly against Roosevelt on many concrete issues—the race suicide banality, the Panama swindle, the war. He was far too much the realist to believe in the American case, either before or after 1917, and the manner in which it was urged, by Roosevelt and others, violated his notions of truth, honor and decency. I assume nothing here; I simply record what he told me himself. Nevertheless, the sheer notoriety of the Rough Rider—his picturesque personality and talent as a mountebank—had its effect on Huneker, and so he was a bit flattered when he was summoned to Oyster Bay, and there accepted gravely the nonsense that was poured into his ear, and even repeated some of it without a cackle in his book. To say that he actually believed in it would be to libel him. It was precisely such hollow tosh that he stood against in his rôle of critic of art and life; it was by exposing its hollowness that he lifted himself above the general. The same weakness induced him to accept membership in the National Institute of Arts and Letters. The offer of it to a man of his age and attainments, after he had been passed over year after year in favor of all sorts of cheapjack novelists and tenth-rate compilers of college textbooks, was intrinsically insulting; it was almost as if the Musical Union had offered to admit a Brahms. But with the insult went a certain gage of respectability, a certain formal forgiveness for old frivolities, a certain abatement of old doubts and self-questionings and so Huneker accepted. Later on, reviewing the episode in his own mind, he found it the spring of doubts that were even more uncomfortable. His last letter to me was devoted to the matter. He was by then eager to maintain that he had got in by a process only partly under his control, and that, being in, he could discover no decorous way of getting out.

But perhaps I devote too much space to the elements in the man that worked against his own free development. They were, after all, grounded upon qualities that are certainly not to be deprecated—modesty, good-will to his fellow-men, a fine sense of team-work, a distaste for acrimonious and useless strife. These qualities gave him great charm. He was not only humorous; he was also good-humored; even when the crushing discomforts of his last illness were upon him his amiability never faltered.

And in addition to humor there was wit, a far rarer thing. His most casual talk was full of this wit, and it bathed everything that he discussed in a new and brilliant light. I have never encountered a man who was further removed from dullness; it seemed a literal impossibility for him to open his mouth without discharging some word or phrase that arrested the attention and stuck in the memory. And under it all, giving an extraordinary quality to the verbal fireworks, there was a solid and apparently illimitable learning. The man knew as much as forty average men, and his knowledge was well-ordered and instantly available. He had read everything and had seen everything and heard everything, and nothing that he had ever read or seen or heard quite passed out of his mind.

Here, in three words, was the main virtue of his criticism—its gigantic richness. It had the dazzling charm of an ornate and intricate design, a blazing fabric of fine silks. It was no mere pontifical statement of one man's reactions to a set of ideas; it was a sort of essence of the reactions of many men—of all the men, in fact, worth hearing. Huneker discarded their scaffolding, their ifs and whereases, and presented only what was important and arresting in their conclusions. It was never a mere *pastiche;* the selection was made delicately, discreetly, with almost unerring taste and judgment. And in the summing up there was always the clearest possible statement of the whole matter. What finally emerged was a body of doctrine that came, I believe, very close to the truth. Into an assembly of national critics who had long wallowed in dogmatic puerilities, Huneker entered with a taste infinitely surer and more civilized, a learning infinitely greater, and an address infinitely more engaging. No man was less the reformer by inclination, and yet he became a reformer beyond compare. He emancipated criticism in America from its old slavery to stupidity, and with it he emancipated all the arts themselves.

III. FOOTNOTE ON CRITICISM

NEARLY all the discussions of criticism that I am acquainted with start off with a false assumption, to wit, that the primary motive of the critic, the impulse which makes a critic of him instead of, say, a politician, or a stockbroker, is pedagogical—that he writes because he is possessed by a passion to advance the enlightenment, to put down error and wrong, to disseminate some specific doctrine: psychological, epistemological, historical, or æsthetic. This is true, it seems to me, only of bad critics, and its degree of truth increases in direct ratio to their badness. The motive of the critic who is really worth reading—the only critic of whom, indeed, it may be said truthfully that it is at all possible to read him, save as an act of mental discipline—is something quite different. That motive is not the motive of the pedagogue, but the motive of the artist. It is no more and no less than the simple desire to function freely and beautifully, to give outward and objective form to ideas that bubble inwardly and have a fascinating lure in them, to get rid of them dramatically and make an articulate noise in the world. It was for this reason that Plato wrote the "Republic," and for this reason that Beethoven wrote the Ninth Symphony, and it is for this reason, to drop a million miles, that I am writing the present essay. Everything else is afterthought, mock-modesty, messianic delusion—in brief, affectation and folly. Is the contrary conception of criticism widely cherished? Is it almost universally held that the thing is a brother to jurisprudence, advertising, laparotomy, chautauqua lecturing and the art of the schoolmarm? Then certainly the fact that it is so held should be sufficient to set up an overwhelming probability of its lack of truth and sense. If I speak with some heat, it is as one who has suffered. When, years ago, I devoted myself diligently to critical pieces upon the writings of Theodore Dreiser, I found that practically every one who took any notice of my proceedings at all fell into either one of two assumptions about my underlying purpose: (*a*) that I had a fanatical devotion for Mr. Dreiser's ideas and desired to propagate them, or (*b*) that I was an ardent patriot, and yearned to lift up American literature. Both assumptions were false. I had then, and I have now, very little interest in many of Mr. Dreiser's main ideas; when we meet, in fact, we usually quarrel about them. And I am wholly devoid of public spirit, and haven't the least lust to improve American literature; if it ever came to what I regard as perfection my job would be gone. What, then, was my motive in writing about Mr. Dreiser so copiously? My motive, well known to Mr. Dreiser himself and to every one else who knew me as intimately as he did, was simply and solely to sort out and give coherence to the ideas of Mr. Mencken, and to put them into suave and ingratiating terms, and to discharge them with a flourish, and maybe with a phrase of pretty song, into the dense fog that blanketed the Republic.

The critic's choice of criticism rather than of what is called creative writing is chiefly a matter of temperament—perhaps, more accurately of hormones—with accidents of education and environment to help. The feelings that happen to be dominant in him at the moment the scribbling frenzy seizes him are feelings inspired, not directly by life itself, but by books, pictures, music, sculpture, architecture, religion, philosophy—in brief, by some other man's feelings about life. They are thus, in a sense, secondhand, and it is no wonder that creative artists so easily fall into the theory that they are also second-rate. Perhaps they usually are. If, indeed, the critic continues on this plane—if he lacks the intellectual agility and enterprise needed to make the leap from the work of art to the vast and mysterious complex of phenomena behind it—then they *always* are, and he remains no more than a fugelman or policeman to his betters. But if a genuine artist is concealed within him—if his feelings are in any sense profound and original, and his capacity for self-expression is above the average of educated men—then he moves inevitably from the work of art to life itself, and begins to take on a dignity that he formerly lacked. It is impossible to think of a man of any actual force and originality, universally recognized as having those qualities, who spent his whole life appraising and describing the work of other men. Did Goethe, or Carlyle, or Matthew Arnold, or Sainte-Beuve, or Macaulay, or even, to come down a few pegs, Lewes, or Lowell, or Hazlitt? Certainly not. The thing that becomes most obvious about the writings of all such men, once they are examined carefully, is that the critic is always being swallowed up by the creative artist—that what starts out as the review of a book, or a play, or other work of art, usually develops very quickly into an independent essay upon the theme of that work of art, or upon some theme that it suggests—in a word, that it becomes a fresh work of art, and only indirectly related to the one that suggested it. This fact, indeed, is so plain that it scarcely needs statement. What the pedagogues always object to in, for example, the *Quarterly* reviewers is that they forgot the books they were supposed to review, and wrote long papers—often, in fact, small books—expounding ideas suggested (or not suggested) by the books under review. Every critic who is worth reading falls inevitably into the same habit. He cannot stick to his task: what is before him is always infinitely less interesting to him than what is within him. If he is genuinely first-rate—if what is within him stands the test of type, and wins an audience, and produces the reactions that every artist craves—then he usually ends by abandoning the criticism of specific works of art altogether, and setting up shop as a general merchant in general ideas, *i. e.*, as an artist working in the materials of life itself.

Mere reviewing, however conscientiously and competently it is done, is plainly a much inferior business. Like writing poetry, it is chiefly a function of intellectual immaturity. The young literatus just out of the university, having as yet no capacity for grappling with the fundamental mysteries of existence, is put to writing reviews of books, or plays, or music, or painting. Very often he does it extremely well; it is, in fact, not hard to do well, for even decayed pedagogues often do it, as such graves of the intellect as the New York *Times* bear witness. But if he continues to do it, whether well or ill, it is a sign to all the world that his growth ceased when they made him *Artium Baccalaureus*. Gradually he becomes, whether in or out of the academic grove, a professor, which is to say, a man devoted to diluting and retailing the ideas of his superiors—not an artist, not even a bad artist, but almost the antithesis of an artist. He is learned, he is sober, he is painstaking and accurate—but he is as hollow as a jug. Nothing is in him save the ghostly echoes of other men's thoughts and feelings. If he were a genuine artist he would have thoughts and feelings of his own, and the impulse to give them objective form would be irresistible. An artist can no more withstand that impulse than a politician can withstand the temptations of a job. There are no mute, inglorious Miltons, save in the hallucinations of poets. The one sound test of a Milton is that he functions as a Milton. His difference from other men lies precisely in the superior vigor of his impulse to self-expression, not in the superior beauty and loftiness of his ideas. Other men, in point of fact, often have the same ideas, or perhaps even loftier ones, but they are able to suppress them, usually on grounds of decorum, and so they escape being artists, and are respected by right-thinking persons, and die with money in the bank, and are forgotten in two weeks.

Obviously, the critic whose performance we are commonly called upon to investigate is a man standing somewhere along the path leading from the beginning that I have described to the goal. He has got beyond being a mere cataloguer and valuer of other men's ideas, but he has not yet become an autonomous artist—he is not yet ready to challenge attention with his own ideas alone. But it is plain that his motion, in so far as he is moving at all, must be in the direction of that autonomy—that is, unless one imagines him sliding backward into senile infantilism: a spectacle not unknown to literary pathology, but too pathetic to be discussed here. Bear this motion in mind, and the true nature of his aims and purposes becomes clear; more, the incurable falsity of the aims and purposes usually credited to him becomes equally clear. He is not actually trying to perform an impossible act of arctic justice upon the artist whose work gives him a text. He is not trying with mathematical passion to find out exactly what was in that artist's mind at the moment of creation, and to display it precisely and in an ecstasy of appreciation. He is not trying to bring the work discussed into accord with some transient theory of æsthetics, or ethics, or truth, or to determine its degree of departure from that theory. He is not trying to lift up the fine arts, or to defend democracy against sense, or to promote happiness at the domestic hearth, or to convert sophomores into right-thinkers, or to serve God. He is not trying to fit a group of novel phenomena into the orderly process of history. He is not even trying to discharge the catalytic office that I myself, in a romantic moment, once sought to force upon him. He is, first and last, simply trying to express himself. He is trying to arrest and challenge a sufficient body of readers, to make them pay attention to him, to impress them with the charm and novelty of his ideas, to provoke them into an agreeable (or shocked) awareness of him, and he is trying to achieve thereby for his own inner ego the grateful feeling of a function performed, a tension relieved, a *katharsis* attained which Wagner achieved when he wrote "Die Walküre," and a hen achieves every time she lays an egg.

Joseph Conrad is moved by that necessity to write romances; Bach was moved to write music; poets are moved to write poetry; critics are moved to write criticism. The form is nothing; the only important thing is the motive power, and it is the same in all cases. It is the pressing yearning of every man who has ideas in him to empty them upon the world, to hammer them into plausible and ingratiating shapes, to compel the attention and respect of his equals, to lord it over his inferiors. So seen, the critic becomes a far more transparent and agreeable fellow than ever he was in the discourses of the psychologists who sought to make him a mere appraiser in an intellectual customs house, a gauger in a distillery of the spirit, a just and infallible judge upon the cosmic bench. Such offices, in point of fact, never fit him. He always bulges over their confines. So labelled and estimated, it inevitably turns out that the specific critic under examination is a very bad one, or no critic at all. But when he is thought of, not as pedagogue, but as artist, then he begins to take on reality, and, what is more, dignity. Carlyle was surely no just and infallible judge; on the contrary, he was full of prejudices, biles, naïvetés, humors. Yet he is read, consulted, attended to. Macaulay was unfair, inaccurate, fanciful, lyrical—yet his essays live. Arnold had his faults too, and so did Sainte-Beauve, and so did Goethe, and so did many another of that line—and yet they are remembered to-day, and all the learned and conscientious critics of their time, laboriously concerned with the precise intent of the artists under review, and passionately determined to set it forth with god-like care and to relate it exactly to this or that great stream of ideas—all these pedants are forgotten. What saved Carlyle, Macaulay and company is as plain as day. They were first-rate artists. They could make the thing charming, and that is always a million times more important than making it true.

Truth, indeed, is something that is believed in completely only by persons who have never tried personally to pursue it to its fastnesses and grab it by the tail. It is the adoration of second-rate men—men who always receive it at second-hand. Pedagogues believe in immutable truths and spend their lives trying to determine them and propagate them; the intellectual progress of man consists largely of a concerted effort to block and destroy their enterprise. Nine times out of ten, in the arts as in life, there is actually no truth to be discovered; there is only error to be exposed. In whole departments of human inquiry it seems to me quite unlikely that the truth ever *will* be discovered. Nevertheless, the rubber-stamp thinking of the world always makes the assumption that the exposure of an error is identical with the discovery of the truth—that error and truth are simple opposites. They are nothing of the sort. What the world turns to, when it has been cured of one error, is usually simply another error, and maybe one worse than the first one. This is the whole history of the intellect in brief. The average man of to-day does not believe in precisely the same imbecilities that the Greek of the fourth century before Christ believed in, but the things that he *does* believe in are often quite as idiotic. Perhaps this statement is a bit too sweeping. There is, year by year, a gradual accumulation of what may be called, provisionally, truths—there is a slow accretion of ideas that somehow manage to meet all practicable human tests, and so survive. But even so, it is risky to call them absolute truths. All that one may safely say of them is that no one, as yet, has demonstrated that they are errors. Soon or late, if experience teaches us anything, they are likely to succumb too. The profoundest truths of the Middle Ages are now laughed at by schoolboys. The profoundest truths of democracy will be laughed at, a few centuries hence, even by school-teachers.

In the department of æsthetics, wherein critics mainly disport themselves, it is almost impossible to think of a so-called truth that shows any sign of being permanently true. The most profound of principles begins to fade and quiver almost as soon as it is stated. But the work of art, as opposed to the theory behind it, has a longer life, particularly if that theory be obscure and questionable, and so cannot be determined accurately. "Hamlet," the Mona Lisa, "Faust," "Dixie," "Parsifal," "Mother Goose," "Annabel Lee," "Huckleberry Finn"—these things, so baffling to pedagogy, so contumacious to the categories, so mysterious in purpose and utility—these things live. And why? Because there is in them the flavor of salient, novel and attractive personality, because the quality that shines from them is not that of correct demeanor but that of creative passion, because they pulse and breathe and speak, because they are genuine works of art. So with criticism. Let us forget all the heavy effort to make a science of it; it is a fine art, or nothing. If the critic, retiring to his cell to concoct his treatise upon a book or play or what-not, produces a piece of writing that shows sound structure, and brilliant color, and the flash of new and persuasive ideas, and civilized manners, and the charm of an uncommon personality in free function, then he has given something to the world that is worth having, and sufficiently justified his existence. Is Carlyle's "Frederick" true? Who cares? As well ask if the Parthenon is true, or the C Minor Symphony, or "Wiener Blut." Let the critic who is an artist leave such necropsies to professors of æsthetics, who can no more determine the truth than he can, and will infallibly make it unpleasant and a bore.

It is, of course, not easy to practice this abstention. Two forces, one within and one without, tend to bring even a Hazlitt or a Huneker under the campus pump. One is the almost universal human susceptibility to messianic delusions—the irresistible tendency of practically every man, once he finds a crowd in front of him, to strut and roll his eyes. The other is the public demand, born of such long familiarity with pedagogical criticism that no other kind is readily conceivable, that the critic teach something as well as say something—in the popular phrase, that he be constructive. Both operate powerfully against his free functioning, and especially the former. He finds it hard to resist the flattery of his customers, however little he may actually esteem it. If he knows anything at all, he knows that his following, like that of every other artist in ideas, is chiefly made up of the congenitally subaltern type of man and woman—natural converts, lodge joiners, me-toos, stragglers after circus parades. It is precious seldom that he ever gets a positive idea out of them; what he usually gets is mere unintelligent ratification. But this troop, despite its obvious failings, corrupts him in various ways. For one thing, it enormously reënforces his belief in his own ideas, and so tends to make him stiff and dogmatic—in brief, precisely everything that he ought not to be. And for another thing, it tends to make him (by a curious contradiction) a bit pliant and politic: he begins to estimate new ideas, not in proportion as they are amusing or beautiful, but in proportion as they are likely to please. So beset, front and rear, he sometimes sinks supinely to the level of a professor, and his subsequent proceedings are interesting no more. The true aim of a critic is certainly not to make converts. He must know that very few of the persons who are susceptible to conversion are worth converting. Their minds are intrinsically flabby and parasitical, and it is certainly not sound sport to agitate minds of that sort. Moreover, the critic must always harbor a grave doubt about most of the ideas that they lap up so greedily—it must occur to him not infrequently, in the silent watches of the night, that much that he writes is sheer buncombe. As I have said, I can't imagine any idea—that is, in the domain of æsthetics—that is palpably and incontrovertibly sound. All that I am familiar with, and in particular all that I announce most vociferously, seem to me to contain a core of quite obvious nonsense. I thus try to avoid cherishing them too lovingly, and it always gives me a shiver to see any one else gobble them at one gulp. Criticism, at bottom, is indistinguishable from skepticism. Both launch themselves, the one by æsthetic presentations and the other by logical presentations, at the common human tendency to accept whatever is approved, to take in ideas ready-made, to be responsive to mere rhetoric and gesticulation. A critic who believes in anything absolutely is bound to that something quite as helplessly as a Christian is bound to the Freudian garbage in the Book of Revelation. To that extent, at all events, he is unfree and unintelligent, and hence a bad critic.

The demand for "constructive" criticism is based upon the same false assumption that immutable truths exist in the arts, and that the artist will be improved by being made aware of them. This notion, whatever the form it takes, is always absurd—as much so, indeed, as its brother delusion that the critic, to be competent, must be a practitioner of the specific art he ventures to deal with, *i. e.*, that a doctor, to cure a belly-ache, must have a belly-ache. As practically encountered, it is disingenuous as well as absurd, for it comes chiefly from bad artists who tire of serving as performing monkeys, and crave the greater ease and safety of sophomores in class. They demand to be taught in order to avoid being knocked about. In their demand is the theory that instruction, if they could get it, would profit them—that they are capable of doing better work than they do. As a practical matter, I doubt that this is ever true. Bad poets never actually grow any better; they invariably grow worse and worse. In all history there has never been, to my knowledge, a single practitioner of any art who, as a result of "constructive" criticism, improved his work. The curse of all the arts, indeed, is the fact that they are constantly invaded by persons who are not artists at all—persons whose yearning to express their ideas and feelings is unaccompanied by the slightest capacity for charming expression—in brief, persons with absolutely nothing to say. This is particularly true of the art of letters, which interposes very few technical obstacles to the vanity and garrulity of such invaders. Any effort to teach them to write better is an effort wasted, as every editor discovers for himself; they are as incapable of it as they are of jumping over the moon. The only sort of criticism that can deal with them to any profit is the sort that employs them frankly as laboratory animals. It cannot cure them, but it can at least make an amusing and perhaps edifying show of them. It is idle to argue that the good in them is thus destroyed with the bad. The simple answer is that there *is* no good in them. Suppose Poe had wasted his time trying to dredge good work out of Rufus Dawes, author of "Geraldine." He would have failed miserably—and spoiled a capital essay, still diverting after three-quarters of a century. Suppose Beethoven, dealing with Gottfried Weber, had tried laboriously to make an intelligent music critic of him. How much more apt, useful and durable the simple note: "Arch-ass! Double-barrelled ass!" Here was absolutely sound criticism. Here was a judgment wholly beyond challenge. Moreover, here was a small but perfect work of art.

Upon the low practical value of so-called constructive criticism I can offer testimony out of my own experience. My books are commonly reviewed at great length, and many critics devote themselves to pointing out what they conceive to be my errors, both of fact and of taste. Well, I cannot recall a case in which any suggestion offered by a constructive critic has helped me in the slightest, or even actively interested me. Every such wet-nurse of letters has sought fatuously to make me write in a way differing from that in which the Lord God Almighty, in His infinite wisdom, impels me to write—that is, to make me write stuff which, coming from me, would be as false as an appearance of decency in a Congressman. All the benefits I have ever got from the critics of my work have come from the destructive variety. A hearty slating always does me good, particularly if it be well written. It begins by enlisting my professional respect; it ends by making me examine my ideas coldly in the privacy of my chamber. Not, of course, that I usually revise them, but I at least examine them. If I decide to hold fast to them, they are all the dearer to me thereafter, and I expound them with a new passion and plausibility. If, on the contrary, I discern holes in them, I shelve them in a *pianissimo* manner, and set about hatching new ones to take their place. But constructive criticism irritates me. I do not object to being denounced, but I can't abide being school-mastered, especially by men I regard as imbeciles.

I find, as a practicing critic, that very few men who write books are even as tolerant as I am—that most of them, soon or late, show signs of extreme discomfort under criticism, however polite its terms. Perhaps this is why enduring friendships between authors and critics are so rare. All artists, of course, dislike one another more or less, but that dislike seldom rises to implacable enmity, save between opera singer and opera singer, and creative author and critic. Even when the latter two keep up an outward show of good-will, there is always bitter antagonism under the surface. Part of it, I daresay, arises out of the impossible demands of the critic, particularly if he be tinged with the constructive madness. Having favored an author with his good opinion, he expects the poor fellow to live up to that good opinion without the slightest compromise or faltering, and this is commonly beyond human power. He feels that any let-down compromises *him*—that his hero is stabbing him in the back, and making him ridiculous—and this feeling rasps his vanity. The most bitter of all literary quarrels are those between critics and creative artists, and most of them arise in just this way. As for the creative artist, he on his part naturally resents the critic's air of pedagogical superiority and he resents it especially when he has an uneasy feeling that he has fallen short of his best work, and that the discontent of the critic is thus justified. Injustice is relatively easy to bear; what stings is justice. Under it all, of course, lurks the fact that I began with: the fact that the critic is himself an artist, and that his creative impulse, soon or late, is bound to make him neglect the punctilio. When he sits down to compose his criticism, his artist ceases to be a friend, and becomes mere raw material for his work of art. It is my experience that artists invariably resent this cavalier use of them. They are pleased so long as the critic confines himself to the modest business of interpreting them—preferably in terms of their own estimate of themselves—but the moment he proceeds to adorn their theme with variations of his own, the moment he brings new ideas to the enterprise and begins contrasting them with their ideas, that moment they grow restive. It is precisely at this point, of course, that criticism becomes genuine criticism; before that it was mere reviewing. When a critic passes it he loses his friends. By becoming an artist, he becomes the foe of all other artists.

But the transformation, I believe, has good effects upon him: it makes him a better critic. Too much *Gemütlichkeit* is as fatal to criticism as it would be to surgery or politics. When it rages unimpeded it leads inevitably either to a dull professorial sticking on of meaningless labels or to log-rolling, and often it leads to both. One of the most hopeful symptoms of the new *Aufklärung* in the Republic is the revival of acrimony in criticism—the renaissance of the doctrine that æsthetic matters are important, and that it is worth the while of a healthy male to take them seriously, as he takes business, sport and amour. In the days when American literature was showing its first vigorous growth, the native criticism was extraordinarily violent and even vicious; in the days when American literature swooned upon the tomb of the Puritan *Kultur* it became flaccid and childish. The typical critic of the first era was Poe, as the typical critic of the second was Howells. Poe carried on his critical jehads with such ferocity that he often got into law-suits, and sometimes ran no little risk of having his head cracked. He regarded literary questions as exigent and momentous. The lofty aloofness of the don was simply not in him. When he encountered a book that seemed to him to be bad, he attacked it almost as sharply as a Chamber of Commerce would attack a fanatic preaching free speech, or the corporation of Trinity Church would attack Christ. His opponents replied in the same Berserker manner. Much of Poe's surviving ill-fame, as a drunkard and dead-beat, is due to their inordinate denunciations of him. They were not content to refute him; they constantly tried to dispose of him altogether. The very ferocity of that ancient row shows that the native literature, in those days, was in a healthy state. Books of genuine value were produced. Literature always thrives best, in fact, in an atmosphere of hearty strife. Poe, surrounded by admiring professors, never challenged, never aroused to the emotions of revolt, would probably have written poetry indistinguishable from the hollow stuff of, say, Prof. Dr. George E. Woodberry. It took the persistent (and often grossly unfair and dishonorable) opposition of Griswold *et al* to stimulate him to his highest endeavors. He needed friends, true enough, but he also needed enemies.

To-day, for the first time in years, there is strife in American criticism, and the Paul Elmer Mores and Hamilton Wright Mabies are no longer able to purr in peace. The instant they fall into stiff professorial attitudes they are challenged, and often with anything but urbanity. The *ex cathedra* manner thus passes out, and free discussion comes in. Heretics lay on boldly, and the professors are forced to make some defense. Often, going further, they attempt counter-attacks. Ears are bitten off. Noses are bloodied. There are wallops both above and below the belt. I am, I need not say, no believer in any magical merit in debate, no matter how free it may be. It certainly does not necessarily establish the truth; both sides, in fact, may be wrong, and they often are. But it at least accomplishes two important effects. On the one hand, it exposes all the cruder fallacies to hostile examination, and so disposes of many of them. And on the other hand, it melodramatizes the business of the critic, and so convinces thousands of bystanders, otherwise quite inert, that criticism is an amusing and instructive art, and that the problems it deals with are important. What men will fight for seems to be worth looking into.

IV. DAS KAPITAL

AFTER a hearty dinner of *potage créole*, planked Chesapeake shad, Guinea hen *en casserole* and some respectable salad, with two or three cocktails made of two-thirds gin, one-third Martini-Rossi vermouth and a dash of absinthe as *Vorspiel* and a bottle of Ruhländer 1903 to wash it down, the following thought often bubbles up from my subconscious: that many of the acknowledged evils of capitalism, now so horribly visible in the world, are not due primarily to capitalism itself but rather to democracy, that universal murrain of Christendom.

What I mean, in brief, is that capitalism, under democracy, is constantly under hostile pressure and often has its back to the wall, and that its barbaric manners and morals, at least in large part, are due to that fact—that they are, in essence, precisely the same manners and morals that are displayed by any other creature or institution so beset. Necessity is not only the mother of invention; it is also the mother of every imaginable excess and infamy. A woman defending her child is notoriously willing to go to lengths that even a Turk or an agent of the Department of Justice would regard as inordinate, and so is a Presbyterian defending his hell, or a soldier defending his fatherland, or a banker defending his gold. It is only when there is no danger that the average human being is honorable, just as it is only when there *is* danger that he is virtuous. He would commit adultery every day if it were safe, and he would commit murder every day if it were necessary.

The essential thing about democracy, as every one must know, is that it is a device for strengthening and heartening the have-nots in their eternal war upon the haves. That war, as every one knows again, has its psychological springs in envy pure and simple—envy of the more fortunate man's greater wealth, the superior pulchritude of his wife or wives, his larger mobility and freedom, his more protean capacity for and command of happiness—in brief, his better chance to lead a bearable life in this worst of possible worlds. It follows that under democracy, which gives a false power and importance to the have-nots by counting every one of them as the legal equal of George Washington or Beethoven, the process of government consists largely, and sometimes almost exclusively, of efforts to spoil that advantage artificially. Trust-busting, free silver, direct elections,

Prohibition, government ownership and all the other varieties of American political quackery are but symptoms of the same general rage. It is the rage of the have-not against the have, of the farmer who must drink hard cider and forty-rod against the city man who may drink Burgundy and Scotch, of the poor fellow who must stay at home looking at a wife who regards the lip-stick as lewd and lascivious against the lucky fellow who may go to Atlantic City or Palm Beach and ride up and down in a wheel-chair with a girl who knows how to make up and has put away the fear of God.

The ignobler sort of men, of course, are too stupid to understand various rare and exhilarating sorts of superiority, and so they do not envy the happiness that goes with them. If they could enter into the mind of a Wagner or a Brahms and begin to comprehend the stupendous joy that such a man gets out of the practice of his art, they would pass laws against it and make a criminal of him, as they have already made criminals, in the United States, of the man with a civilized taste for wines, the man so attractive to women that he can get all the wives he wants without having to marry them, and the man who can make pictures like Félicien Rops, or books like Flaubert, Zola, Dreiser, Cabell or Rabelais. Wagner and Brahms escape, and their arts with them, because the great masses of men cannot understand the sort of thing they try to do, and hence do not envy the man who does it well, and gets joy out of it. It is much different with, say, Rops. Every American Congressman, as a small boy, covered the fence of the Sunday-School yard with pictures in the manner of Rops. What he now remembers of the business is that the pictures were denounced by the superintendent, and that he was cowhided for making them; what he hears about Rops, when he hears at all, is that the fellow is vastly esteemed, and hence probably full of a smug æsthetic satisfaction. In consequence, it is unlawful in the United States to transmit the principal pictures of Rops by mail, or, indeed, "to have and possess" them. The man who owns them must conceal them from the *okhrána* of the Department of Justice just as carefully as he conceals the wines and whiskeys in his cellar, or the poor working girl he transports from the heat and noise of New York to the salubrious calm of the Jersey coast, or his hand-tooled library set of the "Contes Drôlatiques," or his precious first edition of "Jurgen."

But, as I say, the democratic pressure in such directions is relatively feeble, for there are whole categories of more or less æsthetic superiority and happiness that the democrat cannot understand at all, and is in consequence virtually unaware of. It is far different with the varieties of superiority and happiness that are the functions of mere money. Here the democrat is extraordinarily alert and appreciative. He can not only imagine hundreds of ways of getting happiness out of money; he devotes almost the whole of his intellectual activity, such as it is, to imagining them, and he seldom if ever imagines anything else. Even his sexual fancies translate themselves instantly into concepts of dollars and cents; the thing that confines him so miserably to one wife, and to one, alas, so unappetizing and depressing, is simply his lack of money; if he only had the wealth of Diamond Jim Brady he too would be the glittering Don Giovanni that Jim was. All the known species of democratic political theory are grounded firmly upon this doctrine that money, and money only, makes the mare go—that all the conceivable varieties of happiness are possible to the man who has it. Even the Socialists, who profess to scorn money, really worship it. Socialism, indeed, is simply the degenerate capitalism of bankrupt capitalists. Its one genuine object is to get more money for its professors; all its other grandiloquent objects are afterthoughts, and most of them are bogus. The democrats of other schools pursue the same single aim—and adorn it with false pretenses even more transparent. In the United States the average democrat, I suppose, would say that the establishment and safeguarding of liberty was the chief purpose of democracy. The theory is mere wind. The average American democrat really cares nothing whatever for liberty, and is always willing to sell it for money. What he actually wants, and strives to get by his politics, is more money. His fundamental political ideas nearly all contemplate restraints and raids upon capital, even when they appear superficially to be quite free from economic flavor, and most of the political banshees and bugaboos that alternately freeze and boil his blood have dollar marks written all over them. There is no need to marshal a long catalogue of examples from English and American political history: I simply defy any critic of my doctrine to find a single issue of genuine appeal to the populace, at any time during the past century, that did not involve a more or less obvious scheme for looting a minority—the slave-owners, Wall Street, the railroads, the dukes, or some other group representing capital. Even the most affecting idealism of the plain people has a thrifty basis. In the United States, during the early part of the late war, they were very cynical about the Allied cause; it was not until the war orders of the Allies raised their wages that they began to believe in the noble righteousness of Lloyd-George and company. And after Dr. Wilson had jockeyed the United States itself into the war, and the cost of living began to increase faster than wages, he faced a hostile country until he restored altruism by his wholesale bribery of labor.

It is my contention that the constant exposure of capitalism to such primitive lusts and forays is what makes it so lamentably extortionate and unconscionable in democratic countries, and particularly in the United States. The capitalist, warned by experience, collars all he can while the getting is good, regardless of the commonest honesty and decorum, because he is haunted by an uneasy feeling that his season will not be long. His dominating passion is to pile up the largest amount of capital possible, by fair means or foul, so that he will have ample reserves when the next raid comes, and he has to use part of it to bribe one part of the proletariat against the other. In the long run, of course, he always wins, for this bribery is invariably feasible; in the United States, indeed, every fresh struggle leaves capital more secure than it was before. But though the capitalist thus has no reason to fear actual defeat and disaster, he is well aware that victory is always expensive, and his natural prudence causes him to discount the cost in advance, even when he has planned to shift it to other shoulders. I point, in example, to the manner in which capital dealt with the discharged American soldiers after the war. Its first effort was to cajole them into its service, as they had been cajoled by the politicians after the Civil War. To this end, it borrowed the machine erected by Dr. Wilson and his agents for debauching the booboisie during the actual war, and by the skillful use of that machine it quickly organized the late conscripts into the American Legion, alarmed them with lies about a Bolshevist scheme to make slaves of them (*i. e.*, to cut off forever their hope of getting money), and put them to clubbing and butchering their fellow proletarians. The business done, the conscripts found themselves out of jobs: their gallant war upon Bolshevism had brought down wages, and paralysed organized labor. They now demanded pay for their work, and capital had to meet the demand. It did so by promising them a bonus—*i. e.*, loot—out of the public treasury, and by straightway inventing a scheme whereby the ultimate cost would fall chiefly upon poor folk.

Throughout the war, indeed, capital exhibited an inordinately extortionate spirit, and thereby revealed its underlying dread. First it robbed the Allies in the manner of bootleggers looting a country distillery, then it swindled the plain people at home by first bribing them with huge wages and then taking away all their profits and therewith all their savings, and then it seized and made away with the impounded property of enemy nationals—property theoretically held in trust for them, and the booty, if it was booty at all, of the whole American people. This triple burglary was excessive, to be sure, but who will say that it was not prudent? The capitalists of the Republic are efficient, and have foresight. They saw some lean and hazardous years ahead, with all sorts of raids threatening. They took measures to fortify their position. To-day their prevision is their salvation. They are losing some of their accumulation, of course, but they still have enough left to finance an effective defense of the remainder. There was never any time in the history of any country, indeed, when capital was so securely intrenched as it is to-day in the United States. It has divided the proletariat into two bitterly hostile halves, it has battered and crippled unionism almost beyond recognition, it has a firm grip upon all three arms of the government, and it controls practically every agency for the influencing of public opinion, from the press to the church. Had it been less prudent when times were good, and put its trust in God alone, the I. W. W. would have rushed it at the end of the war.

As I say, I often entertain the thought that it would be better, in the long run, to make terms with a power so hard to resist, and thereby purge it of its present compulsory criminality. I doubt that capitalists, as a class, are naturally vicious; certainly they are no more vicious than, say, lawyers and politicians—upon whom the plain people commonly rely, in their innocence, to save them. I have known a good many men of great wealth in my time, and most of them have been men showing all the customary decencies. They deplore the harsh necessities of their profession quite as honestly as a judge deplores the harsh necessities of his. You will never convince me that the average American banker, during the war, got anything properly describable as professional satisfaction out of selling Liberty bonds at 100 to poor stenographers, and then buying them back at 83. He knew that he'd need his usurious profit against the blue day when the boys came home, and so he took it, but it would have given him ten times as much pleasure if it had come from the reluctant gizzard of some other banker. In brief, there is a pride of workmanship in capitalists, just as there is in all other men above the general. They get the same spiritual lift out of their sordid swindles that Swinburne got out of composing his boozy dithyrambs, and I often incline to think that it is quite as worthy of respect. In a democratic society, with the arts adjourned and the sciences mere concubines of money, it is chiefly the capitalists, in fact, who keep pride of workmanship alive. In their principal enemies, the trades-unionists, it is almost extinct. Unionism seldom, if ever, uses such power as it has to insure better work; almost always it devotes a large part of that power to safeguarding bad work. A union man who, moved by professional pride, put any extra effort into his job would probably be punished by his union as a sort of scab. But a capitalist is still able to cherish some of the old spirit of the guildsman. If he invents a new device for corralling the money of those who have earned it, or operates an old device in some new and brilliant way, he is honored and envied by his colleagues. The late J. Pierpont Morgan was thus honored and envied, not because he made more actual money than any other capitalist of his time—in point of fact, he made a good deal less than some, and his own son, a much inferior man, has made more since his death than he did during his whole life—but because his operations showed originality, daring, coolness, and imagination—in brief, because he was a great virtuoso in the art he practiced.

What I contend is that the democratic system of government would be saner and more effective in its dealings with capital if it ceased to regard all capitalists as criminals *ipso facto*, and thereby ceased to make their armed pursuit the chief end of practical politics—if it gave over this vain effort to put them down by force, and tried to bring them to decency by giving greater play and confidence to the pride of workmanship that I have described. They would be less ferocious and immoderate, I think, if they were treated with less hostility, and put more upon their conscience and honor. No doubt the average democrat, brought up upon the prevailing superstitions and prejudices of his faith, will deny at once that they are actually capable of conscience or honor, or that they have any recognizable pride of workmanship. Well, let him deny it. He will make precisely the same denial with respect to kings. Nevertheless, it must be plain to every one who has read history attentively that the majority of the kings of the past, even when no criticism could reach them, showed a very great pride of workmanship—that they tried to be good kings even when it was easier to be bad ones. The same thing is true of the majority of capitalists —the kings of to-day. They are criminals by our democratic law, but their criminality is chiefly artificial and theoretical, like that of a bootlegger. If it were abolished by repealing the laws which create it—if it became legally just as virtuous to organize and operate a great industrial corporation, or to combine and rehabilitate railroads, or to finance any other such transactions as it is to organize a trades-union, a *Bauverein,* or a lodge of Odd Fellows—then I believe that capitalists would forthwith abandon a great deal of the scoundrelism which now marks their proceedings, that they could be trusted to police their order at least as vigilantly as physicians or lawyers police theirs, and that the activities of those members of it who showed no pride of workmanship at all would be effectively curbed.

The legal war upon them under democracy is grounded upon the false assumption that it would be possible, given laws enough, to get rid of them altogether. The *Ur*-Americanos, who set the tone of our legislation and provided examples for the legislation of every other democratic country, were chiefly what would be called Bolsheviki to-day. They dreamed of a republic wholly purged of capitalism—and taxes. They were have-nots of the most romantic and ambitious variety, and saw Utopia before them. Every man of their time who thought capitalistically—that is, who believed that things consumed had to be paid for—was a target for their revilings: for example, Alexander Hamilton. But they were wrong, and their modern heirs and assigns are wrong just as surely. That wrongness of theirs, in truth, has grown enormously since it was launched, for the early Americans were a pastoral people, and could get along with very little capital, whereas the Americans of to-day lead a very complex life, and need the aid of capitalism at almost every breath they draw. Most of their primary necessities—the railroad, the steamship lines, the trolley car, the telephone, refrigerated meats, machine-made clothes, phonograph records, moving-picture shows, and so on—are wholly unthinkable save as the products of capital in large aggregations. No man of to-day can imagine doing without them, or getting them without the aid of such aggregations. The most even the wildest Socialist can think of is to take the capital away from the capitalists who now have it and hand it over to the state—in other words, to politicians. A century ago there were still plenty of men who, like Thoreau, proposed to abolish it altogether. But now even the radicals of the extreme left assume as a matter of course that capital is indispensible, and that abolishing it or dispersing it would cause a collapse of civilization.

What ails democracy, in the economic department, is that it proceeds upon the assumption that the contrary is true—that it seeks to bring capitalism to a state of innocuous virtue by grossly exaggerating its viciousness—that it penalizes ignorantly what is, at bottom, a perfectly natural and legitimate aspiration, and one necessary to society. Such penalizings, I need not argue, never destroy the impulse itself; surely the American experience with Prohibition should make even a democrat aware of that. What they do is simply to make it evasive, intemperate, and relentless. If it were legally as hazardous in the United States to play a string quartette as it is to build up a great bank or industrial enterprise—if the performers, struggling with their parts, had to watch the windows in constant fear that a Bryan, a Roosevelt, a Lloyd-George or some other such predatory mountebank would break in, armed with a club and followed by a rabble—then string quartette players would become as devious and anti-social in their ways as the average American capitalist is today, and when, by a process of setting one part of the mob against the rest, they managed to get a chance to play quartettes in temporary peace, despite the general mob hatred of them, they would forget the lovely music of Haydn and Mozart altogether, and devote their whole time to a *fortissimo* playing of the worst musical felonies of Schönberg, Ravel and Strawinsky.

V. AD IMAGINEM DEI CREAVIT ILLUM

I

The Life of Man

THE old anthropomorphic notion that the life of the whole universe centers in the life of man—that human existence is the supreme expression of the cosmic process—this notion seems to be on its way toward the Sheol of exploded delusions. The fact is that the life of man, as it is more and more studied in the light of general biology, appears to be more and more empty of significance. Once apparently the chief concern and masterpiece of the gods, the human race now begins to bear the aspect of an accidental by-product of their vast, inscrutable and probably nonsensical operations. A blacksmith making a horse-shoe produces something almost as brilliant and mysterious—the shower of sparks. But his eye and thought, as we know, are not on the sparks, but on the horse-shoe. The sparks, indeed, constitute a sort of disease of the horse-shoe; their existence depends upon a wasting of its tissue. In the same way, perhaps, man is a local disease of the cosmos—a kind of pestiferous eczema or urethritis. There are, of course, different grades of eczema, and so are there different grades of men. No doubt a cosmos afflicted with nothing worse than an infection of Beethovens would not think it worth while to send for the doctor. But a cosmos infested by prohibitionists, Socialists, Scotsmen and stockbrokers must suffer damnably. No wonder the sun is so hot and the moon is so diabetically green!

2

The Anthropomorphic Delusion

As I say, the anthropomorphic theory of the world is made absurd by modern biology—but that is not saying, of course, that it will ever be abandoned by the generality of men. To the contrary, they will cherish it in proportion as it becomes more and more dubious. To-day, indeed, it is cherished as it was never cherished in the Ages of Faith, when the doctrine that man was god-like was at least ameliorated by the doctrine that woman was vile. What else is behind charity, philanthropy, pacifism, Socialism, the uplift, all the rest of the current sentimentalities? One and all, these sentimentalities are based upon the notion that man is a glorious and ineffable animal, and that his continued existence in the world ought to be facilitated and insured. But this notion is obviously full of fatuity. As animals go, even in so limited a space as our world, man is botched and ridiculous. Few other brutes are so stupid or so cowardly. The commonest yellow dog has far sharper senses and is infinitely more courageous, not to say more honest and dependable. The ants and the bees are, in many ways, far more intelligent and ingenious; they manage their government with vastly less quarreling, wastefulness and imbecility. The lion is more beautiful, more dignified, more majestic. The antelope is swifter and more graceful. The ordinary house-cat is cleaner. The horse, foamed by labor, has a better smell. The gorilla is kinder to his children and more faithful to his wife. The ox and the ass are more industrious and serene. But most of all, man is deficient in courage, perhaps the noblest quality of them all. He is not only mortally afraid of all other animals of his own weight or half his weight—save a few that he has debased by artificial inbreeding—; he is even mortally afraid of his own kind—and not only of their fists and hooves, but even of their sniggers.

No other animal is so defectively adapted to its environment. The human infant, as it comes into the world, is so puny that if it were neglected for two days running it would infallibly perish, and this congenital infirmity, though more or less concealed later on, persists until death. Man is ill far more than any other animal, both in his savage state and under civilization. He has more different diseases and he suffers from them oftener. He is easier exhausted and injured. He dies more horribly and usually sooner. Practically all the other higher vertebrates, at least in their wild state, live longer and retain their faculties to a greater age. Here even the anthropoid apes are far beyond their human cousins. An orang-outang marries at the age of seven or eight, raises a family of seventy or eighty children, and is still as hale and hearty at eighty as a European at forty-five.

All the errors and incompetencies of the Creator reach their climax in man. As a piece of mechanism he is the worst of them all; put beside him, even a salmon or a staphylococcus is a sound and efficient machine. He has the worst kidneys known to comparative zoölogy, and the worst lungs, and the worst heart. His eye, considering the work it is called upon to do, is less efficient than the eye of an earthworm; an optical instrument maker who made an instrument so clumsy would be mobbed by his customers. Alone of all animals, terrestrial, celestial or marine, man is unfit by nature to go abroad in the world he inhabits. He must clothe himself, protect himself, swathe himself, armor himself. He is eternally in the position of a turtle born without a shell, a dog without hair, a fish without fins. Lacking his heavy and cumbersome trappings, he is defenseless even against flies. As God made him he hasn't even a tail to switch them off.

I now come to man's one point of unquestionable natural superiority: he has a soul. This is what sets him off from all other animals, and makes him, in a way, their master. The exact nature of that soul has been in dispute for thousands of years, but regarding its function it is possible to speak with some authority. That function is to bring man into direct contact with God, to make him aware of God, above all, to make him resemble God. Well, consider the colossal failure of the device! If we assume that man actually does resemble God, then we are forced into the impossible theory that God is a coward, an idiot and a bounder. And if we assume that man, after all these years, does *not* resemble God, then it appears at once that the human soul is as inefficient a machine as the human liver or tonsil, and that man would probably be better off, as the chimpanzee undoubtedly *is* better off, without it.

Such, indeed, is the case. The only practical effect of having a soul is that it fills man with anthropomorphic and anthropocentric vanities—in brief with cocky and preposterous superstitions.

He struts and plumes himself because he has this soul—and overlooks the fact that it doesn't work. Thus he is the supreme clown of creation, the *reductio ad absurdum* of animated nature. He is like a cow who believed that she could jump over the moon, and ordered her whole life upon that theory. He is like a bullfrog boasting eternally of fighting lions, of flying over the Matterhorn, and of swimming the Hellespont. And yet this is the poor brute we are asked to venerate as a gem in the forehead of the cosmos! This is the worm we are asked to defend as God's favorite on earth, with all its millions of braver, nobler, decenter quadrupeds—its superb lions, its lithe and gallant leopards, its imperial elephants, its honest dogs, its courageous rats! This is the insect we are besought, at infinite trouble, labor and expense, to reproduce!

3

Meditation on Meditation.

Man's capacity for abstract thought, which most other mammals seem to lack, has undoubtedly given him his present mastery of the land surface of the earth—a mastery disputed only by several hundred species of microscopic organisms. It is responsible for his feeling of superiority, and under that feeling there is undoubtedly a certain measure of reality, at least within narrow limits. But what is too often overlooked is that the capacity to perform an act is by no means synonymous with its salubrious exercise. The simple fact is that most of man's thinking is stupid, pointless, and injurious to him. Of all animals, indeed, he seems the least capable of arriving at accurate judgments in the matters that most desperately affect his welfare. Try to imagine a rat, in the realm of rat ideas, arriving at a notion as violently in contempt of plausibility as the notion, say, of Swedenborgianism, or that of homeopathy, or that of infant damnation, or that of mental telepathy. Try to think of a congregation of educated rats gravely listening to such disgusting intellectual rubbish as was in the public bulls of Dr. Woodrow Wilson. Man's natural instinct, in fact, is never toward what is sound and true; it is toward what is specious and false. Let any great nation of modern times be confronted by two conflicting propositions, the one grounded upon the utmost probability and reasonableness and the other upon the most glaring error, and it will almost invariably embrace the latter. It is so in politics, which consists wholly of a succession of unintelligent crazes, many of them so idiotic that they exist only as battle-cries and shibboleths and are not reducible to logical statement at all. It is so in religion, which, like poetry, is simply a concerted effort to deny the most obvious realities. It is so in nearly every field of thought. The ideas that conquer the race most rapidly and arouse the wildest enthusiasm and are held most tenaciously are precisely the ideas that are most insane. This has been true since the first "advanced" gorilla put on underwear, cultivated a frown and began his first lecture tour in the first chautauqua, and it will be so until the high gods, tired of the farce at last, obliterate the race with one great, final blast of fire, mustard gas and streptococci.

No doubt the imagination of man is to blame for this singular weakness. That imagination, I daresay, is what gave him his first lift above his fellow primates. It enabled him to visualize a condition of existence better than that he was experiencing, and bit by bit he was able to give the picture a certain crude reality. Even to-day he keeps on going ahead in the same manner. That is, he thinks of something that he would like to be or to get, something appreciably better than what he is or has, and then, by the laborious, costly method of trial and error, he gradually moves toward it. In the process he is often severely punished for his discontent with God's ordinances. He mashes his thumb, he skins his shin; he stumbles and falls; the prize he reaches out for blows up in his hands. But bit by bit he moves on, or, at all events, his heirs and assigns move on. Bit by bit he smooths the path beneath his remaining leg, and achieves pretty toys for his remaining hand to play with, and accumulates delights for his remaining ear and eye.

Alas, he is not content with this slow and sanguinary progress! Always he looks further and further ahead. Always he imagines things just over the sky-line. This body of imaginings constitutes his stock of sweet beliefs, his corpus of high faiths and confidences—in brief, his burden of errors. And that burden of errors is what distinguishes man, even above his capacity for tears, his talents as a liar, his excessive hypocrisy and poltroonery, from all the other orders of mammalia. Man is the yokel *par excellence,* the booby unmatchable, the king dupe of the cosmos. He is chronically and unescapably deceived, not only by the other animals and by the delusive face of nature herself, but also and more particularly by himself—by his incomparable talent for searching out and embracing what is false, and for overlooking and denying what is true.

The capacity for discerning the essential truth, in fact, is as rare among men as it is common among crows, bullfrogs and mackerel. The man who shows it is a man of quite extraordinary quality—perhaps even a man downright diseased. Exhibit a new truth of any natural plausibilty before the great masses of men, and not one in ten thousand will suspect its existence, and not one in a hundred thousand will embrace it without a ferocious resistance. All the durable truths that have come into the world within historic times have been opposed as bitterly as if they were so many waves of smallpox, and every individual who has welcomed and advocated them, absolutely without exception, has been denounced and punished as an enemy of the race. Perhaps "absolutely without exception" goes too far. I substitute "with five or six exceptions." But who were the five or six exceptions? I leave you to think of them; myself, I can't. . . . But I think at once of Charles Darwin and his associates, and of how they were reviled in their time. This reviling, of course, is less vociferous than it used to be, chiefly because later victims are in the arena, but the underlying hostility remains. Within the past two years the principal Great Thinker of Britain, George Bernard Shaw, has denounced the hypothesis of natural selection to great applause, and a three-times candidate for the American Presidency, William Jennings Bryan, has publicly advocated prohibiting the teaching of it by law. The great majority of Christian ecclesiastics in both English-speaking countries, and with them the great majority of their catachumens, are still committed to the doctrine that Darwin was a scoundrel, and Herbert Spencer another, and Huxley a third—and that Nietzsche is to the three of them what Beelzebub himself is to a trio of bad boys.

This is the reaction of the main body of respectable folk in two puissant and idealistic Christian nations to the men who will live in history as the intellectual leaders of the Nineteenth Century. This is the immemorial attitude of men in the mass, and of their chosen prophets, to whatever is honest, and important, and most probably true.

But if truth thus has hard sledding, error is given a loving welcome. The man who invents a new imbecility is hailed gladly, and bidden to make himself at home; he is, to the great masses of men, the *beau ideal* of mankind. Go back through the history of the past thousand years and you will find that nine-tenths of the popular idols of the world—not the heroes of small sects, but the heroes of mankind in the mass—have been merchants of palpable nonsense. It has been so in politics, it has been so in religion, and it has been so in every other department of human thought. Every such hawker of the not-true has been opposed, in his time, by critics who denounced and refuted him; his contention has been disposed of immediately it was uttered. But on the side of every one there has been the titanic force of human credulity, and it has sufficed in every case to destroy his foes and establish his immortality.

4

Man and His Soul

Of all the unsound ideas thus preached by great heroes and accepted by hundreds of millions of their eager dupes, probably the most patently unsound is the one that is most widely held, to wit, the idea that man has an immortal soul—that there is a part of him too ethereal and too exquisite to die. Absolutely the only evidence supporting this astounding notion lies in the hope that it is true—which is precisely the evidence underlying the late theory that the Great War would put an end to war, and bring in an era of democracy, freedom, and peace. But even archbishops, of course, are too intelligent to be satisfied permanently by evidence so unescapably dubious; in consequence, there have been efforts in all ages to give it logical and evidential support. Well, all I ask is that you give some of that corroboration your careful scrutiny. Examine, for example, the proofs amassed by five typical witnesses in five widely separated ages: St. John, St. Augustine, Martin Luther, Emanuel Swedenborg and Sir Oliver Lodge. Approach these proofs prayerfully, and study them well. Weigh them in the light of the probabilities, the ordinary intellectual decencies. And then ask yourself if you could imagine a mud-turtle accepting them gravely.

5

Coda

To sum up:

1. The cosmos is a gigantic fly-wheel making 10,000 revolutions a minute.
2. Man is a sick fly taking a dizzy ride on it.
3. Religion is the theory that the wheel was designed and set spinning to give him the ride.

VI. STAR-SPANGLED MEN

I OPEN the memoirs of General Grant, Volume II, at the place where he is describing the surrender of General Lee, and find the following:

> I was without a sword, as I usually was when on horseback on (*sic*) the field, and wore a soldier's blouse for a coat, with the shoulder straps of my rank to indicate to the army who I was.

Anno 1865. I look out of my window and observe an officer of the United States Army passing down the street. Anno 1922. Like General Grant, he is without a sword. Like General Grant, he wears a sort of soldier's blouse for a coat. Like General Grant, he employs shoulder straps to indicate to the army who he is. But there is something more. On the left breast of this officer, apparently a major, there blazes so brilliant a mass of color that, as the sun strikes it and the flash bangs my eyes, I wink, catch my breath and sneeze. There are two long strips, each starting at the sternum and disappearing into the shadows of the axillia—every hue in the rainbow, the spectroscope, the kaleidoscope—

imperial purples, *sforzando* reds, wild Irish greens, romantic blues, loud yellows and oranges, rich maroons, sentimental pinks, all the half-tones from ultra-violet to infra-red, all the vibrations from the impalpable to the unendurable. A gallant *Soldat,* indeed! How he would shame a circus ticketwagon if he wore all the medals and badges, the stars and crosses, the pendants and lavallières, that go with those ribbons! . . . I glance at his sleeves. A simple golden stripe on the one—six months beyond the raging main. None on the other—the Kaiser's cannon missed him.

Just what all these ribbons signify I am sure I don't know; probably they belong to campaign medals and tell the tale of butcheries in foreign and domestic parts—mountains of dead Filipinos, Mexicans, Haitians, Dominicans, West Virginia miners, perhaps even Prussians. But in addition to campaign medals and the Distinguished Service Medal there are now certainly enough foreign orders in the United States to give a distinct brilliance to the national scene, viewed, say, from Mars. The Frederician tradition, borrowed by the ragged Continentals and embodied in Article I, Section 9, of the Constitution, lasted until 1918, and then suddenly blew up; to mention it to-day is a sort of indecorum, and to-morrow, no doubt, will be a species of treason. Down with Frederick; up with John Philip Sousa! Imagine what General Pershing would look like at a state banquet of his favorite American order, the Benevolent and Protective one of Elks, in all the Byzantine splendor of his casket of ribbons, badges, stars, garters, sunbursts and cockades—the lordly Bath of the grateful motherland, with its somewhat disconcerting "Ich dien"; the gorgeous tricolor baldrics, sashes and festoons of the Légion d'Honneur; the grand cross of SS. Maurizio e Lazzaro of Italy; the sinister Danilo of Montenegro, with its cabalistic monogram of Danilo I and its sinister hieroglyphics; the breastplate of the Paulownia of Japan, with its rising sun of thirty-two white rays, its blood-red heart, its background of green leaves and its white ribbon edged with red; the mystical St. Saviour of Greece, with its Greek motto and its brilliantly enameled figure of Christ; above all, the Croix de Guerre of Czecho-Slovakia, a new one and hence not listed in the books, but surely no shrinking violet! Alas, Pershing was on the wrong side—that is, for one with a fancy for gauds of that sort. The most blinding of all known orders is the Medijie of Turkey, which not only entitles the holder to four wives, but also absolutely requires him to wear a red fez and a frozen star covering his whole façade. I was offered this order by Turkish spies during the war, and it wabbled me a good deal. The Alexander of Bulgaria is almost as seductive. The badge consists of an eight-pointed white cross, with crossed swords between the arms and a red Bulgarian lion over the swords. The motto is "Za Chrabrost!" Then there are the Prussian orders—the Red and Black Eagles, the Pour le Mérite, the Prussian Crown, the Hohenzollern and the rest. And the Golden Fleece of Austria—the noblest of them all. Think of the Golden Fleece on a man born in Linn County, Missouri! . . . I begin to doubt that the General would have got it, even supposing him to have taken the other side. The Japs, I note, gave him only the grand cordon of the Paulownia, and the Belgians and Montenegrins were similarly cautious. There are higher classes. The highest of the Paulownia is only for princes, which is to say, only for non-Missourians.

Pershing is the champion, with General March a bad second. March is a K. C. M. G., and entitled to wear a large cross of white enamel bearing a lithograph of the Archangel Michael and the motto, "Auspicium Melioris Aevi," but he is not a K. C. B. Admirals Benson and Sims are also grand crosses of Michael and George, and like most other respectable Americans, members of the Legion of Honor, but they seem to have been forgotten by the Greeks, the Montenegrins, the Italians and the Belgians. The British-born and extremely Anglomaniacal Sims refused the Distinguished Service Medal of his adopted country, but is careful to mention in "Who's

Who in America" that his grand cross of Michael and George was conferred upon him, not by some servile gold-stick, but by "King George of England"; Benson omits mention of His Majesty, as do Pershing and March. It would be hard to think of any other American officer, real or bogus, who would refuse the D. S. M., or, failing it, the grand decoration of chivalry of the Independent Order of Odd Fellows. I once saw the latter hung, with ceremonies of the utmost magnificence, upon a bald-headed tinner who had served the fraternity long and faithfully; as he marched down the hall toward the throne of the Supreme Exalted Pishposh a score of little girls, the issue of other tinners, strewed his pathway with roses, and around the stem of each rose was a piece of glittering tinfoil. The band meanwhile played "The Rosary," and, at the conclusion of the spectacle, as fried oysters were served, "Wien Bleibt Wien."

It was, I suspect, by way of the Odd Fellows and other such gaudy heirs to the Deutsche Ritter and Rosicrucians that the lust to gleam and jingle got into the arteries of the American people. For years the austere tradition of Washington's day served to keep the military bosom bare of spangles, but all the while a weakness for them was growing in the civil population. Rank by rank, they became Knights of Pythias, Odd Fellows, Red Men, Nobles of the Mystic Shrine, Knights Templar, Patriarchs Militant,

Elks, Moose, Woodmen of the World, Foresters, Hoo-Hoos, Ku Kluxers—and in every new order there were thirty-two degrees, and for every degree there was a badge, and for every badge there was a yard of ribbon. The Nobles of the Mystic Shrine, chiefly paunchy wholesalers of the Rotary Club species, are not content with swords, baldrics, stars, garters and jewels; they also wear red fezes. The Elks run to rubies. The Red Men array themselves like Sitting Bull. The patriotic ice-wagon drivers and Methodist deacons of the Ku Klux Klan carry crosses set with incandescent lights. An American who is forced by his profession to belong to many such orders—say a life insurance solicitor, a bootlegger or a dealer in Oklahoma oil stock—accumulates a trunk full of decorations, many of them weighing a pound. There is an undertaker in Hagerstown, Md., who has been initiated eighteen times. When he robes himself to plant a fellow joiner he weighs three hundred pounds and sparkles and flashes like the mouth of hell itself. He is entitled to bear seven swords, all jeweled, and to hang his watch chain with the golden busts of nine wild animals, all with precious stones for eyes. Put beside this lowly washer of the dead, Pershing newly polished would seem almost like a Trappist.

But even so the civil arm is robbed of its just dues in the department of gauds and radioactivity, no doubt by the direct operation of military vanity and jealousy. Despite a million proofs (and perhaps a billion eloquent arguments) to the contrary, it is still the theory at the official ribbon counter that the only man who serves in a war is the man who serves in uniform. This is soft for the Bevo officer, who at least has his service stripes and the spurs that gnawed into his desk, but it is hard upon his brother Irving, the dollar-a-year man, who worked twenty hours a day for fourteen months buying soap-powder, canned asparagus and raincoats for the army of God. Irving not only labored with inconceivable diligence; he also faced hazards of no mean order, for on the one hand was his natural prejudice in favor of a very liberal rewarding of commercial enterprise, and on the other hand were his patriotism and his fear of Atlanta Penitentiary. I daresay that many and many a time, after working his twenty hours, he found it difficult to sleep the remaining four hours. I know, in fact, survivors of that obscure service who are far worse wrecks to-day than Pershing is. Their reward is—what? Winks, sniffs, innuendos. If they would indulge themselves in the now almost universal American yearning to go adorned, they must join the Knights of Pythias. Even the American Legion fails them, for though it certainly does not bar non-combatants, it insists that they shall have done their non-combatting in uniform.

What I propose is a variety of the Distinguished Service Medal for civilians,—perhaps, better still, a distinct order for civilians, closed to the military and with badges of different colors and areas, to mark off varying services to democracy. Let it run, like the Japanese Paulownia, from high to low—the lowest class for the patriot who sacrificed only time, money and a few nights' sleep; the highest for the great martyr who hung his country's altar with his dignity, his decency and his sacred honor. For Irving and his nervous insomnia, a simple rosette, with an iron badge bearing the national motto, "Safety First"; for the university president who prohibited the teaching of the enemy language in his learned grove, heaved the works of Goethe out of the university library, cashiered every professor unwilling to support Woodrow for the first vacancy in the Trinity, took to the stump for the National Security League, and made two hundred speeches in moving picture theaters—for this giant of loyal endeavor let no 100 per cent. American speak of anything less than the grand cross of the order, with a gold badge in polychrome enamel and stained glass, a baldric of the national colors, a violet plug hat with a sunburst on the side, the privilege of the floor of Congress, and a pension of $10,000 a year. After all, the cost would not be excessive; there are not many of them. Such prodigies of patriotism are possible only to rare and gifted men. For the grand cordons of the order, *e. g.*, college professors who spied upon and reported the seditions of their associates, state presidents of the American Protective League, alien property custodians, judges whose sentences of conscientious objectors mounted to more than 50,000 years, members of Dr. Creel's herd of 2,000 American historians, the authors of the Sisson documents, etc.—pensions of $10 a day would be enough, with silver badges and no plug hats. For the lower ranks, bronze badges and the legal right to the title of "the Hon.," already every true American's by courtesy.

Not, of course, that I am insensitive to the services of the gentlemen of those lower ranks, but in such matters one must go by rarity rather than by intrinsic value. If the grand cordon or even the nickel-plated eagle of the third class were given to every patriot who bored a hole through the floor of his flat to get evidence against his neighbors, the Krausmeyers, and to every one who visited the Hofbräuhaus nightly, denounced the Kaiser in searing terms, and demanded assent from Emil and Otto, the waiters, and to every one who notified the catchpolls of the Department of Justice when the wireless plant was open in the garret of the Arion Liedertafel, and to all who took a brave and forward part in slacker raids, and to all who lent their stenographers funds at 6 per cent. to buy Liberty bonds at 4¼ per cent., and to all who sold out at 99 and then bought in again at 83.56 and to all who served as jurors or perjurers in cases against members and ex-members of the I. W. W., and to the German-American members of the League for German Democracy, and to all the Irish who snitched upon the Irish—if decorations were thrown about with any such lavishness, then there would be no nickel left for our bathrooms. On the civilian side as on the military side the great rewards of war go, not to mere dogged industry and fidelity, but to originality—to the unprecedented, the arresting, the bizarre. The New York *Tribune* liar who invented the story about the German plant for converting the corpses of the slain into soap did more for democracy and the Wilsonian idealism, and hence deserves a more brilliant recognition, than a thousand uninspired hawkers of atrocity stories supplied by Viscount Bryce and his associates. For that great servant of righteousness the grand cordon, with two silver badges and the chair of history at Columbia, would be scarcely enough; for the ordinary hawkers any precious metal would be too much.

Whether or not the Y. M. C. A. has decorated its chocolate pedlars and soul-snatchers I do not know; since the chief Y. M. C. A. lamassary in my town of Baltimore became the scene of a homo-sexual scandal I have ceased to frequent evangelical society. If not, then there should be some governmental recognition of those highly characteristic heroes of the war for democracy. The veterans of the line, true enough, dislike them excessively, and have a habit of denouncing them obscenely when the corn-juice flows. They charged too much for cigarettes; they tried to discourage the amiability of the ladies of France; they had a habit of being absent when the shells burst in air. Well, some say this and some say that. A few, at least, of the pale and oleaginous brethren must have gone into the Master's work because they thirsted to save souls, and not simply because they desired to escape the trenches. And a few, I am told, were anything but unpleasantly righteous, as a round of Wassermanns would show. If, as may be plausibly argued, these Soldiers of the Double Cross deserve to live at all, then they surely deserve to be hung with white enameled stars of the third class, with gilt dollar marks superimposed. Motto: "Glory, glory, hallelujah!"

But what of the vaudeville actors, the cheer leaders, the doughnut fryers, the camp librarians, the press agents? I am not forgetting them. Let them be distributed among all the classes from the seventh to the eighth, according to their sufferings for the holy cause. And the agitators against Beethoven, Bach, Brahms, Wagner, Richard Strauss, all the rest of the cacophonous Huns? And the specialists in the crimes of the German professors? And the collectors for the Belgians, with their generous renunciation of all commissions above 80 per cent.? And the pathologists who denounced Johannes Müller as a fraud, Karl Ludwig as an imbecile, and Ehrlich as a thief? And the patriotic chemists who discovered arsenic in dill pickles, ground glass in pumpernickel, bichloride tablets in Bismarck herring, pathogenic organisms in aniline dyes? And the inspired editorial writers of the New York *Times* and *Tribune*, the Boston *Transcript*, the Philadelphia *Ledger*, the Mobile *Register*, the Jones Corners *Eagle?* And the headline writers? And the Columbia, Yale and Princeton professors? And the authors of books describing how the Kaiser told them the whole plot in 1913, while they were pulling his teeth or shining his shoes? And the ex-ambassadors? And the *Nietzschefresser?* And the chautauqua orators? And the four-minute men? And the Methodist pulpit pornographers who switched so facilely from vice-crusading to German atrocities? And Dr. Newell Dwight Hillis? And Dr. Henry van Dyke? And the master minds of the *New Republic?* And Tumulty? And the Vigilantes? Let no grateful heart forget them!

Palmer and Burleson I leave for special legislation. If mere university presidents, such as Nicholas Murray Butler, are to have the grand cross, then Palmer deserves to be rolled in malleable gold from head to foot, and polished until he blinds the cosmos —then Burleson must be hung with diamonds like Mrs. Warren and bathed in spotlights like Gaby Deslys. . . . Finally, I reserve a special decoration, to be conferred in camera and worn only in secret chapter, for husbands who took chances and refused to read anonymous letters from Paris: the somber badge of the Ordre de la Cuculus Canorus, first and only class.

VII. THE POET AND HIS ART

1

"A GOOD prose style," says Prof. Dr. Otto Jerpersen in his great work, "Growth and Structure of the English Language," "is everywhere a late acquirement, and the work of whole generations of good authors is needed to bring about the easy flow of written prose." The learned *Sprachwissenschaftler* is here speaking of Old English, or, as it used to be called when you and I were at the breast of enlightenment, Anglo-Saxon. An inch or so lower down the page he points out that what he says of prose is by no means true of verse—that poetry of very respectable quality is often written by peoples and individuals whose prose is quite as crude and graceless as that, say of the Hon. Warren Gamaliel Harding—that even the so-called Anglo-Saxons of Beowulf's time, a race as barbarous as the modern Jugo-Slavs or Mississippians, were yet capable, on occasion, of writing dithyrambs of an indubitable sweet gaudiness.

The point needs no laboring. A glance at the history of any literature will prove its soundness.

Moreover, it is supported by what we see around us every day—that is, if we look in literary directions. Some of the best verse in the modern movement, at home and abroad, has been written by intellectual adolescents who could no more write a first-rate paragraph in prose then they could leap the Matterhorn—girls just out of Vassar and Newnham, young army officers, chautauqua orators, New England old maids, obscure lawyers and doctors, newspaper reporters, all sorts of hollow dilettanti, male and female. Nine-tenths of the best poetry of the world has been written by poets less than thirty years old; a great deal more than half of it has been written by poets under twenty-five. One always associates poetry with youth, for it deals chiefly with the ideas that are peculiar to youth, and its terminology is quite as youthful as its content. When one hears of a poet past thirty-five, he seems somehow unnatural and even a trifle obscene; it is as if one encountered a graying man who still played the Chopin waltzes and believed in elective affinities. But prose, obviously, is a sterner and more elderly matter. All the great masters of prose (and especially of English prose, for its very resilience and brilliance make it extraordinarily hard to write) have had to labor for years before attaining to their mastery of it. The early prose of Abraham Lincoln was remarkable only for its badness; it was rhetorical and bombastic, and full of supernumerary words; in brief, it was a kind of poetry. It took years and years of hard striving for Abe to develop the simple and exquisite prose of his last half-decade. So with Thomas Henry Huxley, perhaps the greatest virtuoso of plain English who has ever lived. His first writings were competent but undistinguished; he was almost a grandfather before he perfected his superb style. And so with Anatole France, and Addison, and T. B. Macaulay, and George Moore, and James Branch Cabell, and Æ., and Lord Dunsany, and Nietzsche, and to go back to antiquity, Marcus Tullius Cicero. I have been told that the average age of the men who made the Authorized Version of the Bible was beyond sixty years. Had they been under thirty they would have made it lyrical; as it was, they made it colossal.

The reason for all this is not far to seek. Prose, however powerful its appeal to the emotions, is always based primarily upon logic, and is thus scientific; poetry, whatever its so-called intellectual content is always based upon mere sensation and emotion, and is thus loose and disorderly. A man must have acquired discipline over his feelings before he can write sound prose; he must have learned how to subordinate his transient ideas to more general and permanent ideas; above all, he must have acquired a good head for words, which is to say, a capacity for resisting their mere lascivious lure. But to write acceptable poetry, or even good poetry, he needs none of these things. If his hand runs away with his head it is actually a merit. If he writes what every one knows to be untrue, in terms that no sane adult would ever venture to use in real life, it is proof of his divine afflation. If he slops over and heaves around in a manner never hitherto observed on land or sea, the fact proves his originality. The so-called forms of verse and the rules of rhyme and rhythm do not offer him difficulties; they offer him refuges. Their purpose is not to keep him in order, but simply to give him countenance by providing him with a formal orderliness when he is most out of order. Using them is like swimming with bladders. The first literary composition of a quick-minded child is always some sort of jingle. It starts out with an inane idea —half an idea. Sticking to prose, it could go no further. But to its primary imbecility it now adds a meaningless phrase which, while logically unrelated, provides an agreeable concord in mere sound —and the result is the primordial tadpole of a sonnet. All the sonnets of the world, save a few of miraculous (and perhaps accidental) quality, partake of this fundamental nonsensicality. In all of them there are ideas that would sound idiotic in prose, and phrases that would sound clumsy and uncouth in prose. But the rhyme scheme conceals this nonsensicality. As a substitute for the missing logical plausibility it provides a sensuous harmony. Reading the thing, one gets a vague effect of agreeable sound, and so the logical feebleness is overlooked. It is, in a sense, like observing a pretty girl, competently dressed and made up, across the footlights. But translating the poem into prose is like meeting and marrying her.

II

Much of the current discussion of poetry—and what, save Prohibition, is more discussed in America? —is corrupted by a fundamental error. That error consists in regarding the thing itself as a simple entity, to be described conveniently in a picturesque phrase. "Poetry," says one critic, "is the statement of overwhelming emotional values." "Poetry," says another, "is an attempt to purge language of everything except its music and its pictures." "Poetry," says a third, "is the entering of delicately imaginative plateaus." "Poetry," says a fourth, "is truth carried alive into the heart by a passion." "Poetry," says a fifth, "is compacted of what seems, not of what is." "Poetry," says a sixth, "is the expression of thought in musical language." "Poetry," says a seventh, "is the language of a state of crisis." And so on, and so on. *Quod est poetica?* They all answer, and yet they all fail to answer. Poetry, in fact, is two quite distinct things. It may be either or both. One is a series of words that are intrinsically musical, in clang-tint and rhythm, as the single word *cellar-door* is musical. The other is a series of ideas, false in themselves, that offer a means of emotional and imaginative escape from the harsh realities of everyday. In brief, (I succumb, like all the rest, to phrase-making), poetry is a comforting piece of fiction set to more or less lascivious music—a slap on the back in waltz time—a grand release of longings and repressions to the tune of flutes, harps, sackbuts, psalteries and the usual strings.

As I say, poetry may be either the one thing or the other—caressing music or caressing assurance. It need not necessarily be both. Consider a familiar example from "Othello":

> Not poppy, nor mandragora,
> Nor all the drowsy syrups of the world
> Shall ever medicine thee to that sweet sleep
> Which thou owed'st yesterday.

Here the sense, at best, is surely very vague. Probably not one auditor in a hundred, hearing an actor recite those glorious lines, attaches any intelligible meaning to the archaic word *owed'st,* the cornerstone of the whole sentence. Nevertheless, the effect is stupendous. The passage assaults and benumbs the faculties like Schubert's "Ständchen" or the slow movement of Schumann's Rhenish symphony; hearing it is a sensuous debauch; the man anæsthetic to it could stand unmoved before Rheims cathedral or the Hofbräuhaus at Munich. One easily recalls many other such bursts of pure music, almost meaningless but infinitely delightful—in Poe, in Swinburne, in Marlowe, even in Joaquin Miller. Two-thirds of the charm of reading Chaucer (setting aside the Rabelaisian comedy) comes out of the mere burble of the words; the meaning, to a modern, is often extremely obscure, and sometimes downright undecipherable. The whole fame of Poe, as a poet, is based upon five short poems. Of them, three are almost pure music. Their intellectual content is of the vaguest. No one would venture to reduce them to plain English. Even Poe himself always thought of them, not as statements of poetic ideas, but as simple utterances of poetic (*i.e.*, musical) sounds.

It was Sidney Lanier, himself a competent poet, who first showed the dependence of poetry upon music. He had little to say, unfortunately, about the clang-tint of words; what concerned him almost exclusively was rhythm. In "The Science of English Verse," he showed that the charm of this rhythm could be explained in the technical terms of music—that all the old gabble about dactyls and spondees was no more than a dog Latin invented by men who were fundamentally ignorant of the thing they discussed.

Lanier's book was the first intelligent work ever published upon the nature and structure of the sensuous content of English poetry. He struck out into such new and far paths that the professors of prosody still lag behind him after forty years, quite unable to understand a poet who was also a shrewd critic and a first-rate musician. But if, so deeply concerned with rhythm, he marred his treatise by forgetting clang-tint, he marred it still more by forgetting content. Poetry that is all music is obviously relatively rare, for only a poet who is also a natural musician can write it, and natural musicians are much rarer in the world than poets. Ordinary poetry, average poetry, thus depends in part upon its ideational material, and perhaps even chiefly. It is the *idea* expressed in a poem, and not the mellifluousness of the words used to express it, that arrests and enchants the average connoisseur. Often, indeed, he disdains this mellifluousness, and argues that the idea ought to be set forth without the customary pretty jingling, or, at most, with only the scant jingling that lies in rhythm—in brief, he wants his ideas in the altogether, and so advocates *vers libre.*

It was another American, this time Prof. Dr. F. C. Prescott, of Cornell University, who first gave scientific attention to the intellectual content of poetry. His book is called "Poetry and Dreams." Its virtue lies in the fact that it rejects all the customary mystical and romantic definitions of poetry, and seeks to account for the thing in straightforward psychological terms. Poetry, says Prescott, is simply the verbal materialization of a day-dream, the statement of a Freudian wish, an attempt to satisfy a subconscious longing by saying that it is satisfied. In brief, poetry represents imagination's bold effort to escape from the cold and clammy facts that hedge us in—to soothe the wrinkled and fevered brow with beautiful balderdash. On the precise nature of this beautiful balderdash you can get all in the information you need by opening at random the nearest book of verse. The ideas you will find in it may be divided into two main divisions. The first consists of denials of objective facts; the second of denials of subjective facts. Specimen of the first sort:

> God's in His heaven,
> All's well with the world.

Specimen of the second:

> I am the master of my fate;
> I am the captain of my soul.

It is my contention that all poetry (forgetting, for the moment, its possible merit as mere sound) may be resolved into either the one or the other of these frightful imbecilities—that its essential character lies in its bold flouting of what every reflective adult knows to be the truth. The poet, imagining him to be sincere, is simply one who disposes of all the horrors of life on this earth, and of all the difficulties presented by his own inner weaknesses no less, by the childish device of denying them. Is it a well-known fact that love is an emotion that is almost as perishable as eggs—that it is biologically impossible for a given male to yearn for a given female more than a few brief years? Then the poet disposes of it by assuring his girl that he will nevertheless love her forever—more, by pledging his word of honor that he believes that *she* will love *him* forever. Is it equally notorious that there is no such thing as justice in the world—that the good are tortured insanely and the evil go free and prosper? Then the poet composes a piece crediting God with a mysterious and unintelligible theory of jurisprudence, whereby the torture of the good is a sort of favor conferred upon them for their goodness. Is it of almost equally widespread report that no healthy man likes to contemplate his own inevitable death—that even in time of war, with a vast pumping up of emotion to conceal the fact, every soldier hopes and believes that he, personally, will escape? Then the poet, first carefully introducing himself into a bomb-proof, achieves strophes declaring that he is free from all such weakness—that he will deliberately seek a rendezvous with death, and laugh ha-ha when the bullet finds him.

The precise nature of the imbecility thus solemnly set forth depends, very largely, of course, upon the private prejudices and yearnings of the poet, and the reception that is given it depends, by the same token, upon the private prejudices and yearnings of the reader. That is why it is often so difficult to get any agreement upon the merits of a definite poem, *i. e.*, to get any agreement upon its capacity to soothe. There is the man who craves only the animal delights of a sort of Moslem-Methodist paradise: to him "The Frost is on the Pumpkin" is a noble poem. There is the man who yearns to get out of the visible universe altogether and tread the fields of asphodel: for him there is delight only in the mystical stuff of Crashaw, Thompson, Yeats and company. There is the man who revolts against the sordid Christian notion of immortality—an eternity to be spent flapping wings with pious greengrocers and oleaginous Anglican bishops; he finds *his* escape in the gorgeous blasphemies of Swinburne. There is, to make an end of examples, the man who, with an inferiority complex eating out his heart, is moved by a great desire to stalk the world in heroic guise: he may go to the sonorous swanking of Kipling, or he may go to something more subtle, to some poem in which the boasting is more artfully concealed, say Christina Rosetti's "When I am Dead." Many men, many complexes, many secret yearnings! They collect, of course, in groups; if the group happens to be large enough the poet it is devoted to becomes famous. Kipling's great fame is thus easily explained. He appeals to the commonest of all types of men, next to the sentimental type—which is to say, he appeals to the bully and braggart type, the chest-slapping type, the patriot type. Less harshly described, to the boy type. All of us have been Kiplingomaniacs at some time or other. I was myself a very ardent one at 17, and wrote many grandiloquent sets of verse in the manner of "Tommy Atkins" and "Fuzzy-Wuzzy." But if the gifts of observation and reflection have been given to us, we get over it. There comes a time when we no longer yearn to be heroes, but seek only peace—maybe even hope for quick extinction. Then we turn to Swinburne and "The Garden of Proserpine"—more false assurances, more mellifluous play-acting, another tinkling make-believe—but how sweet on blue days!

III

One of the things to remember here (too often it is forgotten, and Dr. Prescott deserves favorable mention for stressing it) is that a man's conscious desires are not always identical with his subconscious longings; in fact, the two are often directly antithetical. No doubt the real man lies in the depths of the subconscious, like a carp lurking in mud. His conscious personality is largely a product of his environment—the reaction of his subconscious to the prevailing notions of what is meet and seemly. Here, of course, I wander into platitude, for the news that all men are frauds was already stale in the days of Hammurabi. The ingenious Freud simply translated the fact into pathological terms, added a bedroom scene, and so laid the foundations for his psychoanalysis. Incidentally, it has always seemed to me that Freud made a curious mistake when he brought sex into the foreground of his new magic. He was, of course, quite right when he set up the doctrine that, in civilized societies, sex impulses were more apt to be suppressed than any other natural impulses, and that the subconscious thus tended to be crowded with their ghosts. But in considering sex impulses, he forgot sex imaginings. Digging out, by painful cross-examination in a darkened room, some startling tale of carnality in his patient's past, he committed the incredible folly of assuming it to be literally true. More often than not, I believe, it was a mere piece of boasting, a materialization of desire—in brief, a poem. It is astonishing that this possibility never occurred to the venerable professor; it is more astonishing that it has never occured to any of his disciples. He should have psychoanalyzed a few poets instead of wasting all his time upon psychopathic women with sclerotic husbands. He would have dredged amazing things out of their subconsciouses, heroic as well as amorous. Imagine the billions of Boers, Germans, Irishmen and Hindus that Kipling would have confessed to killing!

But here I get into morbid anatomy, and had better haul up. What I started out to say was that a man's preferences in poetry constitute an excellent means of estimating his inner cravings and credulities. The music disarms his critical sense, and he confesses to chershing ideas that he would repudiate with indignation if they were put into plain words. I say he cherishes those ideas. Maybe he simply tolerates them unwillingly; maybe they are no more than inescapable heritages from his barbarous ancestors, like his vermiform appendix. Think of the poems you like, and you will come upon many such intellectual fossils—ideas that you by no means subscribe to openly, but that nevertheless give you a strange joy. I put myself on the block as Exhibit A. There is my delight in Lizette Woodworth Reese's sonnet, "Tears." Nothing could do more violence to my conscious beliefs. Put into prose, the doctrine in the poem would exasperate and even enrage me. There is no man in Christendom who is less a Christian than I am. But here the dead hand grabs me by the ear. My ancestors were converted to Christianity in the year 1535, and remained of that faith until near the middle of the eighteenth century. Observe, now, the load I carry; more than two hundred years of Christianity, and perhaps a thousand years (maybe even two, or three thousand years) of worship of heathen gods before that—at least twelve hundred years of uninterrupted belief in the immortality of the soul. Is it any wonder that, betrayed by the incomparable music of Miss Reese's Anglo-Saxon monosyllables, my conscious faith is lulled to sleep, thus giving my subconscious a chance to wallow in its immemorial superstition?

Even so, my vulnerability to such superstitions is very low, and it tends to grow less as I increase in years and sorrows. As I have said, I once throbbed to the drum-beat of Kipling; later on, I was responsive to the mellow romanticism of Tennyson; now it takes one of the genuinely fundamental delusions of the human race to move me. But progress is not continuous; it has interludes. There are days when every one of us experiences a sort of ontogenetic back-firing, and returns to an earlier stage of development. It is on such days that grown men break down and cry like children; it is then that they play games, or cheer the flag, or fall in love. And it is then that they are in the mood for poetry, and get comfort out of its asseverations of the obviously not true. A truly civilized man, when he is wholly himself, derives no pleasure from hearing a poet state, as Browning stated, that this world is perfect. Such tosh not only does not please him; it definitely offends him, as he is offended by an idiotic article in a newspaper; it roils him to encounter so much stupidity in Christendom. But he may like it when he is drunk, or suffering from some low toxemia, or staggering beneath some great disaster. Then, as I say, the ontogenetic process reverses itself, and he slides back into infancy. Then he goes to poets, just as he goes to women, "glad" books, and dogmatic theology. The very highest orders of men, perhaps, never suffer from such malaises of the spirit, or, if they suffer from them, never succumb to them. These are men who are so thoroughly civilized that even the most severe attack upon the emotions is not sufficient to dethrone their reason. Charles Darwin was such a man. There was never a moment in his life when he sought religious consolation, and there was never a moment when he turned to poetry; in fact, he regarded all poetry as silly. Other first-rate men, more sensitive to the possible music in it, regard it with less positive aversion, but I have never heard of a truly first-rate man who got any permanent satisfaction out of its content. The Browning Societies of the latter part of the nineteenth century (and I choose the Browning Societies because Browning's poetry was often more or less logical in content, and thus above the ordinary intellectually) were not composed of such men as Huxley, Spencer, Lecky, Buckle and Travelyn, but of third-rate school-masters, moony old maids, candidates for theosophy, literary vicars, collectors of Rogers groups, and other such Philistines. The chief propagandist for Browning in the United States was not Henry Adams, or William Summer, or Daniel C. Gilman, but an obscure professor of English who was also an ardent spook-chaser. And what is thus true ontogenetically is also true phylogenetically. That is to say, poetry is chiefly produced and esteemed by peoples that have not yet come to maturity. The Romans had a dozen poets of the first talent before they had a single prose writer of any skill whatsoever. So did the English. So did the Germans. In our own day we see the negroes of the South producing religious and secular verse of such quality that it is taken over by the whites, and yet the number of negroes who show a decent prose style is still very small, and there is no sign of it increasing. Similarly, the white authors of America, during the past ten or fifteen years, have produced a great mass of very creditable poetry, and yet the quality of our prose remains very low, and the Americans with prose styles of any distinction could be counted on the fingers of two hands.

IV

So far I have spoken chiefly of the content of poetry. In its character as a sort of music it is plainly a good deal more respectable, and makes an appeal to a far higher variety of reader, or, at all events, to a reader in a state of greater mental clarity. A capacity for music—by which I mean melody, harmony and clang-tint—comes late in the history of every race. The savage can apprehend rhythm, but he is quite incapable of carrying a tune in any intelligible scale. The negro roustabouts of our own South, who are commonly regarded as very musical, are actually only rhythmical; they never invent melodies, but only rhythms. And the whites to whom their barbarous dance-tunes chiefly appeal are in their own stage of culture. When one observes a room full of well-dressed men and women swaying and wriggling to the tune of some villainous mazurka from the Mississippi levees, one may assume very soundly that they are all the sort of folk who play golf and bridge, and prefer "The Sheik" to "Heart of Darkness" and believe in the League of Nations. A great deal of superficial culture is compatible with that pathetic barbarism, and even a high degree of æsthetic sophistication in other directions. The Greeks who built the Parthenon knew no more about music than a hog knows of predestination; they were almost as ignorant in that department as the modern Iowans or New Yorkers. It was not, indeed, until the Renaissance that music as we know it appeared in the world, and it was not until less than two centuries ago that it reached a high development. In Shakespeare's day music was just getting upon its legs in England; in Goethe's day it was just coming to full flower in Germany; in France and America it is still in the savage state. It is thus the youngest of the arts, and the most difficult, and hence the noblest. Any sane young man of twenty-two can write an acceptable sonnet, or design a habitable house or draw a horse that will not be mistaken for an automobile, but before he may write even a bad string quartet he must go through a long and arduous training, just as he must strive for years before he may write prose that is instantly recognizable as prose, and not as a string of mere words.

The virtue of such great poets as Shakespeare does not lie in the content of their poetry, but in its music. The content of the Shakespearean plays, in fact, is often puerile, and sometimes quite incomprehensible. No scornful essays by George Bernard Shaw and Frank Harris were needed to demonstrate the fact; it lies plainly in the text. One snickers sourly over the spectacle of generations of pedants debating the question of Hamlet's mental processes; the simple fact is that Shakespeare gave him no more mental processes than a Fifth avenue rector has, but merely employed him as a convenient spout for some of the finest music ever got into words. Assume that he has all the hellish sagacity of a Nietzsche, and that music remains unchanged; assume that he is as idiotic as a Grand Worthy Flubdub of the Freemasons, and it still remains unchanged. As it is intoned on the stage by actors, the poetry of Shakespeare commonly loses content altogether. One cannot make out what the *cabotin* is saying; one can only observe that it is beautiful. There are whole speeches in the Shakespearean plays whose meaning is unknown ever to scholars—and yet they remain favorites, and well deserve to. Who knows, again, what the sonnets are about? Is the bard talking about the inn-keeper's wife at Oxford, or about a love affair of a pathological, Y. M. C. A. character? Some say one thing, and some say the other. But all who have ears must agree that the sonnets are extremely beautiful stuff—that the English language reaches in them the topmost heights of conceivable beauty. Shakespeare thus ought to be ranked among the musicians, along with Beethoven. As a philosopher he was a ninth-rater—but so was old Ludwig. I wonder what he would have done with prose? I can't make up my mind about it. One day I believe that he would have written prose as good as Dryden's, and the next day I begin to fear that he would have produced something as bad as Swinburne's. He had the ear, but he lacked the logical sense. Poetry has done enough when it charms, but prose must also convince.

I do not forget, of course, that there is a borderland in which it is hard to say, of this or that composition, whether it is prose or poetry. Lincoln's Gettysburg speech is commonly reckoned as prose, and yet I am convinced that it is quite as much poetry as the Queen Mab speech or Marlowe's mighty elegy on Helen of Troy. More, it is so read and admired by the great masses of the American people. It is an almost perfect specimen of a comforting but unsound asseveration put into rippling and hypnotizing words; done into plain English, the statements of fact in it would make even a writer of school history-books laugh. So with parts of the Declaration of Independence. No one believes seriously that they are true, but nearly everyone agrees that it would be a nice thing if they *were* true—and meanwhile Jefferson's eighteenth century rhetoric, by Johnson out of John Lyly's "Euphues," completes the enchantment. In the main, the test is to be found in the audience rather than in the poet. If it is naturally intelligent and in a sober and critical mood, demanding sense and proofs, then nearly all poetry becomes prose; if, on the contrary, it is congenitally maudlin, or has a few drinks aboard, or is in love, or is otherwise in a soft and believing mood, then even the worst of prose, if it has a touch of soothing sing-song in it, becomes moving poetry—for example, the diplomatic and political gospel-hymns of the late Dr. Wilson, a man constitutionally unable to reason clearly or honestly, but nevertheless one full of the burbling that caresses the ears of simple men. Most of his speeches, during the days of his divine appointment, translated into intelligible English, would have sounded as idiotic as a prose version of "The Blessed Damozel." Read by his opponents, they sounded so without the translation.

But at the extremes, of course, there are indubitable poetry and incurable prose, and the difference is not hard to distinguish. Prose is simply a form of writing in which the author intends that his statements shall be accepted as conceivably true, even when they are about imaginary persons and events; its appeal is to the fully conscious and alertly reasoning man. Poetry is a form of writing in which the author attempts to disarm reason and evoke emotion, partly by presenting images that awaken a powerful response in the subconscious and partly by the mere sough and blubber of words. Poetry is not distinguished from prose, as Prof. Dr. Lowes says in his "Convention and Revolt in Poetry," by an exclusive phraseology, but by a peculiar attitude of mind—an attitude of self-delusion, of fact-denying, of saying what isn't true. It is essentially an effort to elude the bitter facts of life, whereas prose is essentially a means of unearthing and exhibiting them. The gap is bridged by sentimental prose, which is half prose and half poetry—Lincoln's Gettysburg speech, the average sermon, the prose of an erotic novelette. Immediately the thing acquires a literal meaning it ceases to be poetry; immediately it becomes capable of convincing an adult and perfectly sober man during the hours between breakfast and luncheon it is indisputably prose.

This quality of untruthfulness pervades all poetry, good and bad. You will find it in the very best poetry that the world has so far produced, to wit, in the sonorous poems of the Jewish Scriptures. The ancient Jews were stupendous poets. Moreover, they were shrewd psychologists, and so knew the capacity of poetry, given the believing mind, to convince and enchant—in other words, its capacity to drug the auditor in such a manner that he accepts it literally, as he might accept the baldest prose. This danger in poetry, given auditors impressionable enough, is too little estimated and understood. It is largely responsible for the persistence of sentimentality in a world apparently designed for the one purpose of manufacturing cynics. It is probably chiefly responsible for the survival of Christianity, despite the hard competition that it has met with from other religions. The theology of Christianity—*i. e.*, its prose—is certainly no more convincing than that of half a dozen other religions that might be named; it is, in fact, a great deal less convincing than the theology of, say, Buddhism. But the poetry of Christianity is infinitely more lush and beautiful than that of any other religion ever heard of. There is more lovely poetry in one of the Psalms than in all of the Non-Christian scriptures of the world taken together. More, this poetry is in both Testaments, the New as well as the Old. Who could imagine a more charming poem than that of the Child in the manger? It has enchanted the world for nearly two thousand years. It is simple, exquisite and overwhelming. Its power to arouse emotion is so great that even in our age it is at the bottom of fully a half of the kindliness, romanticism and humane sentimentality that survive in Christendom. It is worth a million syllogisms.

Once, after plowing through sixty or seventy volumes of bad verse, I described myself as a poetry-hater. The epithet was and is absurd. The truth is that I enjoy poetry as much as the next man—when the mood is on me. But what mood? The mood, in a few words, of intellectual and spiritual fatigue, the mood of revolt against the insoluble riddle of existence, the mood of disgust and despair. Poetry, then, is a capital medicine. First its sweet music lulls, and then its artful presentation of the beautifully improbable soothes and gives surcease. It is an escape from life, like religion, like enthusiasm, like glimpsing a pretty girl. And to the mere sensuous joy in it, to the mere low delight in getting away from the world for a bit, there is added, if the poetry be good, something vastly better, something reaching out into the realm of the intelligent, to wit, appreciation of good workmanship. A sound sonnet is almost as pleasing an object as a well-written fugue. A pretty lyric, deftly done, has all the technical charm of a fine carving. I think it is craftsmanship that I admire most in the world. Brahms enchants me because he knew his trade perfectly. I like Richard Strauss because he is full of technical ingenuities, because he is a master-workman. Well, who ever heard of a finer craftsman than William Shakespeare? His music was magnificent, he played superbly upon all the common emotions—and he did it magnificently, he did it with an air. No, I am no poetry-hater. But even Shakespeare I most enjoy, not on brisk mornings when I feel fit for any deviltry, but on dreary evenings when my old wounds are troubling me, and some fickle one has just sent back the autographed set of my first editions, and bills are piled up on my desk, and I am too sad to work. Then I mix a stiff dram—and read poetry.

VIII. FIVE MEN AT RANDOM

1

Abraham Lincoln

THE backwardness of the art of biography in These States is made shiningly visible by the fact that we have yet to see a first-rate life of either Lincoln or Whitman. Of Lincolniana, of course, there is no end, nor is there any end to the hospitality of those who collect it. Some time ago a publisher told me that there are four kinds of books that never, under any circumstances, lose money in the United States—first, detective stories; secondly, novels in which the heroine is forcibly debauched by the hero; thirdly, volumes on spiritualism, occultism and other such claptrap, and fourthly, books on Lincoln. But despite all the vast mass of Lincolniana and the constant discussion of old Abe in other ways, even so elemental a problem as that of his religious faith—surely an important matter in any competent biography—is yet but half solved. Here, for example, is the Rev. William E.

Barton, grappling with it for more than four hundred large pages in "The Soul of Abraham Lincoln." It is a lengthy inquiry—the rev. pastor, in truth, shows a good deal of the habitual garrulity of his order—but it is never tedious. On the contrary, it is curious and amusing, and I have read it with steady interest, including even the appendices. Unluckily, the author, like his predecessors, fails to finish the business before him. Was Lincoln a Christian? Did he believe in the Divinity of Christ? I am left in doubt. He was very polite about it, and very cautious, as befitted a politician in need of Christian votes, but how much genuine conviction was in that politeness? And if his occasional references to Christ were thus open to question, what of his rather vague avowals of belief in a personal God and in the immortality of the soul? Herndon and some of his other close friends always maintained that he was an atheist, but Dr. Barton argues that this atheism was simply disbelief in the idiotic Methodist and Baptist dogmas of his time—that nine Christian churches out of ten, if he were alive to-day, would admit him to their high privileges and prerogatives without anything worse than a few warning coughs. As for me, I still wonder.

The growth of the Lincoln legend is truly amazing. He becomes the American solar myth, the chief butt of American credulity and sentimentality. Washington, of late years, has been perceptibly humanized; every schoolboy now knows that he used to swear a good deal, and was a sharp trader, and had a quick eye for a pretty ankle. But meanwhile the varnishers and veneerers have been busily converting Abe into a plaster saint, thus making him fit for adoration in the chautauquas and Y. M. C. A.'s. All the popular pictures of him show him in his robes of state, and wearing an expression fit for a man about to be hanged. There is, so far as I know, not a single portrait of him showing him smiling—and yet he must have cackled a good deal, first and last: who ever heard of a storyteller who didn't? Worse, there is an obvious effort to pump all his human weaknesses out of him, and so leave him a mere moral apparition, a sort of amalgam of John Wesley and the Holy Ghost. What could be more absurd? Lincoln, in point of fact, was a practical politician of long experience and high talents, and by no means cursed with inconvenient ideals. On the contrary, his career in the Illinois Legislature was that of a good organization man, and he was more than once denounced by reformers. Even his handling of the slavery question was that of a politician, not that of a fanatic. Nothing alarmed him more than the suspicion that he was an Abolitionist. Barton tells of an occasion when he actually fled town to avoid meeting the issue squarely. A genuine

Abolitionist would have published the Emancipation Proclamation the day after the first battle of Bull Run. But Lincoln waited until the time was more favorable—until Lee had been hurled out of Pennsylvania, and, more important still, until the political currents were safely running his way. Always he was a wary fellow, both in his dealings with measures and in his dealings with men. He knew how to keep his mouth shut.

Nevertheless, it was his eloquence that probably brought him to his great estate. Like William Jennings Bryan, he was a dark horse made suddenly formidable by fortunate rhetoric. The Douglas debate launched him, and the Cooper Union speech got him the presidency. This talent for emotional utterance, this gift for making phrases that enchanted the plain people, was an accomplishment of late growth. His early speeches were mere empty fireworks—the childish rhodomontades of the era. But in middle life he purged his style of ornament and it became almost baldly simple—and it is for that simplicity that he is remembered to-day. The Gettysburg speech is at once the shortest and the most famous oration in American history. Put beside it, all the whoopings of the Websters, Sumners and Everetts seem gaudy and silly. It is eloquence brought to a pellucid and almost child-like perfection—the highest emotion reduced to one graceful and irresistible gesture. Nothing else precisely like it is to be found in the whole range of oratory. Lincoln himself never even remotely approached it. It is genuinely stupendous.

But let us not forget that it is oratory, not logic; beauty, not sense. Think of the argument in it! Put it into the cold words of everyday! The doctrine is simply this: that the Union soldiers who died at Gettysburg sacrificed their lives to the cause of self-determination—"that government of the people, by the people, for the people," should not perish from the earth. It is difficult to imagine anything more untrue. The Union soldiers in that battle actually fought against self-determination; it was the Confederates who fought for the right of their people to govern themselves. What was the practical effect of the battle of Gettysburg? What else than the destruction of the old sovereignty of the States, *i. e.*, of the people of the States? The Confederates went into battle an absolutely free people; they came out with their freedom subject to the supervision and vote of the rest of the country—and for nearly twenty years that vote was so effective that they enjoyed scarcely any freedom at all. Am I the first American to note the fundamental nonsensicality of the Gettysburg address? If so, I plead my æsthetic joy in it in amelioration of the sacrilege.

2

Paul Elmer More

Nothing new is to be found in the latest volume of Paul Elmer More's Shelburne Essays. The learned author, undismayed by the winds of anarchic doctrine that blow down his Princeton stovepipe, continues to hold fast to the notions of his earliest devotion. He is still the gallant champion sent against the Romantic Movement by the forces of discipline and decorum. He is still the eloquent fugleman of the Puritan ethic and æsthetic. In so massive a certainty, so resolute an immovability there is something almost magnificent. These are somewhat sad days for the exponents of that ancient correctness. The Goths and the Huns are at the gate, and as they batter wildly they throw dead cats, perfumed lingerie, tracts against predestination, and the bound files of the *Nation,* the *Freeman* and the *New Republic* over the fence. But the din does not flabbergast Dr. More. High above the blood-bathed battlements there is a tower, of ivory within and solid ferro-concrete without, and in its austere upper chamber he sits undaunted, solemnly composing an elegy upon Jonathan Edwards, "the greatest theologian and philosopher yet produced in this country."

Magnificent, indeed—and somehow charming.

On days when I have no nobler business I sometimes join the barbarians and help them to launch their abominable bombs against the embattled blue-noses. It is, in the main, fighting that is too easy, too Anglo-Saxon to be amusing. Think of the decayed professors assembled by Dr. Franklin for the *Profiteers' Review;* who could get any genuine thrill out of dropping *them?* They come out on crutches, and are as much afraid of what is behind them as they are of what is in front of them. Facing all the horrible artillery of Nineveh and Tyre, they arm themselves with nothing worse than the pedagogical birch. The janissaries of Adolph Ochs, the Anglo-Saxon supreme archon, are even easier. One has but to blow a *shofar*, and down they go. Even Prof. Dr. Stuart P. Sherman is no antagonist to delight a hard-boiled heretic. Sherman is at least honestly American, of course, but the trouble with him is that he is *too* American. The Iowa hayseed remains in his hair; he can't get rid of the smell of the chautauqua; one inevitably sees in him a sort of *reductio ad absurdum* of his fundamental theory—to wit, the theory that the test of an artist is whether he hated the Kaiser in 1917, and plays his honorable part in Christian Endeavor, and prefers Coca-Cola to Scharlachberger 1911, and has taken to heart the great lessons of sex hygiene. Sherman is game, but he doesn't offer sport in the grand manner. Moreover, he has been showing sad signs of late of a despairing heart: he tries to be ingratiating, and begins to hug in the clinches.

The really tempting quarry is More. To rout him out of his armored tower, to get him out upon the glacis for a duel before both armies, to bring him finally to the wager of battle—this would be an enterprise to bemuse the most audacious and give pause to the most talented. More has a solid stock of learning in his lockers; he is armed and outfitted as none of the pollyannas who trail after him is armed and outfitted; he is, perhaps, the nearest approach to a genuine scholar that we have in America, God save us all! But there is simply no truculence in him, no flair for debate, no lust to do execution upon his foes. His method is wholly *ex parte*. Year after year he simply iterates and reiterates his misty protests, seldom changing so much as a word. Between his first volume and his last there is not the difference between Gog and Magog. Steadily, ploddingly, vaguely, he continues to preach the gloomy gospel of tightness and restraint. He was against "the electric thrill of freer feeling" when he began, and he will be against it on that last gray day —I hope it long post-dates my own hanging—when the ultimate embalmer sneaks upon him with velvet tread, and they haul down the flag to half-staff at Princeton, and the readers of the New York *Evening*

Journal note that an obscure somebody named Paul E. More is dead.

3

Madison Cawein

A vast and hefty tome celebrates this dead poet, solemnly issued by his mourning friends in Louisville. The editor is Otto A. Rothert, who confesses that he knew Cawein but a year or two, and never read his poetry until after his death. The contributors include such local *literati* as Reuben Post Halleck, Leigh Gordon Giltner, Anna Blanche McGill and Elvira S. Miller Slaughter. Most of the ladies gush over the departed in the manner of high-school teachers paying tribute to Plato, Montaigne or Dante Alighieri. His young son, seventeen years old, contributes by far the most vivid and intelligent account of him; it is, indeed, very well written, as, in a different way, is the contribution of Charles Hamilton Musgrove, an old newspaper friend. The ladies, as I hint, simply swoon and grow lyrical. But it is a fascinating volume, all the same, and well worth the room it takes on the shelf. Mr. Rothert starts off with what he calls a "picturography" of Cawein—the poet's father and mother in the raiment of 1865, the coat-of-arms of his mother's great-grandfather's uncle, the house which now stands on the site of the house in which he was born, the rock spring from which he used to drink as a boy, a group showing him with his three brothers, another showing him with one brother and their cousin Fred, Cawein himself with sideboards, the houses he lived in, the place where he worked, the walks he liked around Louisville, his wife and baby, the hideous bust of him in the Louisville Public Library, the church from which he was buried, his modest grave in Cave Hill Cemetery—in brief, all the photographs that collect about a man as he staggers through life, and entertain his ribald grandchildren after he is gone. Then comes a treatise on the ancestry and youth of the poet, then a collection of newspaper clippings about him, then a gruesomely particular account of his death, then a fragment of autobiography, then a selection from his singularly dull letters, then some prose pieces from his pen, then the aforesaid tributes of his neighbors, and finally a bibliography of his works, and an index to them.

As I say, a volume of fearful bulk and beam, but nevertheless full of curious and interesting things. Cawein, of course, was not a poet of the first rank, nor is it certain that he has any secure place in the second rank, but in the midst of a great deal of obvious and feeble stuff he undoubtedly wrote some nature lyrics of excellent quality. The woods and the fields were his delight. He loved to roam through them, observing the flowers, the birds, the tall trees, the shining sky overhead, the green of Spring, the reds and browns of Autumn, the still whites of Winter. There were times when he got his ecstasy into words—when he wrote poems that were sound and beautiful. These poems will not be forgotten; there will be no history of American literature written for a hundred years that does not mention Madison Cawein. But what will the literary historians make of the man himself? How will they explain his possession, however fitfully, of the divine gift—his genuine kinship with Wordsworth and Shelly? Certainly no more unlikely candidate for the bays ever shinned up Parnassus. His father was a quack doctor; his mother was a professional spiritualist; he himself, for years and years, made a living as cashier in a gambling-house! Could anything be more grotesque? Is it possible to imagine a more improbable setting for a poet? Yet the facts are the facts, and Mr. Rothert makes no attempt whatever to conceal them. Add a final touch of the bizarre: Cawein fell over one morning while shaving in his bathroom, and cracked his head on the bathtub, and after his death there was a row over his life insurance. Mr. Rothert presents all of the documents. The autopsy is described; the death certificate is quoted. . . . A strange, strange tale, indeed!

4

Frank Harris

Though, so far as I know, this Harris is a perfectly reputable man, fearing God and obeying the laws, it is not to be gainsaid that a certain flavor of the sinister hangs about his aspect. The first time I ever enjoyed the honor of witnessing him, there bobbed up in my mind (instantly put away as unworthy and unseemly) a memory of the handsome dogs who used to chain shrieking virgins to railway tracks in the innocent, pre-Ibsenish dramas of my youth, the while a couple of stage hands imitated the rumble of the Empire State Express in the wings. There was the same elegance of turn-out, the same black mustachios, the same erect figure and lordly air, the same agate glitter in the eyes, the same aloof and superior smile. A sightly fellow, by all the gods, and one who obviously knew how to sneer. That afternoon, in fact, we had a sneering match, and before it was over most of the great names in the letters and politics of the time, *circa* 1914, had been reduced to faint hisses and ha-has. . . . Well, a sneerer has his good days and his bad days. There are times when his gift gives him such comfort that it can be matched only by God's grace, and there are times when it launches upon him such showers of darts that he is bound to feel a few stings. Harris got the darts first, for the year that he came back to his native land, after a generation of exile, was the year in which Anglomania rose to the dignity of a national religion—and what he had to say about the English, among whom he had lived since the early 80's, was chiefly of a very waspish and disconcerting character. Worse, he not only said it, twirling his mustache defiantly; he also wrote it down, and published it in a book. This book was full of shocks for the rapt worshippers of the Motherland, and particularly for the literary *Kanonendelicatessen* who followed the pious leadership of Woodrow and Ochs, Putnam and Roosevelt, Wister and Cyrus Curtis, young Reid and Mrs. Jay. So they called a special meeting of the American Academy of Arts and Letters, sang "God Save the King," kissed the Union Jack, and put Harris into Coventry. And there he remained for five or six long years. The literary reviews never mentioned him. His books were expunged from the minutes. When he was heard of at all, it was only in whispers, and the general burden of those whispers was that he was in the pay of the Kaiser, and plotting to garrot the Rev. Dr. William T. Manning. . . .

So down to 1921. Then the English, with characteristic lack of delicacy, played a ghastly trick upon all those dutiful and well-meaning colonists. That is to say, they suddenly forgave Harris his criminal refusal to take their war buncombe seriously, exhumed him from his long solitude among the Anglo-Ashkenazim, and began praising him in rich, hearty terms as a literary gentleman of the first water, and even as the chief adornment of American letters! The English notices of his "Contemporary Portraits: Second Series" were really quite amazing. The London *Times* gave him two solid columns, and where the *Times* led, all the other great organs of English literary opinion followed. The book itself was described as something extraordinary, a piece of criticism full of shrewdness and originality, and the author was treated with the utmost politeness. . . . One imagines the painful sensation in the New York *Times* office, the dismayed groups around far-flung campus pumps, the special meetings of the Princeton, N. J., and Urbana, Ill., American Legions, the secret conference between the National Institute of Arts and Letters and the Ku Klux Klan. But though there was tall talk by hot heads, nothing could be done. Say "Wo!" and the dutiful jackass turns to the right; say "Gee!" and he turns to the left. It is too much, of course, to ask him to cheer as well as turn—but he nevertheless turns. Since 1921 I have heard no more whispers against Harris from professors and Vigilantes. But on two or three occasions, the subject coming up, I have heard him sneer his master sneer, and each time my blood has run cold.

Well, what is in him? My belief, frequently expressed, is that there is a great deal. His "Oscar Wilde" is, by long odds, the best literary biography ever written by an American—an astonishingly frank, searching and vivid reconstruction of character—a piece of criticism that makes all ordinary criticism seem professorial and lifeless. The Comstocks, I need not say, tried to suppress it; a brilliant light is thrown upon Harris by the fact that they failed ignominiously. All the odds were in favor of the Comstocks; they had patriotism on their side and the help of all the swine who flourished in those days; nevertheless, Harris gave them a severe beating, and scared them half to death. In brief, a man of the most extreme bellicosity, enterprise and courage—a fellow whose ideas are expressed absolutely regardless of tender feelings, whether genuine or bogus. In "The Man Shakespeare" and "The Women of Shakespeare" he tackled the whole body of academic English critics *en masse*—and routed them *en masse*. The two books, marred perhaps by a too bombastic spirit, yet contain some of the soundest, shrewdest and most convincing criticism of Shakespeare that has ever been written. All the old hocus-pocus is thrown overboard. There is an entirely new examination of the materials, and to the business is brought a knowledge of the plays so ready and so vast that that of even the most learned don begins to seem a mere smattering. The same great grasp of facts and evidences is visible in the sketches which make up the three volumes of "Contemporary Portraits." What one always gets out of them is a feeling that the man knows the men he is writing about—that he not only knows what he sets down, but a great deal more. There is here nothing of the cold correctness of the usual literary "estimate." Warts are not forgotten, whether of the nose or of the immortal soul. The subject, beginning as a political shibboleth or a row of books, gradually takes on all the colors of life, and then begins to move, naturally and freely. I know of no more brilliant evocations of personality in any literature—and most of them are personalities of sharp flavor, for Harris, in his day, seems to have known almost everybody worth knowing, and whoever he knew went into his laboratory for vivisection.

The man is thus a first rate critic of his time, and what he has written about his contemporaries is certain to condition the view of them held in the future. What gives him his value in this difficult field is, first of all and perhaps most important of all, his cynical detachment—his capacity for viewing men and ideas objectively. In his life, of course, there have been friendships and some of them have been strong and long-continued, but when he writes it is with a sort of surgical remoteness, as if the business in hand were vastly more important than the man. He was lately protesting violently that he was and is quite devoid of malice. Granted. But so is a surgeon. To write of George Moore as he has written may be writing devoid of malice, but nevertheless the effect is precisely that which would follow if some malicious enemy were to drag poor George out of his celibate couch in the dead of night, and chase him naked down Shaftsbury avenue. The thing is appallingly revelatory—and I believe that it is true. The Moore that he depicts may not be absolutely the real Moore, but he is unquestionably far nearer to the real Moore than the Moore of the Moore books. The method, of course, has its defects. Harris is far more interested, fundamentally, in men than in their ideas: the catholic sweep of his "Contemporary Portraits" proves it. In consequence his judgments of books are often colored by his opinions of their authors. He dislikes Mark Twain as his own antithesis: a trimmer and poltroon. *Ergo,* "A Connecticut Yankee" is drivel, which leads us, as Euclid hath it, to absurdity. He once had a row with Dreiser. *Ergo,* "The Titan" is nonsense, which is itself nonsense. But I know of no critic who is wholly free from that quite human weakness. In the academic bunkophagi it is everything; they are willing to swallow anything so long as the author is sound upon the League of Nations. It seems to me that such aberrations are rarer in Harris than in most. He may have violent prejudices, but it is seldom that they play upon a man who is honest.

I judge from his frequent discussions of himself—he is happily free from the vanity of modesty—that the pets of his secret heart are his ventures into fiction, and especially, "The Bomb" and "Montes the Matador." The latter has been greatly praised by Arnold Bennett, who has also praised Leonard Merrick. I have read it four or five times, and always with enjoyment. It is a powerful and adept tale; well constructed and beautifully written; it recalls some of the best of the shorter stories of Thomas Hardy. Alongside it one might range half a dozen other Harris stories—all of them carefully put together, every one the work of a very skillful journeyman. But despite Harris, the authentic Harris is not the story-writer: he has talents, of course, but it would be absurd to put "Montes the Matador" beside "Heart of Darkness." In "Love in Youth" he descends to unmistakable fluff and feebleness. The real Harris is the author of the Wilde volumes, of the two books about Shakespeare, of the three volumes of "Contemporary Portraits." Here there is stuff that lifts itself clearly and brilliantly above the general—criticism that has a terrific vividness and plausibility, and all the gusto that the professors can never pump up. Harris makes his opinions not only interesting, but important. What he has to say always seems novel, ingenious, and true. Here is the chief lifework of an American who, when all values are reckoned up, will be found to have been a sound artist and an extremely intelligent, courageous and original man—and infinitely the superior of the poor dolts who once tried so childishly to dispose of him.

5

Havelock Ellis

If the test of the personal culture of a man be the degree of his freedom from the banal ideas and childish emotions which move the great masses of men, then Havelock Ellis is undoubtedly the most civilized Englishman of his generation. He is a man of the soundest and widest learning, but it is not his positive learning that gives him distinction; it is his profound and implacable skepticism, his penetrating eye for the transient, the disingenuous, and the shoddy. So unconditioned a skepticism, it must be plain, is not an English habit. The average Englishman of science, though he may challenge the Continentals within his speciality, is only too apt to sink to the level of a politician, a green grocer, or a suburban clergyman outside it. The examples of Wallace, Crookes, and Lodge are anything but isolated. Scratch an English naturalist and you are likely to discover a spiritualist; take an English metaphysician to where the band is playing, and if he begins to snuffle patriotically you need not be surprised. The late war uncovered this weakness in a wholesale manner. The English *Gelehrten,* as a class, not only stood by their country; they also stood by the Hon. David Lloyd George, the *Daily Mail,* and the mob in Trafalgar Square. Unluckily, the asinine manifestations ensuing—for instance, the "proofs" of the eminent Oxford philologist that the Germans had never contributed anything to philology—are not to be described with good grace by an American, for they were far surpassed on this side of the water. England at least had Ellis, with Bertrand Russell, Wilfrid Scawen Blunt, and a few others in the background. We had, on that plane, no one.

Ellis, it seems to me, stood above all the rest, and precisely because his dissent from the prevailing imbecilities was quite devoid of emotion and had nothing in it of brummagen moral purpose. Too many of the heretics of the time were simply orthodox witch-hunters off on an unaccustomed tangent. In their disorderly indignation they matched the regular professors; it was only in the objects of their ranting that they differed. But Ellis kept his head throughout. An Englishman of the oldest native stock, an unapologetic lover of English scenes and English ways, an unshaken believer in the essential soundness and high historical destiny of his people, he simply stood aside from the current clown-show and waited in patience for sense and decency to be restored. His "Impressions and Comments," the record of his war-time reflections, is not without its note of melancholy; it was hard to look on without depression. But for the man of genuine culture there were at least some resources remaining within himself, and what gives this volume its chief value is its picture of how such a man made use of them. Ellis, facing the mob unleashed, turned to concerns and ideas beyond its comprehension—to the humanism that stands above all such sordid conflicts. There is something almost of Renaissance dignity in his chronicle of his speculations. The man that emerges is not a mere scholar immured in a cell, but a man of the world superior to his race and his time—a philosopher viewing the childish passion of lesser men disdainfully and yet not too remote to understand it, and even to see in it a certain cosmic use. A fine air blows through the book. It takes the reader into the company of one whose mind is a rich library and whose manner is that of a gentleman. He is the complete anti-Kipling. In him the Huxleian tradition comes to full flower.

His discourse ranges from Beethoven to Comstockery and from Spanish architecture to the charm of the English village. The extent of the man's knowledge is really quite appalling. His primary work in the world has been that of a psychologist, and in particular he has brought a great erudition and an extraordinarily sound judgment to the vexatious problems of the psychology of sex, but that professional concern, extending over so many years, has not prevented him from entering a dozen other domains of speculation, nor has it dulled his sensitiveness to beauty nor his capacity to evoke it. His writing was never better than in this volume. His style, especially towards the end, takes on a sort of glowing clarity. It is English that is as transparent as a crystal, and yet it is English that is full of fine colors and cadences. There could be no better investiture for the questionings and conclusions of so original, so curious, so learned, and, above all, so sound and hearty a man.

IX. THE NATURE OF LIBERTY

EVERY time an officer of the constabulary, in the execution of his just and awful powers under American law, produces a compound fracture of the occiput of some citizen in his custody, with hemorrhage, shock, coma and death, there comes a feeble, falsetto protest from specialists in human liberty. Is it a fact without significance that this protest is never supported by the great body of American freemen, setting aside the actual heirs and creditors of the victim? I think not. Here, as usual, public opinion is very realistic. It does not rise against the policeman for the plain and simple reason that it does not question his right to do what he has done. Policemen are not given night-sticks for ornament. They are given them for the purpose of cracking the skulls of the recalcitrant plain people, Democrats and Republicans alike. When they execute that high duty they are palpably within their rights.

The specialists aforesaid are the same fanatics who shake the air with sobs every time the Postmaster-General of the United States bars a periodical from the mails because its ideas do not please him, and every time some poor Russian is deported for reading Karl Marx, and every time a Prohibition enforcement officer murders a bootlegger who resists his levies, and every time agents of the Department of Justice throw an Italian out of the window, and every time the Ku Klux Klan or the American Legion tars and feathers a Socialist evangelist. In brief, they are Radicals, and to scratch one with a pitchfork is to expose a Bolshevik. They are men standing in contempt of American institutions and in enmity to American idealism. And their evil principles are no less offensive to right-thinking and red-blooded Americans when they are United States Senators or editors of wealthy newspapers than when they are degraded I. W. W.'s throwing dead cats and infernal machines into meetings of the Rotary Club.

What ails them primarily is the ignorant and uncritical monomania that afflicts every sort of fanatic, at all times and everywhere. Having mastered with their limited faculties the theoretical principles set forth in the Bill of Rights, they work themselves into a passionate conviction that those principles are identical with the rules of law and justice, and ought to be enforced literally, and without the slightest regard for circumstance and expediency. It is precisely as if a High Church rector, accidentally looking into the Book of Chronicles, and especially Chapter II, should suddenly issue a mandate from his pulpit ordering his parishioners, on penalty of excommunication and the fires of hell, to follow exactly the example set forth, to wit: "And Jesse begat his first born Eliab, and Abinadab the second, and Shimma the third, Netheneel the fourth, Raddai the fifth, Ozen the sixth, David the seventh," and so on. It might be very sound theoretical theology, but it would surely be out of harmony with modern ideas, and the rev. gentleman would be extremely lucky if the bishop did not give him 10 days in the diocesan hoosegow.

So with the Bill of Rights. As adopted by the Fathers of the Republic, it was gross, crude, inelastic, a bit fanciful and transcendental. It specified the rights of a citizen, but it said nothing whatever about his duties. Since then, by the orderly processes of legislative science and by the even more subtle and beautiful devices of juridic art, it has been kneaded and mellowed into a far greater pliability and reasonableness. On the one hand, the citizen still retains the great privilege of membership in the most superb free nation ever witnessed on this earth. On the other hand, as a result of countless shrewd enactments and sagacious decisions, his natural lusts and appetites are held in laudable check, and he is thus kept in order and decorum. No artificial impediment stands in the way of his highest aspiration. He may become anything, including even a policeman.

But once a policeman, he is protected by the legislative and judicial arms in the peculiar rights and prerogatives that go with his high office, including especially the right to jug the laity at his will, to sweat and mug them, to subject them to the third degree, and to subdue their resistance by beating out their brains. Those who are unaware of this are simply ignorant of the basic principles of American jurisprudence, as they have been exposed times without number by the courts of first instance and ratified in lofty terms by the Supreme Court of the United States. The one aim of the controlling decisions, magnificently attained, is to safeguard public order and the public security, and to substitute a judicial process for the inchoate and dangerous interaction of discordant egos.

Let us imagine an example. You are, say, a peaceable citizen on your way home from your place of employment. A police sergeant, detecting you in the crowd, approaches you, lays his hand on your collar, and informs you that you are under arrest for killing a trolley conductor in Altoona, Pa., in 1917. Amazed by the accusation, you decide hastily that the officer has lost his wits, and take to your heels. He pursues you. You continue to run. He draws his revolver and fires at you. He misses you. He fires again and fetches you in the leg. You fall and he is upon you. You prepare to resist his apparently maniacal assault. He beats you into insensibility with his espantoon, and drags you to the patrol box.

Arrived at the watch house you are locked in a room with five detectives, and for six hours they question you with subtle art. You grow angry—perhaps robbed of your customary politeness by the throbbing in your head and leg—and answer tartly. They knock you down. Having failed to wring a confession from you, they lock you in a cell, and leave you there all night. The next day you are taken to police headquarters, your photograph is made for the Rogues' Gallery, and a print is duly deposited in the section labeled "Murderers." You are then carted to jail and locked up again. There you remain until the trolley conductor's wife comes down from Altoona to identify you. She astonishes the police by saying that you are not the man. The actual murderer, it appears, was an Italian. After holding you a day or two longer, to search your house for stills, audit your income tax returns, and investigate the premarital chastity of your wife, they let you go.

You are naturally somewhat irritated by your experience and perhaps your wife urges you to seek redress. Well, what are your remedies? If you are a firebrand, you reach out absurdly for those of a preposterous nature: the instant jailing of the sergeant, the dismissal of the Police Commissioner, the release of Mooney, a fair trial for Sacco and Vanzetti, free trade with Russia, One Big Union. But if you are a 100 per cent. American and respect the laws and institutions of your country, you send for your solicitor—and at once he shows you just how far your rights go, and where they end. You cannot cause the arrest of the sergeant, for you resisted him when he attempted to arrest you, and when you resisted him he acquired an instant right to take you by force. You cannot proceed against him for accusing you falsely, for he has a right to make summary arrests for felony, and the courts have many times decided that a public officer, so long as he cannot be charged with corruption or malice, is not liable for errors of judgment made in the execution of his sworn duty. You cannot get the detectives on the mat, for when they questioned you you were a prisoner accused of murder, and it was their duty and their right to do so. You cannot sue the turnkey at the watch house or the warden at the jail for locking you up, for they received your body, as the law says, in a lawful and regular manner, and would have been liable to penalty if they had turned you loose.

But have you no redress whatever, no rights at all? Certainly you have a right, and the courts have jealously guarded it. You have a clear right, guaranteed to you under the Constitution, to go into a court of equity and apply for a mandamus requiring the *Polizei* to cease forthwith to expose your portrait in the

Rogues' Gallery among the murderers. This is your inalienable right, and no man or men on earth can take it away from you. You cannot prevent them cherishing your portrait in their secret files, but you can get an order commanding them to refrain forever from exposing it to the gaze of idle visitors, and if you can introduce yourself unseen into their studio and prove that they disregard that order, you can have them haled into court for contempt and fined by the learned judge.

Thus the law, statute, common and case, protects the free American against injustice. It is ignorance of that subtle and perfect process and not any special love of liberty *per se* that causes radicals of anti-American kidney to rage every time an officer of the *gendarmerie,* in the simple execution of his duty, knocks a citizen in the head. The *gendarme* plainly has an inherent and inalienable right to knock him in the head: it is an essential part of his general prerogative as a sworn officer of the public peace and a representative of the sovereign power of the state. He may, true enough, exercise that prerogative in a manner liable to challenge on the ground that it is imprudent and lacking in sound judgment. On such questions reasonable men may differ. But it must be obvious that the sane and decorous way to settle differences of opinion of that sort is not by public outcry and florid appeals to sentimentality, not by ill-disguised playing to class consciousness and anti-social prejudice, but by an orderly resort to the checks and remedies superimposed upon the Bill of Rights by the calm deliberation and austere logic of the courts of equity.

The law protects the citizen. But to get its protection he must show due respect for its wise and delicate processes.

X. THE NOVEL

AN unmistakable flavor of effeminacy hangs about the novel, however heroic its content. Even in the gaudy tales of a Rex Beach, with their bold projections of the Freudian dreams of go-getters, ice-wagon drivers, Ku Kluxers, Rotary Club presidents and other such carnivora, there is a subtle something that suggests water-color painting, lip-sticks and bon-bons. Well, why not? When the novel, in the form that we know to-day, arose in Spain toward the end of the sixteenth century, it was aimed very frankly at the emerging women of the Castilian seraglios—women who were gradually emancipating themselves from the *Küche-Kinder-Kirche* darkness of the later Middle Ages, but had not yet come to anything even remotely approaching the worldly experience and intellectual curiosity of men. They could now read and they liked to practice the art, but the grand literature of the time was too profound for them, and too somber. So literary confectioners undertook stuff that would be more to their taste, and the modern novel was born. A single plot served most of these confectioners; it became and remains one of the conventions of the form. Man and maid meet, love, and proceed to kiss—but the rest must wait. The buss remains chaste through long and harrowing chapters; not until the very last scene do fate and Holy Church license anything more. This plot, as I say, still serves, and Arnold Bennett is authority for the doctrine that it is the safest known. Its appeal is patently to the feminine fancy, not to the masculine. Women like to be wooed endlessly before they loose their girdles and are wooed no more. But a man, when he finds a damsel to his taste, is eager to get through the preliminary hocus-pocus as soon as possible.

That women are still the chief readers of novels is known to every book clerk: Joseph Hergesheimer, a little while back, was bemoaning the fact as a curse to his craft. What is less often noted is that women themselves, as they have gradually become fully literate, have forced their way to the front as makers of the stuff they feed on, and that they show signs of ousting the men, soon or late, from the business. Save in the department of lyrical verse, which demands no organization of ideas but only fluency of feeling, they have nowhere else done serious work in literature. There is no epic poem of any solid value by a woman, dead or alive; and no drama, whether comedy or tragedy; and no work of metaphysical speculation;

and no history; and no basic document in any other realm of thought. In criticism, whether of works of art or of the ideas underlying them, few women have ever got beyond the *Schwärmerei* of Madame de Staël's "L'Allemagne." In the essay, the most competent woman barely surpasses the average Fleet Street *causerie* hack or Harvard professor. But in the novel the ladies have stood on a level with even the most accomplished men since the day of Jane Austen, and not only in Anglo-Saxondom, but also everywhere else—save perhaps in Russia. To-day it would be difficult to think of a contemporary German novelist of sounder dignity than Clara Viebig, Helene Böhlau or Ricarda Huch, or a Scandinavian novelist clearly above Selma Lagerlöf, or an Italian above Mathilda Serao, or, for that matter, more than two or three living Englishmen above May Sinclair, or more than two Americans equal to Willa Cather. Not only are women writing novels quite as good as those written by men—setting aside, of course, a few miraculous pieces by such fellows as Joseph Conrad: most of them not really novels at all, but metaphysical sonatas disguised as romances—; they are actually surpassing men in their experimental development of the novel form. I do not believe that either Evelyn Scott's "The Narrow House" or May Sinclair's "Life and Death of Harriet Frean" has the depth and beam of, say, Dreiser's "Jennie Gerhardt" or Arnold Bennett's "Old Wives' Tale," but it is certainly to be argued plausibly that both books show a far greater venturesomeness and a far finer virtuosity in the novel form—that both seek to free that form from artificialities which Dreiser and Bennett seem to be almost unaware of. When men exhibit any discontent with those artificialities it usually takes the shape of a vain and uncouth revolt against the whole inner spirit of the novel—that is, against the characteristics which make it what it is. Their lusher imagination tempts them to try to convert it into something that it isn't—for example, an epic, a political document, or a philosophical work. This fact explains, in one direction, such dialectical parables as Dreiser's "The 'Genius,'" H. G. Wells' "Joan and Peter" and Upton Sinclair's "King Coal," and, in a quite different direction, such rhapsodies as Cabell's "Jurgen," Meredith's "The Shaving of Shagpat" and Jacob Wassermann's "The World's Illusion." These things are novels only in the very limited sense that Beethoven's "Vittoria" and Goldmarck's "Ländliche Hochzeit" are symphonies. Their chief purpose is not that of prose fiction; it is either that of argumentation or that of poetry. The women novelists, with very few exceptions, are far more careful to remain within the legitimate bounds of the form; they do not often abandon representation to exhort or exult. Miss Cather's "My Antonía" shows a great deal of originality in its method; the story it tells is certainly not a conventional one, nor is it told in a conventional way. But it remains a novel none the less, and as clearly so, in fact, as "The Ordeal of Richard Feverel" or "Robinson Crusoe."

Much exertion of the laryngeal and respiratory muscles is wasted upon a discussion of the differences between realistic novels and romantic novels. As a matter of fact, every authentic novel is realistic in its method, however fantastic it may be in its fable. The primary aim of the novel, at all times and everywhere, is the representation of human beings at their follies and villainies, and no other art form clings to that aim so faithfully. It sets forth, not what might be true, or what ought to be true, but what actually *is* true. This is obviously not the case with poetry. Poetry is the product of an effort to invent a world appreciably better than the one we live in; its essence is not the representation of the facts, but the deliberate concealment and denial of the facts. As for the drama, it vacillates, and if it touches the novel on one side it also touches the epic on the other. But the novel is concerned solely with human nature as it is practically revealed and with human experience as men actually know it. If it departs from that representational fidelity ever so slightly, it becomes to that extent a bad novel; if it departs violently it ceases to be a novel at all. Cabell, who shows all the critical deficiencies of a sound artist, is one who has spent a good deal of time questioning the uses of realism. Yet it is a plain fact that his own stature as an artist depends almost wholly upon his capacity for accurate observation and realistic representation. The stories in "The Line of Love," though they may appear superficially to be excessively romantic, really owe all of their charm to their pungent realism. The pleasure they give is the pleasure of recognition; one somehow delights in seeing a mediæval baron acting precisely like a New York stockbroker. As for "Jurgen," it is as realistic in manner as Zola's "La Terre," despite its grotesque fable and its burden of political, theological and epistemological ideas. No one not an idiot would mistake the dialogue between Jurgen and Queen Guinevere's father for romantic, in the sense that Kipling's "Mandalay" is romantic; it is actually as mordantly realistic as the dialogue between Nora and Helmer in the last act of "A Doll's House."

It is my contention that women succeed in the novel—and that they will succeed even more strikingly as they gradually throw off the inhibitions that have hitherto cobwebbed their minds—simply because they are better fitted for this realistic representation than men—because they see the facts of life more sharply, and are less distracted by mooney dreams. Women seldom have the pathological faculty vaguely called imagination. One doesn't often hear of them groaning over colossal bones in their sleep, as dogs do, or constructing heavenly hierarchies or political utopias, as men do. Their concern is always with things of more objective substance—roofs, meals, rent, clothes, the birth and upbringing of children. They are, I believe, generally happier than men, if only because the demands they make of life are more moderate and less romantic. The chief pain that a man normally suffers in his progress through this vale is that of disillusionment; the chief pain that a woman suffers is that of parturition. There is enormous significance in the difference. The first is artificial and self-inflicted; the second is natural and unescapable. The psychological history of the differentiation I need not go into here: its springs lie obviously in the greater physical strength of man and his freedom from child-bearing, and in the larger mobility and capacity for adventure that go therewith. A man dreams of utopias simply because he feels himself free to construct them; a woman must keep house. In late years, to be sure, she has toyed with the idea of escaping that necessity, but I shall not bore you with arguments showing that she never will. So long as children are brought into the world and made ready for the trenches, the sweatshops and the gallows by the laborious method ordained of God she will never be quite as free to roam and dream as man is. It is only a small minority of her sex who cherish a contrary expectation, and this minority, though anatomically female, is spiritually male. Show me a woman who has visions comparable, say, to those of Swedenborg, Woodrow Wilson, Strindberg or Dr. Ghandi, and I'll show you a woman who is a very powerful anaphrodisiac.

Thus women, by their enforced preoccupation with the harsh facts of life, are extremely well fitted to write novels, which must deal with the facts or nothing. What they need for the practical business, in addition, falls under two heads. First, they need enough sense of social security to make them free to set down what they see. Secondly, they need the modest technical skill, the formal mastery of words and ideas, necessary to do it. The latter, I believe, they have had ever since they learned to read and write, say three hundred years ago; it comes to them more readily than to men, and is exercised with greater ease. The former they are fast acquiring. In the days of Aphra Behn and Ann Radcliffe it was almost as scandalous for a woman to put her observations and notions into print as it was for her to show her legs; even in the days of Jane Austen and Charlotte Brontë the thing was regarded as decidedly unladylike. But now, within certain limits, she is free to print whatever she pleases, and before long even those surviving limits will be obliterated. If I live to the year 1950 I expect to see a novel by a women that will describe a typical marriage under Christianity, from the woman's standpoint, as realistically as it is treated from the man's standpoint in Upton Sinclair's "Love's Pilgrimage." That novel, I venture to predict, will be a cuckoo. At one stroke it will demolish superstitions that have prevailed in the Western World since the fall of the Roman Empire. It will seem harsh, but it will be true. And, being true, it will be a good novel. There can be no good one that is not true.

What ailed the women novelists, until very recently, was a lingering ladyism—a childish prudery inherited from their mothers. I believe that it is being rapidly thrown off; indeed, one often sees a concrete woman novelist shedding it. I give you two obvious examples: Zona Gale and Willa Cather. Miss Gale started out by trying to put into novels the conventional prettiness that is esteemed along the Main Streets of her native Wisconsin. She had skill and did it well, and so she won a good deal of popular success. But her work was intrinsically as worthless as a treatise on international politics by the Hon. Warren Gamaliel Harding or a tract on the duties of a soldier and a gentleman by a state president of the American Legion. Then, of a sudden, for some reason quite unknown to the deponent, she threw off all that flabby artificiality, and began describing the people about her as they really were. The result was a second success even more pronounced than her first, and on a palpably higher level. The career of Miss Cather has covered less ground, for she began far above Main Street. What she tried to do at the start was to imitate the superficial sophistication of Edith Wharton and Henry James—a deceptive thing, apparently realistic in essence, but actually as conventional as table manners or the professional buffooneries of a fashionable rector. Miss Cather had extraordinary skill as a writer, and so her imitation was scarcely to be distinguished from the original, but in the course of time she began to be aware of its hollowness. Then she turned to first-hand representation—to pictures of the people she actually knew. There ensued a series of novels that rose step by step to the very distinguished quality of "My Antonía." That fine piece is a great deal more than simply a good novel. It is a document in the history of American literature. It proves, once and for all time, that accurate representation is not, as the campus critics of Dreiser seem to think, inimical to beauty. It proves, on the contrary, that the most careful and penetrating representation is itself the source of a rare and wonderful beauty. No romantic novel ever written in America, by man or woman, is one-half so beautiful as "My Antonía."

As I have said, the novel, in the United States as elsewhere, still radiates an aroma of effeminacy, in the conventional sense. Specifically, it deals too monotonously with the varieties of human transactions which chiefly interest the unintelligent women who are its chief patrons and the scarcely less intelligent women who, until recently, were among its chief commercial manufacturers, to wit, the transactions that revolve around the ensnarement of men by women—the puerile tricks and conflicts of what is absurdly called romantic love. But I believe that the women novelists, as they emerge into the fullness of skill, will throw overboard all that old baggage, and leave its toting to such male artisans as Chambers, Beach, Coningsby Dawson and Emerson Hough, as they have already left the whole flag-waving and "red-blooded" buncombe. True enough, the snaring of men will remain the principal business of women in this world for many generations, but it would be absurd to say that intelligent women, even to-day, view it romantically—that is, as it is viewed by bad novelists. They see it realistically, and they see it, not as an end in itself, but as a means to other ends. It is, speaking generally, after she has got her man that a woman begins to live. The novel of the future, I believe, will show her thus living. It will depict the intricate complex of forces that conditions her life and generates her ideas, and it will show, against a background of actuality, her conduct in the eternal struggle between her aspiration and her destiny. Women, as I have argued, are not normally harassed by the grandiose and otiose visions that inflame the gizzards of men, but they too discover inevitably that life is a conflict, and that it is the harsh fate of *Homo sapiens* to get the worst of it. I should like to read a "Main Street" by an articulate Carol Kennicott, or a "Titan" by one of Cowperwood's mistresses, or a "Cytherea" by a Fanny Randon—or a Savina Grove! It would be sweet stuff, indeed. . . . And it will come.

XI. THE FORWARD-LOOKER

WHEN the history of the late years in America is written, I suspect that their grandest, gaudiest gifts to *Kultur* will be found in the incomparable twins: the right-thinker and the forward-looker. No other nation can match them, at any weight. The right-thinker is privy to all God's wishes, and even whims; the forward-looker is the heir to all His promises to the righteous. The former is never wrong; the latter is never despairing. Sometimes the two are amalgamated into one man, and we have a Bryan, a Wilson, a Dr. Frank Crane. But more often there is a division: the forward-looker thinks wrong, and the right-thinker looks backward. I give you Upton Sinclair and Nicholas Murray Butler as examples. Butler is an absolute masterpiece of correct thought; in his whole life, so far as human records show, he has not cherished a single fancy that might not have been voiced by a Fifth Avenue rector or spread upon the editorial page of the New York *Times*. But he has no vision, alas, alas! All the revolutionary inventions for lifting up humanity leave him cold. He is against them all, from the initiative and referendum to birth control, and from Fletcherism to osteopathy. Now turn to Sinclair. He believes in every one of them, however daring and fantoddish; he grasps and gobbles all the new ones the instant they are announced. But the man simply cannot think right. He is wrong on politics, on economics, and on theology. He glories in and is intensely vain of his wrongness. Let but a new article of correct American thought get itself stated by the constituted ecclesiastical and secular authorities—by Bishop Manning, or Judge Gary, or Butler, or Adolph Ochs, or Dr. Fabian Franklin, or Otto Kahn, or Dr. Stephen S. Wise, or Roger W. Babson, or any other such inspired omphalist—and he is against it almost before it is stated.

On the whole, as a neutral in such matters, I prefer the forward-looker to the right-thinker, if only because he shows more courage and originality. It takes nothing save lack of humor to believe what Butler, or Ochs, or Bishop Manning believes, but it takes long practice and a considerable natural gift to get down the beliefs of Sinclair. I remember with great joy the magazine that he used to issue during the war. In the very first issue he advocated Socialism, the single tax, birth control, communism, the League of Nations, the conscription of wealth, government ownership of coal mines, sex hygiene and free trade. In the next issue he added the recall of judges, Fletcherism, the Gary system, the Montessori method, paper-bag cookery, war gardens and the budget system. In the third he came out for sex hygiene, one big union, the initiative and referendum, the city manager plan, chiropractic and Esperanto. In the fourth he went to the direct primary, fasting, the Third International, a federal divorce law, free motherhood, hot lunches for school children, Prohibition, the vice crusade, *Expressionismus*, the government control of newspapers, deep breathing, international courts, the Fourteen Points, freedom for the Armenians, the limitation of campaign expenditures, the merit system, the abolition of the New York Stock Exchange, psychoanalysis, crystal-gazing, the Little Theater movement, the recognition of Mexico, *vers libre*, old age pensions, unemployment insurance, coöperative stores, the endowment of motherhood, the Americanization of the immigrant, mental telepathy, the abolition of grade crossings, federal labor exchanges, profit-sharing in industry, a prohibitive tax on Poms, the clean-up-paint-up campaign, relief for the Jews, osteopathy, mental mastery, and the twilight sleep. And so on, and so on. Once I had got into the swing of the Sinclair monthly I found that I could dispense with at least twenty other journals of the uplift. When he abandoned it I had to subscribe for them anew, and the gravel has stuck in my craw ever since.

In the first volume of his personal philosophy, "The Book of Life: Mind and Body," he is estopped from displaying whole categories of his ideas, for his subject is not man the political and economic machine, but man and mammal. Nevertheless, his characteristic hospitality to new revelations is abundantly visible. What does the mind suggest? The mind suggests its dark and fascinating functions and powers, some of them very recent. There is, for example, psychoanalysis. There is mental telepathy. There is crystal-gazing. There is double personality. Out of each springs a scheme for the uplift of the race—in each there is something for a forward-looker to get his teeth into. And if mind, then why not also spirit? Here even a forward-looker may hesitate; here, in fact, Sinclair himself hesitates. The whole field of spiritism is barred to him by his theological heterodoxy; if he admits that man has an immortal soul, he may also have to admit that the soul can suffer in hell. Thus even forward-looking may turn upon and devour itself. But if the meadow wherein spooks and poltergeists disport is closed, it is at least possible to peep over the fence. Sinclair sees materializations in dark rooms, under red, satanic lights. He is, perhaps, not yet convinced, but he is looking pretty hard. Let a ghostly hand reach out and grab him, and he will be over the fence! The body is easier. The new inventions for dealing with it are innumerable and irresistible; no forward-looker can fail to succumb to at least some of them. Sinclair teeters dizzily. On the one hand he stoutly defends surgery—that is, provided the patient is allowed to make his own diagnosis!—on the other hand he is hot for fasting, teetotalism, and the avoidance of drugs, coffee and tobacco, and he begins to flirt with osteopathy and chiropractic. More, he has discovered a new revelation in San Francisco—a system of diagnosis and therapeutics, still hooted at by the Medical Trust, whereby the exact location of a cancer may be determined by examining a few drops of the patient's blood, and syphilis may be cured by vibrations, and whereby, most curious of all, it can be established that odd numbers, written on a sheet of paper, are full of negative electricity, and even numbers are full of positive electricity.

The book is written with great confidence and address, and has a good deal of shrewdness mixed with its credulities; few licensed medical practitioners could give you better advice. But it is less interesting than its author, or, indeed, than forward-lookers in general. Of all the known orders of men they fascinate me the most. I spend whole days reading their pronunciamentos, and am an expert in the ebb and flow of their singularly bizarre ideas. As I have said, I have never encountered one who believed in but one sure cure for all the sorrows of the world, and let it go at that. Nay, even the most timorous of them gives his full faith and credit to at least two. Turn, for example, to the official list of eminent single taxers issued by the Joseph Fels Fund. I defy you to find one solitary man on it who stops with the single tax. There is David Starr Jordan: he is also one of the great whales of pacifism. There is B. O. Flower: he is the emperor of anti-vaccinationists. There is Carrie Chapman Catt: she is hot for every peruna that the suffragettes brew. There is W. S. U'Ren: he is in general practise as a messiah. There is Hamlin Garland: he also chases spooks. There is Jane Addams: vice crusader, pacifist, suffragist, settlement worker. There is Prof. Dr. Scott Nearing: Socialist and martyr. There is Newt Baker: heir of the Wilsonian idealism. There is Gifford Pinchot: conservationist, Prohibitionist, Bull Moose, and professional Good Citizen. There is Judge Ben B. Lindsey: forward-looking's Jack Horner, forever sticking his thumb into new pies. I could run the list to columns, but no need. You know the type as well as I do. Give the forward-looker the direct primary, and he demands the short ballot. Give him the initiative and referendum, and he bawls for the recall of judges. Give him Christian Science, and he proceeds to the swamis and yogis. Give him the Mann Act, and he wants laws providing for the castration of fornicators. Give him Prohibition, and he launches a new crusade against cigarettes, coffee, jazz, and custard pies.

I have a wide acquaintance among such sad, mad, glad folks, and know some of them very well. It is my belief that the majority of them are absolutely honest—that they believe as fully in their baroque gospels as I believe in the dishonesty of politicians—that their myriad and amazing faiths sit upon them as heavily as the fear of hell sits upon a Methodist deacon who has degraded the vestry-room to carnal uses. All that may be justly said against them is that they are chronically full of hope, and hence chronically uneasy and indignant—that they belong to the less sinful and comfortable of the two grand divisions of the human race. Call them the tender-minded, as the late William James used to do, and you have pretty well described them. They are, on the one hand, pathologically sensitive to the sorrows of the world, and, on the other hand, pathologically susceptible to the eloquence of quacks. What seems to lie in all of them is the doctrine that evils so vast as those they see about them *must* and *will* be laid—that it would be an insult to a just God to think of them as permanent and irremediable. This notion, I believe, is at the bottom of much of the current pathetic faith in Prohibition. The thing itself is obviously a colossal failure—that is, when viewed calmly and realistically. It has not only not cured the rum evil in the United States; it has plainly made that evil five times as bad as it ever was before. But to confess that bald fact would be to break the forward-looking heart: it simply refuses to harbor the concept of the incurable. And so, being debarred by the legal machinery that supports Prohibition from going back to any more feasible scheme of relief, it cherishes the sorry faith that somehow, in some vague and incomprehensible way, Prohibition will yet work. When the truth becomes so horribly evident that even forward-lookers are daunted, then some new quack will arise to fool them again, with some new and worse scheme of super-Prohibition. It is their destiny to wobble thus endlessly between quack and quack. One pulls them by the right arm and one by the left arm. A third is at their coat-tail pockets, and a fourth beckons them over the hill.

The rest of us are less tender-minded, and, in consequence, much happier. We observe quite clearly that the world, as it stands, is anything but perfect—that injustice exists, and turmoil, and tragedy, and bitter suffering of ten thousand kinds—that human life at its best, is anything but a grand, sweet song. But instead of ranting absurdly against the fact, or weeping over it maudlinly, or trying to remedy it with inadequate means, we simply put the thought of it out of our minds, just as a wise man puts away the thought that alcohol is probably bad for his liver, or that his wife is a shade too fat. Instead of mulling over it and suffering from it, we seek contentment by pursuing the delights that are so strangely mixed with the horrors—by seeking out the soft spots and endeavoring to avoid the hard spots. Such is the intelligent habit of practical and sinful men, and under it lies a sound philosophy. After all, the world is not our handiwork, and we are not responsible for what goes on in it, save within very narrow limits. Going outside them with our protests and advice tends to become contumacy to the celestial hierarchy. Do the poor suffer in the midst of plenty? Then let us thank God politely that we are not that poor. Are rogues in offices? Well, go call a policeman, thus setting rogue upon rogue. Are taxes onerous, wasteful, unjust? Then let us dodge as large a part of them as we can. Are whole regiments and army corps of our fellow creatures doomed to hell? Then let them complain to the archangels, and, if the archangels are too busy to hear them, to the nearest archbishop.

Unluckily for the man of tender mind, he is quite incapable of any such easy dismissal of the great plagues and conundrums of existence. It is of the essence of his character that he is too sensitive and sentimental to put them ruthlessly out of his mind: he cannot view even the crunching of a cockroach without feeling the snapping of his own ribs. And it is of the essence of his character that he is unable to escape the delusion of duty—that he can't rid himself of the notion that, whenever he observes anything in the world that might conceivably be improved, he is commanded by God to make every effort to improve it. In brief, he is a public-spirited man, and the ideal citizen of democratic states. But Nature, it must be obvious, is opposed to democracy—and whoso goes counter to nature must expect to pay the penalty. The tender-minded man pays it by hanging forever upon the cruel hooks of hope, and by fermenting inwardly in incessant indignation. All this, perhaps, explains the notorious ill-humor of uplifters—the wowser touch that is in even the best of them. They dwell so much upon the imperfections of the universe and the weaknesses of man that they end by believing that the universe is altogether out of joint and that every man is a scoundrel and every woman a vampire. Years ago I had a combat with certain eminent reformers of the sex hygiene and vice crusading species, and got out of it a memorable illumination of their private minds. The reform these strange creatures were then advocating was directed against sins of the seventh category, and they proposed to put them down by forcing through legislation of a very harsh and fantastic kind—statutes forbidding any woman, however forbidding, to entertain a man in her apartment without the presence of a third party, statutes providing for the garish lighting of all dark places in the public parks, and so on. In the course of my debates with them I gradually jockeyed them into abandoning all of the arguments they started with, and so brought them down to their fundamental doctrine, to wit, that no woman, without the aid of the police, could be trusted to protect her virtue. I pass as a cynic in Christian circles, but this notion certainly gave me pause. And it was voiced by men who were the fathers of grown and unmarried daughters!

It is no wonder that men who cherish such ideas are so ready to accept any remedy for the underlying evils, no matter how grotesque. A man suffering from hay-fever, as every one knows, will take any medicine that is offered to him, even though he knows the compounder to be a quack; the infinitesimal chance that the quack may have the impossible cure gives him a certain hope, and so makes the disease itself more bearable. In precisely the same way a man suffering from the conviction that the whole universe is hell-bent for destruction—that the government he lives under is intolerably evil, that the rich are growing richer and the poor poorer, that no man's word can be trusted and no woman's chastity, that another and worse war is hatching, that the very regulation of the weather has fallen into the hands of rogues—such a man will grab at anything, even birth control, osteopathy or the Fourteen Points, rather than let the foul villainy go on. The apparent necessity of finding a remedy without delay transforms itself, by an easy psychological process, into a belief that the remedy has been found; it is almost impossible for most men, and particularly for tender-minded men, to take in the concept of the insoluble. Every problem that remains unsolved, including even the problem of evil, is in that state simply because men of strict virtue and passionate altruism have not combined to solve it—because the business has been neglected by human laziness and rascality. All that is needed to dispatch it is the united effort of enough pure hearts: the accursed nature of things will yield inevitably to a sufficiently desperate battle; mind (usually written Mind) will triumph over matter (usually written Matter—or maybe Money Power, or Land Monopoly, or Beef Trust, or Conspiracy of Silence, or Commercialized Vice, or Wall Street, or the Dukes, or the Kaiser), and the Kingdom of God will be at hand. So, with the will to believe in full function, the rest is easy. The eager forward-looker is exactly like the man with hay-fever, or arthritis, or nervous dyspepsia, or diabetes. It takes time to try each successive remedy—to search it out, to take it, to observe its effects, to hope, to doubt, to shelve it. Before the process is completed another is offered; new ones are always waiting before their predecessors have been discarded. Here, perhaps, we get a glimpse of the causes behind the protean appetite of the true forward-looker—his virtuosity in credulity. He is in all stages simultaneously—just getting over the initiative and referendum, beginning to have doubts about the short ballot, making ready for a horse doctor's dose of the single tax, and contemplating an experimental draught of Socialism tomorrow.

What is to be done for him? How is he to be cured of his great thirst for sure-cures that do not cure, and converted into a contented and careless backward-looker, peacefully snoozing beneath his fig tree while the oppressed bawl for succor in forty abandoned lands, and injustice stalks the world, and taxes mount higher and higher, and poor working-girls are sold into white slavery, and Prohibition fails to prohibit, and cocaine is hawked openly, and jazz drags millions down the primrose way, and the trusts own the legislatures of all Christendom, and judges go to dinner with millionaires, and Europe prepares for another war, and children of four and five years work as stevedores and locomotive firemen, and guinea pigs and dogs are vivisected, and Polish immigrant women have more children every year, and divorces multiply, and materialism rages, and the devil runs the cosmos? What is to be done to save the forward-looker from his torturing indignations, and set him in paths of happy dalliance? Answer: nothing. He was born that way, as men are born with hare lips or bad livers, and he will remain that way until the angels summon him to eternal rest. Destiny has laid upon him the burden of seeing unescapably what had better not be looked at, of believing what isn't so. There is no way to help him. He must suffer vicariously for the carnal ease of the rest of us. He must die daily that we may live in peace, corrupt and contented,

As I have said, I believe fully that this child of sorrow is honest—that his twinges and malaises are just as real to him as those that rack the man with arthritis, and that his trusting faith in quacks is just as natural. But this, of course, is not saying that the quacks themselves are honest. On the contrary, their utter dishonesty must be quite as obvious as the simplicity of their dupes. Trade is good for them in the United States, where hope is a sort of national vice, and so they flourish here more luxuriously than anywhere else on earth. Some one told me lately that there are now no less than 25,000 national organizations in the United States for the uplift of the plain people and the snaring and shaking down of forward-lookers—societies for the Americanization of immigrants, for protecting poor working-girls against

Jews and Italians, for putting Bibles into the bedrooms of week-end hotels, for teaching Polish women how to wash their babies, for instructing school-children in ring-around-a-rosy, for crusading against the cigarette, for preventing accidents in rolling-mills, for making street-car conductors more polite, for testing the mentality of Czecho-Slovaks, for teaching folk-songs, for restoring the United States to Great Britain, for building day-nurseries in the devastated regions of France, for training deaconesses, for fighting the house-fly, for preventing cruelty to mules and Tom-cats, for forcing householders to clean their backyards, for planting trees, for saving the Indian, for sending colored boys to Harvard, for opposing Sunday movies, for censoring magazines, for God knows what else. In every large American city such organizations swarm, and every one of them has an executive secretary who tries incessantly to cadge space in the newspapers. Their agents penetrate to the remotest hamlets in the land, and their circulars, pamphlets and other fulminations swamp the mails. In Washington and at every state capital they have their lobbyists, and every American legislator is driven half frantic by their innumerable and preposterous demands. Each of them wants a law passed to make its crusade official and compulsory; each is forever hunting for forward-lookers with money.

One of the latest of these uplifting vereins to score a ten-strike is the one that sponsored the so-called Maternity Bill. That measure is now a law, and the over-burdened American taxpayer, at a cost of $3,-000,000 a year, is supporting yet one more posse of perambulating gabblers and snouters. The influences behind the bill were exposed in the Senate by Senator Reed, of Missouri, but to no effect: a majority of the other Senators, in order to get rid of the propagandists in charge of it, had already promised to vote for it. Its one intelligible aim, as Senator Reed showed, is to give government jobs at good salaries to a gang of nosey old maids. These virgins now traverse the country teaching married women how to have babies in a ship-shape and graceful manner, and how to keep them alive after having them. Only one member of the corps has ever been married herself; nevertheless, the old gals are authorized to go out among the Italian and Yiddish women, each with ten or twelve head of kids to her credit, and tell them all about it. According to Senator Reed, the ultimate aim of the forward-lookers who sponsored the scheme is to provide for the official registration of expectant mothers, that they may be warned what to eat, what movies to see, and what midwives to send for when the time comes. Imagine a young bride going down to the County Clerk's office to report herself! And imagine an elderly and anthropopagous spinster coming around next day to advise her! Or a boozy political doctor!

All these crazes, of course, are primarily artificial. They are set going, not by the plain people spontaneously, nor even by the forward-lookers who eventually support them, but by professionals. The Anti-Saloon League is their archetype. It is owned and operated by gentlemen who make excellent livings stirring up the tender-minded; if their salaries were cut off to-morrow, all their moral passion would ooze out, and Prohibition would be dead in two weeks. So with the rest of the uplifting camorras. Their present enormous prosperity, I believe, is due in large part to a fact that is never thought of, to wit, the fact that the women's colleges of the country, for a dozen years past, have been turning out far more graduates than could be utilized as teachers. These supernumerary lady Ph.D's almost unanimously turn to the uplift—and the uplift saves them. In the early days of higher education for women in the United States, practically all the graduates thrown upon the world got jobs as teachers, but now a good many are left over. Moreover, it has been discovered that the uplift is easier than teaching, and that it pays a great deal better. It is a rare woman professor who gets more than $5,000 a year, but there are plenty of uplifting jobs at $8,000 and $10,000 a year, and in the future there will be some prizes at twice as much. No wonder the learned girls fall upon them so eagerly!

The annual production of male Ph.D's is also far beyond the legitimate needs of the nation, but here the congestion is relieved by the greater and more varied demand for masculine labor. If a young man emerging from Columbia or Ohio Wesleyan as *Philosophiæ Doctor* finds it impossible to get a job teaching he can always go on the road as a salesman of dental supplies, or enlist in the marines, or study law, or enter the ministry, or go to work in a coal-mine, or a slaughter-house, or a bucket-shop, or begin selling Oklahoma mine-stock to widows and retired clergymen. The women graduate faces far fewer opportunities. She is commonly too old and too worn by meditation to go upon the stage in anything above the grade of a patent-medicine show, she has been so poisoned by instruction in sex hygiene that she shies at marriage, and most of the standard professions and grafts of the world are closed to her. The invention of the uplift came as a godsend to her. Had not some mute, inglorious Edison devised it at the right time, humanity would be disgraced to-day by the spectacle of hordes of Lady Ph.D's going to work in steam-laundries, hooch shows and chewing-gum factories. As it is, they are all taken care of by the innumerable societies for making the whole world virtuous and happy. One may laugh at the aims and methods of many such societies—for example, at the absurd vereins for Americanizing immigrants, *i. e.*, degrading them to the level of the native peasantry. But one thing, at least, they accomplish: they provide comfortable and permanent jobs for hundreds and thousands of deserving women, most of whom are far more profitably employed trying to make Methodists out of Sicilians than they would be if they were trying to make husbands out of bachelors. It is for this high purpose also that the forward-looker suffers.

XII. MEMORIAL SERVICE

WHERE is the grave-yard of dead gods? What lingering mourner waters their mounds? There was a day when Jupiter was the king of the gods, and any man who doubted his puissance was *ipso facto* a barbarian and an ignoramus. But where in all the world is there a man who worships Jupiter to-day? And what of Huitzilopochtli? In one year—and it is no more than five hundred years ago—50,000 youths and maidens were slain in sacrifice to him. To-day, if he is remembered at all, it is only by some vagrant savage in the depths of the Mexican forest. Huitzilopochtli, like many other gods, had no human father; his mother was a virtuous widow; he was born of an apparently innocent flirtation that she carried on with the sun. When he frowned, his father, the sun, stood still. When he roared with rage, earthquakes engulfed whole cities. When he thirsted he was watered with 10,000 gallons of human blood. But to-day Huitzilopochtli is as magnificently forgotten as Allen G. Thurman. Once the peer of Allah, Buddha and Wotan, he is now the peer of General

Coxey, Richmond P. Hobson, Nan Patterson, Alton B. Parker, Adelina Patti, General Weyler and Tom Sharkey.

Speaking of Huitzilopochtli recalls his brother, Tezcatilpoca. Tezcatilpoca was almost as powerful: he consumed 25,000 virgins a year. Lead me to his tomb: I would weep, and hang a *couronne des perles*. But who knows where it is? Or where the grave of Quitzalcoatl is? Or Tialoc? Or Chalchihuitlicue? Or Xiehtecutli? Or Centeotl, that sweet one? Or Tlazolteotl, the goddess of love? Or Mictlan? Or Ixtlilton? Or Omacatl? Or Yacatecutli? Or Mixcoatl? Or Xipe? Or all the host of Tzitzimitles? Where are their bones? Where is the willow on which they hung their harps? In what forlorn and unheard-of hell do they await the resurrection morn? Who enjoys their residuary estates? Or that of Dis, whom Cæsar found to be the chief god of the Celts? Or that of Tarves, the bull? Or that of Moccos, the pig? Or that of Epona, the mare? Or that of Mullo, the celestial jack-ass? There was a time when the Irish revered all these gods as violently as they now hate the English. But to-day even the drunkest Irishman laughs at them.

But they have company in oblivion: the hell of dead gods is as crowded as the Presbyterian hell for babies. Damona is there, and Esus, and Drunemeton, and Silvana, and Dervones, and Adsalluta, and Deva, and Belisama, and Axona, and Vintios, and Taranuous, and Sulis, and Cocidius, and Adsmerius, and Dumiatis, and Caletos, and Moccus, and Ollovidius, and Albiorix, and Leucitius, and Vitucadrus, and Ogmios, and Uxellimus, and Borvo, and Grannos, and Mogons. All mighty gods in their day, worshiped by millions, full of demands and impositions, able to bind and loose—all gods of the first class, not dilettanti. Men labored for generations to build vast temples to them—temples with stones as large as hay-wagons. The business of interpreting their whims occupied thousands of priests, wizards, archdeacons, evangelists, haruspices, bishops, archbishops. To doubt them was to die, usually at the stake. Armies took to the field to defend them against infidels: villages were burned, women and children were butchered, cattle were driven off. Yet in the end they all withered and died, and to-day there is none so poor to do them reverence. Worse, the very tombs in which they lie are lost, and so even a respectful stranger is debarred from paying them the slightest and politest homage.

What has become of Sutekh, once the high god of the whole Nile Valley? What has become of:

Resheph	Baal
Anath	Astarte
Ashtoreth	Hadad

El	Addu
Nergal	Shalem
Nebo	Dagon
Ninib	Sharrab
Melek	Yau
Ahijah	Amon-Re
Isis	Osiris
Ptah	Sebek
Anubis	Molech?

All these were once gods of the highest eminence. Many of them are mentioned with fear and trembling in the Old Testament. They ranked, five or six thousand years ago, with Jahveh himself; the worst of them stood far higher than Thor. Yet they have all gone down the chute, and with them the following:

Bilé	Gwydion
Lêr	Manawyddan
Arianrod	Nuada Argetlam
Morrigu	Tagd
Govannon	Goibniu
Gunfled	Odin
Sokk-mimi	Llaw Gyffes
Memetona	Lleu
Dagda	Ogma
Kerridwen	Mider
Pwyll	Rigantona
Ogyrvan	Marzin
Dea Dia	Mars

Ceros
Vaticanus
Edulia
Adeona
Iuno Lucina
Saturn
Furrina
Vediovis
Consus
Cronos
Enki
Engurra
Belus
Dimmer
Mu-ul-lil
Ubargisi
Ubilulu
Gasan-lil
U-dimmer-an-kia
Enurestu
U-sab-sib
U-Mersi
Tammuz
Venus
Bau
Mulu-hursang
Anu
Beltis
Nusku
Ni-zu
Sahi
Aa
Allatu

Jupiter
Cunina
Potina
Statilinus
Diana of Ephesus
Robigus
Pluto
Ops
Meditrina
Vesta
Tilmun
Zer-panitu
Merodach
U-ki
Dauke
Gasan-abzu
Elum
U-Tin-dir ki
Marduk
Nin-lil-la
Nin
Persephone
Istar
Lagas
U-urugal
Sirtumu
Ea
Nirig
Nebo
Samas
Ma-banba-anna
En-Mersi
Amurru

Sin
AbilAddu
Apsu
Dagan
Elali
Isum
Mami
Nin-man
Zaraqu
Suqamunu
Zagaga

Assur
Aku
Beltu
Dumu-zi-abzu
Kuski-banda
Kaawanu
Nin-azu
Lugal-Amarada
Qarradu
Ura-gala
Ueras

You may think I spoof. That I invent the names. I do not. Ask the rector to lend you any good treatise on comparative religion: you will find them all listed. They were gods of the highest standing and dignity—gods of civilized peoples—worshipped and believed in by millions. All were theoretically omnipotent, omniscient and immortal. And all are dead.

XIII. EDUCATION

I

NEXT to the clerk in holy orders, the fellow with the worst job in the world is the schoolmaster. Both are underpaid, both fall steadily in authority and dignity, and both wear out their hearts trying to perform the impossible. How much the world asks of them, and how little they can actually deliver! The clergyman's business is to save the human race from hell: if he saves one-eighth of one per cent., even within the limits of his narrow flock, he does magnificently. The schoolmaster's is to spread the enlightenment, to make the great masses of the plain people intelligent—and intelligence is precisely the thing that the great masses of the plain people are congenitally and eternally incapable of.

Is it any wonder that the poor birchman, facing this labor that would have staggered Sisyphus Æolusohn, seeks refuge from its essential impossibility in a Chinese maze of empty technic? The ghost of Pestalozzi, once bearing a torch and beckoning toward the heights, now leads down stairways into black and forbidding dungeons. Especially in America, where all that is bombastic and mystical is most esteemed, the art of pedagogics becomes a sort of puerile magic, a thing of preposterous secrets, a grotesque compound of false premises and illogical conclusions. Every year sees a craze for some new solution of the teaching enigma, at once simple and infallible—manual training, playground work, song and doggerel lessons, the Montessori method, the Gary system—an endless series of flamboyant arcanums. The worst extravagances of *privat dozent* experimental psychology are gravely seized upon; the uplift pours in its ineffable principles and discoveries; mathematical formulæ are worked out for every emergency; there is no sure-cure so idiotic that some superintendent of schools will not swallow it.

A couple of days spent examining the literature of the New Thought in pedagogy are enough to make the judicious weep. Its aim seems to be to reduce the whole teaching process to a sort of automatic reaction, to discover some master formula that will not only take the place of competence and resourcefulness in the teacher but that will also create an artificial receptivity in the child. The merciless application of this formula (which changes every four days) now seems to be the chief end and aim of pedagogy. Teaching becomes a thing in itself, separable from and superior to the thing taught. Its mastery is a special business, a transcendental art and mystery, to be acquired in the laboratory. A teacher well grounded in this mystery, and hence privy to every detail of the new technic (which changes, of course, with the formula), can teach anything to any child, just as a sound dentist can pull any tooth out of any jaw.

All this, I need not point out, is in sharp contrast to the old theory of teaching. By that theory mere technic was simplified and subordinated. All that it demanded of the teacher told off to teach, say, geography, was that he master the facts in the geography book and provide himself with a stout rattan. Thus equipped, he was ready for a test of his natural pedagogical genius. First he exposed the facts in the book, then he gilded them with whatever appearance of interest and importance he could conjure up, and then he tested the extent of their transference to the minds of his pupils. Those pupils who had ingested them got apples; those who had failed got fanned with the rattan. Followed the second round, and the same test again, with a second noting of results. And then the third, and fourth, and the fifth, and so on until the last and least pupil had been stuffed to his subnormal and perhaps moronic brim.

I was myself grounded in the underlying delusions of what is called knowledge by this austere process, and despite the eloquence of those who support newer ideas, I lean heavily in favor of it, and regret to hear that it is no more. It was crude, it was rough, and it was often not a little cruel, but it at least had two capital advantages over all the systems that have succeeded it. In the first place, its machinery was simple; even the stupidest child could understand it; it hooked up cause and effect with the utmost clarity. And in the second place, it tested the teacher as and how he ought to be tested—that is, for his actual capacity to teach, not for his mere technical virtuosity. There was, in fact, no technic for him to master, and hence none for him to hide behind. He could not conceal a hopeless inability to impart knowledge beneath a correct professional method.

That ability to impart knowledge, it seems to me, has very little to do with technical method. It may operate at full function without any technical method at all, and contrariwise, the most elaborate of technical methods, whether out of Switzerland, Italy or Gary, Ind., cannot make it operate when it is not actually present. And what does it consist of? It consists, first, of a natural talent for dealing with children, for getting into their minds, for putting things in a way that they can comprehend. And it consists, secondly, of a deep belief in the interest and importance of the thing taught, a concern about it amounting to a sort of passion. A man who knows a subject thoroughly, a man so soaked in it that he eats it, sleeps it and dreams it—this man can always teach it with success, no matter how little he knows of technical pedagogy. That is because there is enthusiasm in him, and because enthusiasm is almost as contagious as fear or the barber's itch. An enthusiast is willing to go to any trouble to impart the glad news bubbling within him. He thinks that it is important and valuable for to know; given the slightest glow of interest in a pupil to start with, he will fan that glow to a flame. No hollow formalism cripples him and slows him down. He drags his best pupils along as fast as they can go, and he is so full of the thing that he never tires of expounding its elements to the dullest.

This passion, so unordered and yet so potent, explains the capacity for teaching that one frequently observes in scientific men of high attainments in their specialties—for example, Huxley, Ostwald, Karl Ludwig, Virchow, Billroth, Jowett, William G. Sumner, Halsted and Osler—men who knew nothing whatever about the so-called science of pedagogy, and would have derided its alleged principles if they had heard them stated. It explains, too, the failure of the general run of high-school and college teachers—men who are undoubtedly competent, by the professional standards of pedagogy, but who nevertheless contrive only to make intolerable bores of the things they presume to teach. No intelligent student ever learns much from the average drover of undergraduates; what he actually carries away has come out of his textbooks, or is the fruit of his own reading and inquiry. But when he passes to the graduate school, and comes among men who really understand the subjects they teach, and, what is more, who really love them, his store of knowledge increases rapidly, and in a very short while, if he has any intelligence at all, he learns to think in terms of the thing he is studying.

So far, so good. But an objection still remains, the which may be couched in the following terms: that in the average college or high school, and especially in the elementary school, most of the subjects taught are so bald and uninspiring that it is difficult to imagine them arousing the passion I have been describing —in brief, that only an ass could be enthusiastic about them. In witness, think of the four elementals: reading, penmanship, arithmetic and spelling. This objection, at first blush, seems salient and dismaying, but only a brief inspection is needed to show that it is really of very small validity. It is made up of a false assumption and a false inference. The false inference is that there is any sound reason for prohibiting teaching by asses, if only the asses know how to do it, and do it well. The false assumption is that there are no asses in our schools and colleges to-day. The facts stand in almost complete antithesis to these notions. The truth is that the average schoolmaster, on all the lower levels, is and always must be essentially an ass, for how can one imagine an intelligent man engaging in so puerile an avocation? And, the truth is that it is precisely his inherent asininity, and not his technical equipment as a pedagogue, that is responsible for whatever modest success he now shows.

I here attempt no heavy jocosity, but mean exactly what I say. Consider, for example, penmanship. A decent handwriting, it must be obvious, is useful to all men, and particularly to the lower orders of men. It is one of the few things capable of acquirement in school that actually helps them to make a living. Well, how is it taught to-day? It is taught, in the main, by schoolmarms so enmeshed in a complex and unintelligible technic that, even supposing them able to write clearly themselves, they find it quite impossible to teach their pupils. Every few years sees a radical overhauling of the whole business. First the vertical hand is to make it easy; then certain curves are the favorite magic; then there is a return to slants and shadings. No department of pedagogy sees a more hideous cavorting of quacks. In none is the natural talent and enthusiasm of the teacher more depressingly crippled. And the result? The result is that our American school children write abominably—that a clerk or stenographer with a simple, legible hand becomes almost as scarce as one with Greek.

Go back, now, to the old days. Penmanship was then taught, not mechanically and ineffectively, by unsound and shifting formulæ, but by passionate penmen with curly patent-leather hair and far-away eyes—in brief, by the unforgettable professors of our youth, with their flourishes, their heavy down-strokes and their lovely birds-with-letters-in-their-bills. You remember them, of course. Asses all! Preposterous popinjays and numskulls! Pathetic idiots! But they loved penmanship, they believed in the glory and beauty of penmanship, they were fanatics, devotees, almost martyrs of penmanship—and so they got some touch of that passion into their pupils. Not enough, perhaps, to make more flourishers and bird-blazoners, but enough to make sound penmen. Look at your old writing book; observe the excellent legibility, the clear strokes of your "Time is money." Then look at your child's.

Such idiots, despite the rise of "scientific" pedagogy, have not died out in the world. I believe that our schools are full of them, both in pantaloons and in skirts. There are fanatics who love and venerate spelling as a tom-cat loves and venerates catnip. There are grammatomaniacs; schoolmarms who would rather parse than eat; specialists in an objective case that doesn't exist in English; strange beings, otherwise sane and even intelligent and comely, who suffer under a split infinitive as you or I would suffer under gastro-enteritis. There are geography cranks, able to bound Mesopotamia and Beluchistan. There are zealots for long division, experts in the multiplication table, lunatic worshipers of the binomial theorem. But the system has them in its grip. It combats their natural enthusiam diligently and mercilessly. It tries to convert them into mere technicians, clumsy machines. It orders them to teach, not by the process of emotional osmosis which worked in the days gone by, but by formulæ that are as baffling to the pupil as they are paralyzing to the teacher. Imagine what would happen to one of them who stepped to the blackboard, seized a piece of chalk, and engrossed a bird that held the class spell-bound—a bird with a thousand flowing feathers, wings bursting with parabolas and epicycloids, and long ribbons streaming from its bill! Imagine the fate of one who began "Honesty is the best policy" with an H as florid and—to a child—as beautiful as the initial of a mediæval manuscript! Such a teacher would be cashiered and handed over to the secular arm; the very enchantment of the assembled infantry would be held as damning proof against him. And yet it is just such teachers that we should try to discover and develop. Pedagogy needs their enthusiasm, their naïve belief in their own grotesque talents, their capacity for communicating their childish passion to the childish.

But this would mean exposing the children of the Republic to contact with monomaniacs, half-wits, defectives? Well, what of it? The vast majority of them are already exposed to contact with half-wits in their own homes; they are taught the word of God by half-wits on Sundays; they will grow up into Knights of Pythias, Odd Fellows, Red Men and other such half-wits in the days to come. Moreover, as I have hinted, they are already face to face with half-wits in the actual schools, at least in three cases out of four. The problem before us is not to dispose of this fact, but to utilize it. We cannot hope to fill the schools with persons of high intelligence, for persons of high intelligence simply refuse to spend their lives teaching such banal things as spelling and arithmetic. Among the teachers male we may safely assume that 95 per cent. are of low mentality, else they would depart for more appetizing pastures. And even among the teachers female the best are inevitably weeded out by marriage, and only the worst (with a few romantic exceptions) survive. The task before us, as I say, is not to make a vain denial of this cerebral inferiority of the pedagogue, nor to try to combat and disguise it by concocting a mass of technical hocus-pocus, but to search out and put to use the value lying concealed in it. For even stupidity, it must be plain, has its uses in the world, and some of them are uses that intelligence cannot meet. One would not tell off a Galileo or a Pasteur to drive an ash-cart or an Ignatius Loyola to be a stock-broker, or a Brahms to lead the orchestra in a Broadway cabaret. By the same token, one would not ask a Herbert Spencer or a Duns Scotus to instruct sucklings. Such men would not only be wasted at the job; they would also be incompetent. The business of dealing with children, in fact, demands a certain childishness of mind. The best teacher, until one comes to adult pupils, is not the one who knows most, but the one who is most capable of reducing knowledge to that simple compound of the obvious and the wonderful which slips easiest into the infantile comprehension. A man of high intelligence, perhaps, may accomplish the thing by a conscious intellectual feat. But it is vastly easier to the man (or woman) whose habits of mind are naturally on the plane of a child's. The best teacher of children, in brief, is one who is essentially childlike.

I go so far with this notion that I view the movement to introduce female bachelors of arts into the primary schools with the utmost alarm. A knowledge of Bergsonism, the Greek aorist, sex hygiene and the dramas of Percy MacKaye is not only no help to the teaching of spelling, it is a positive handicap to the teaching of spelling, for it corrupts and blows up that naive belief in the glory and portentousness of spelling which is at the bottom of all successful teaching of it. If I had my way, indeed, I should expose all candidates for berths in the infant grades to the Binet-Simon test, and reject all those who revealed the mentality of more than fifteen years. Plenty would still pass. Moreover, they would be secure against contamination by the new technic of pedagogy. Its vast wave of pseudo-psychology would curl and break against the hard barrier of their innocent and passionate intellects—as it probably does, in fact, even now. They would know nothing of cognition, perception, attention, the sub-conscious and all the other half-fabulous fowl of the pedagogic aviary. But they would see in reading, writing and arithmetic the gaudy charms of profound and esoteric knowledge, and they would teach these ancient branches, now so abominably in decay, with passionate gusto, and irresistible effectiveness, and a gigantic success.

II

Two great follies corrupt the present pedagogy, once it gets beyond the elementals. One is the folly of overestimating the receptivity of the pupil; the other is the folly of overestimating the possible efficiency of the teacher. Both rest upon that tendency to put too high a value upon mere schooling which characterizes democratic and upstart societies—a tendency born of the theory that a young man who has been "educated," who has "gone through college," is in some subtle way more capable of making money than one who hasn't. The nature of the schooling on tap in colleges is but defectively grasped by the adherents of the theory. They view it, I believe, as a sort of extension of the schooling offered in elementary schools—that is, as an indefinite multiplication of training in such obviously valuable and necessary arts as reading, writing and arithmetic. It is, of course, nothing of the sort. If the pupil, as he climbs the educational ladder, is fortunate enough to come into contact with a few Huxleys or Ludwigs, he may acquire a great deal of extremely sound knowledge, and even learn how to think for himself. But in the great majority of cases he is debarred by two things: the limitations of his congenital capacity and the limitations of the teachers he actually encounters. The latter is usually even more brilliantly patent than the former. Very few professional teachers, it seems to me, really know anything worth knowing, even about the subjects they essay to teach. If you doubt it, simply examine their contributions to existing knowledge. Several years ago, while engaged upon my book, "The American Language," I had a good chance to test the matter in one typical department, that of philology. I found a truly appalling condition of affairs. I found that in the whole

United States there were not two dozen teachers of English philology—in which class I also include the innumerable teachers of plain grammar—who had ever written ten lines upon the subject worth reading. It was not that they were indolent or illiterate: in truth, they turned out to be enormously diligent. But as I plowed through pyramid after pyramid of their doctrines and speculations, day after day and week after week, I discovered little save a vast laboring of the obvious, with now and then a bold flight into the nonsensical. A few genuinely original philologians revealed themselves—pedagogues capable of observing accurately and reasoning clearly. The rest simply wasted time and paper. Whole sections of the field were unexplored, and some of them appeared to be even unsuspected. The entire life-work of many an industrious professor, boiled down, scarcely made a footnote in my book, itself a very modest work.

This tendency to treat the superior pedagogue too seriously—to view him as, *ipso facto*, a learned man, and one thus capable of conveying learning to others —is supported by the circumstance that he so views himself, and is, in fact, very pretentious and even bombastic. Nearly all discussions of the educational problem, at least in the United States, are carried on by schoolmasters or ex-schoolmasters—for example, college presidents, deans, and other such magnificoes—and so they assume it to be axiomatic that such fellows are genuine bearers of the enlightenment, and hence capable of transmitting it to others. This is true sometimes, as I have said, but certainly not usually. The average high-school or college pedagogue is not one who has been selected because of his uncommon knowledge; he is simply one who has been stuffed with formal ideas and taught to do a few conventional intellectual tricks. Contact with him, far from being inspiring to any youth of alert mentality, is really quite depressing; his point of view is commonplace and timorous; his best thought is no better than that of any other fourth-rate professional man, say a dentist or an advertisement writer. Thus it is idle to talk of him as if he were a Socrates, an Aristotle, or even a Leschetizky. He is actually much more nearly related to a barber or a lieutenant of marines. A worthy man, industrious and respectable—but don't expect too much of him. To ask him to struggle out of his puddle of safe platitudes and plunge into the whirlpool of surmise and speculation that carries on the fragile shallop of human progress—to do this is as absurd as to ask a neighborhood doctor to undertake major surgery.

In the United States his low intellectual status is kept low, not only by the meager rewards of his trade in a country where money is greatly sought and esteemed, but also by the democratic theory of education—that is, by the theory that mere education can convert a peasant into an intellectual aristocrat, with all of the peculiar superiorities of an aristocrat—in brief, that it is possible to make purses out of sow's ears. The intellectual collapse of the American *Gelehrten* during the late war—a collapse so nearly unanimous that those who did not share it attained to a sort of immortality overnight—was perhaps largely due to this error. Who were these bawling professors, so pathetically poltroonish and idiotic? In an enormous number of cases they were simply peasants in frock coats—oafs from the farms and villages of Iowa, Kansas, Vermont, Alabama, the Dakotas and other such backward states, horribly stuffed with standardized learning in some fresh-water university, and then set to teaching. To look for a civilized attitude of mind in such Strassburg geese is to look for honor in a valet; to confuse them with scholars is to confuse the Knights of Pythias with the Knights Hospitaller. In brief, the trouble with them was that they had no sound tradition behind them, that they had not learned to think clearly and decently, that they were not gentlemen. The youth with a better background behind him, passing through an American university, seldom acquires any yearning to linger as a teacher. The air is too thick for him; the rewards are too trivial; the intrigues are too old-maidish and degrading. Thus the chairs, even in the larger universities, tend to be filled more and more by yokels who have got themselves what is called an education only by dint of herculean effort. Exhausted by the cruel process, they are old men at 26 or 28, and so, hugging their Ph.D's, they sink into convenient instructorships, and end at 60 as *ordentliche Professoren.* The social status of the American pedagogue helps along the process. Unlike in Europe, where he has a secure and honorable position, he ranks, in the United States, somewhere between a Methodist preacher and a prosperous brickyard owner—certainly clearly below the latter. Thus the youth of civilized upbringings feels that it would be stooping a bit to take up the rattan. But the plow-hand obviously makes a step upward, and is hence eager for the black gown. Thereby a vicious circle is formed. The plow-hand, by entering the ancient guild, drags it down still further, and so makes it increasingly difficult to snare apprentices from superior castes.

A glance at "Who's Who in America" offers a good deal of support for all this theorizing. There was a time when the typical American professor came from a small area in New England—for generations the seat of a high literacy, and even of a certain austere civilization. But to-day he comes from the region of silos, revivals, and saleratus. Behind him there is absolutely no tradition of aristocratic aloofness and urbanity, or even of mere civilized decency. He is a hind by birth, and he carries the smell of the dunghill into the academic grove—and not only the smell, but also some of the dung itself. What one looks for in such men is dullness, superficiality, a great credulity, an incapacity for learning anything save a few fly-blown rudiments, a passionate yielding to all popular crazes, a malignant distrust of genuine superiority, a huge megalomania. These are precisely the things that one finds in the typical American pedagogue of the new dispensation. He is not only a numskull; he is also a boor. In the university president he reaches his heights. Here we have a so-called learned man who spends his time making speeches before chautauquas, chambers of commerce and Rotary Clubs, and flattering trustees who run both universities and street-railways, and cadging money from such men as Rockefeller and Carnegie.

III

The same educational fallacy which fills the groves of learning with such dunces causes a huge waste of energy and money on lower levels—those, to wit, of the secondary schools. The theory behind the lavish multiplication of such schools is that they outfit the children of the mob with the materials of reasoning, and inculcate in them a habit of indulging in it. I have never been able to discover any evidence in support of that theory. The common people of America—at least the white portion of them—are rather above the world's average in literacy, but there is no sign that they have acquired thereby any capacity for weighing facts or comparing ideas. The school statistics show that the average member of the American Legion can read and write after a fashion, and is able to multiply eight by seven after four trials, but they tell us nothing about his actual intelligence. The returns of the Army itself, indeed, indicate that he is stupid almost beyond belief—that there is at least an even chance that he is a moron. Is such a fellow appreciably superior to the villein of the Middle Ages? Sometimes I am tempted to doubt it. I suspect, for example, that the belief in witchcraft is still almost as widespread among the plain people of the United States, at least outside the large cities, as it was in Europe in the year 1500. In my own state of Maryland all of the negroes and mulattoes believe absolutely in witches, and so do most of the whites. The belief in ghosts penetrates to quite high levels. I know very few native-born Americans, indeed, who reject it without reservation. One constantly comes upon grave defenses of spiritism in some form or other by men theoretically of learning; in the two houses of Congress it would be difficult to muster fifty men willing to denounce the thing publicly. It would not only be politically dangerous for them to do so; it would also go against their consciences.

What is always forgotten is that the capacity for knowledge of the great masses of human blanks is very low—that, no matter how adroitly pedagogy tackles them with its technical sorceries, it remains a practical impossibility to teach them anything beyond reading and writing, and the most elementary arithmetic. Worse, it is impossible to make any appreciable improvement in their congenitally ignoble tastes, and so they devote even the paltry learning that they acquire to degrading uses. If the average American read only the newspapers, as is frequently alleged, it would be bad enough, but the truth is that he reads only the most imbecile *parts* of the newspapers. Nine-tenths of the matter in a daily paper of the better sort is almost as unintelligible to him as the theory of least squares. The words lie outside his vocabulary; the ideas are beyond the farthest leap of his intellect. It is, indeed, a sober fact that even an editorial in the New York *Times* is probably incomprehensible to all Americans save a small minority—and not, remember, on the ground that it is too nonsensical but on the ground that it is too subtle. The same sort of mind that regards Rubinstein's Melody in F as too "classical" to be agreeable is also stumped by the most transparent English.

Like most other professional writers I get a good many letters from my customers. Complaints, naturally, are more numerous than compliments; it is only indignation that can induce the average man to brave the ardors of pen and ink. Well, the complaint that I hear most often is that my English is unintelligible—that it is too full of "hard" words. I can imagine nothing more astounding. My English is actually almost as bald and simple as the English of a college yell. My sentences are short and plainly constructed: I resolutely cultivate the most direct manner of statement; my vocabulary is deliberately composed of the words of everyday. Nevertheless, a great many of my readers in my own country find reading me an uncomfortably severe burden upon their linguistic and intellectual resources. These readers are certainly not below the American average in intelligence; on the contrary, they must be a good deal above the average, for they have at least got to the point where they are willing to put out of the safe harbor of the obvious and respectable, and to brave the seas where more or less novel ideas rage and roar. Think of what the ordinary newspaper reader would make of my compositions! There is, in fact, no need to think; I have tried them on him. His customary response, when, by mountebankish devices, I forced him to read—or, at all events, to try to read—, was to demand resolutely that the guilty newspaper cease printing me, and to threaten to bring the matter to the attention of the *Polizei.* I do not exaggerate in the slightest; I tell the literal truth.

It is such idiots that the little red schoolhouse operates upon, in the hope of unearthing an occasional first-rate man. Is that hope ever fulfilled? Despite much testimony to the effect that it is, I am convinced that it really isn't. First-rate men are never begotten by Knights of Pythias; the notion that they sometimes are is due to an optical delusion. When they appear in obscure and ignoble circles it is no more than a proof that only an extremely wise sire knows his own son. Adultery, in brief, is one of nature's devices for keeping the lowest orders of men from sinking to the level of downright simians: sometimes for a few brief years in youth, their wives and daughters are comely—and now and then the baron drinks more than he ought to. But it is foolish to argue that the gigantic machine of popular education is needed to rescue such hybrids from their environment. The truth is that all the education rammed into the average pupil in the average American public school could be acquired by the larva of any reasonably intelligent man in no more than six weeks of ordinary application, and that where schools are unknown it actually *is* so acquired. A bright child, in fact, can learn to read and write without any save the most casual aid a great deal faster than it can learn to read and write in a classroom, where the difficulties of the stupid retard it enormously and it is further burdened by the crazy formulæ invented by pedagogues. And once it can read and write, it is just as well equipped to acquire further knowledge as nine-tenths of the teachers it will subsequently encounter in school or college.

IV

I know a good many men of great learning—that is, men born with an extraordinary eagerness and capacity to acquire knowledge. One and all, they tell me that they can't recall learning anything of any value in school. All that schoolmasters managed to accomplish with them was to test and determine the amount of knowledge that they had already acquired independently—and not infrequently the determination was made clumsily and inaccurately. In my own nonage I had a great desire to acquire knowledge in certain limited directions, to wit, those of the physical sciences. Before I was ever permitted, by the regulations of the secondary seminary I was penned in, to open a chemistry book I had learned a great deal of chemistry by the simple process of reading the texts and then going through the processes described. When, at last, I was introduced to chemistry officially, I found the teaching of it appalling. The one aim of that teaching, in fact, seemed to be to first purge me of what I already knew and then refill me with the same stuff in a formal, doltish, unintelligible form. My experience with physics was even worse. I knew nothing about it when I undertook its study in class, for that was before the days when physics swallowed chemistry. Well, it was taught so abominably that it immediately became incomprehensible to me, and hence extremely distasteful, and to this day I know nothing about it. Worse, it remains unpleasant to me, and so I am shut off from the interesting and useful knowledge that I might otherwise acquire by reading.

One extraordinary teacher I remember who taught me something: a teacher of mathematics. I had a dislike for that science, and knew little about it. Finally, my neglect of it brought me to bay: in transferring from one school to another I found that I was hopelessly short in algebra. What was needed, of course, was not an actual knowledge of algebra, but simply the superficial smattering needed to pass an examination. The teacher that I mention, observing my distress, generously offered to fill me with that smattering after school hours. He got the whole year's course into me in exactly six lessons of half an hour each. And how? More accurately, why? Simply because he was an algebra fanatic—because he believed that algebra was not only a science of the utmost importance, but also one of the greatest fascination. He was the penmanship professor of years ago, lifted to a higher level. A likable and plausible man, he convinced me in twenty minutes that ignorance of algebra was as calamitous, socially and intellectually, as ignorance of table manners—that acquiring its elements was as necessary as washing behind the ears. So I fell upon the book and gulped it voraciously, greatly to the astonishment of my father, whose earlier mathematical teaching had failed to set me off because it was too pressing—because it bombarded me, not when I was penned in a school and so inclined to make the best of it, but when I had got through a day's schooling, and felt inclined to play. To this day I comprehend the binomial theorem, a very rare accomplishment in an author. For many years, indeed, I was probably the only American newspaper editor who knew what it was.

Two other teachers of that school I remember pleasantly as fellows whose pedagogy profitted me—both, it happens, were drunken and disreputable men. One taught me to chew tobacco, an art that has done more to give me an evil name, perhaps, than even my Socinianism. The other introduced me to Shakespeare, Congreve, Wycherly, Marlowe and Sheridan, and so filled me with that taste for coarseness which now offends so many of my customers, lay and clerical. Neither ever came to a dignified position in academic circles. One abandoned pedagogy for the law, became involved in causes of a dubious nature, and finally disappeared into the shades which engulf third-rate attorneys. The other went upon a fearful drunk one Christmastide, got himself shanghaied on the water-front and is supposed to have fallen overboard from a British tramp, bound east for Cardiff. At all events, he has never been heard from since. Two evil fellows, and yet I hold their memories in affection, and believe that they were the best teachers I ever had. For in both there was something a good deal more valuable than mere pedagogical skill and diligence, and even more valuable than correct demeanor, and that was a passionate love of sound literature. This love, given reasonably receptive soil, they knew how to communicate, as a man can nearly always communicate whatever moves him profoundly. Neither ever made the slightest effort to "teach" literature, as the business is carried on by the usual idiot schoolmaster. Both had a vast contempt for the text-books that were official in their school, and used to entertain the boys by pointing out the nonsense in them. Both were full of derisory objections to the principal heroes of such books in those days: Scott, Irving, Pope, Jane Austen, Dickens, Trollope, Tennyson. But both, discoursing in their disorderly way upon heroes of their own, were magnificently eloquent and persuasive. The boy who could listen to one of them intoning Whitman and stand unmoved was a dull fellow indeed. The boy who could resist the other's enthusiasm for the old essayists was intellectually deaf, dumb and blind.

I often wonder if their expoundings of their passions and prejudices would have been half so charming if they had been wholly respectable men, like their colleagues of the school faculty. It is not likely. A healthy boy is in constant revolt against the sort of men who surround him at school. Their puerile pedantries, their Christian Endeavor respectability, their sedentery pallor, their curious preference for the dull and uninteresting, their general air of so many Y. M. C. A. secretaries—these things infallibly repel the youth who is above milksoppery. In every boys' school the favorite teacher is one who occasionally swears like a cavalryman, or is reputed to keep a jug in his room, or is known to receive a scented note every morning. Boys are good judges of men, as girls are good judges of women. It is not by accident that most of them, at some time or other, long to be cowboys or ice-wagon drivers, and that none of them, not obviously diseased in mind, ever longs to be a Sunday-school superintendent. Put that judgment to a simple test. What would become of a nation in which all of the men were, at heart, Sunday-school superintendents—or Y. M. C. A. secretaries, or pedagogues? Imagine it in conflict with a nation of cowboys and ice-wagon drivers. Which would be the stronger, and which would be the more intelligent, resourceful, enterprising and courageous?

XIV. TYPES OF MEN

1

The Romantic

THERE is a variety of man whose eye inevitably exaggerates, whose ear inevitably hears more than the band plays, whose imagination inevitably doubles and triples the news brought in by his five senses. He is the enthusiast, the believer, the romantic. He is the sort of fellow who, if he were a bacteriologist, would report the streptoccocus pyogenes to be as large as a St. Bernard dog, as intelligent as Socrates, as beautiful as Beauvais Cathedral and as respectable as a Yale professor.

2

The Skeptic

No man ever quite believes in any other man. One may believe in an idea absolutely, but not in a man. In the highest confidence there is always a flavor of doubt—a feeling, half instinctive and half logical, that, after all, the scoundrel *may* have something up his sleeve. This doubt, it must be obvious, is always more than justified, for no man is worthy of unlimited reliance—his treason, at best, only waits for sufficient temptation. The trouble with the world is not that men are too suspicious in this direction, but that they tend to be too confiding—that they still trust themselves too far to other men, even after bitter experience. Women, I believe, are measurably less sentimental, in this as in other things. No married woman ever trusts her husband absolutely, nor does she ever act as if she *did* trust him. Her utmost confidence is as wary as an American pickpocket's confidence that the policeman on the beat will stay bought.

3

The Believer

Faith may be defined briefly as an illogical belief in the occurrence of the improbable. Or, psychoanalytically, as a wish neurose. There is thus a flavor of the pathological in it; it goes beyond the normal intellectual process and passes into the murky domain of transcendental metaphysics. A man full of faith is simply one who has lost (or never had) the capacity for clear and realistic thought. He is not a mere ass: he is actually ill. Worse, he is incurable, for disappointment, being essentially an objective phenomenon, cannot permanently affect his subjective infirmity. His faith takes on the virulence of a chronic infection. What he usually says, in substance, is this: "Let us trust in God, *who has always fooled us in the past.*"

4

The Worker

All democratic theories, whether Socialistic or bourgeois, necessarily take in some concept of the dignity of labor. If the have-not were deprived of this delusion that his sufferings in the sweat-shop are somehow laudable and agreeable to God, there would be little left in his ego save a belly-ache. Nevertheless, a delusion is a delusion, and this is one of the worst. It arises out of confusing the pride of workmanship of the artist with the dogged, painful docility of the machine. The difference is important and enormous. If he got no reward whatever, the artist would go on working just the same; his actual reward, in fact, is often so little that he almost starves. But suppose a garment-worker got nothing for his labor: would he go on working just the same? Can one imagine him submitting voluntarily to hardship and sore want that he might express his soul in 200 more pairs of pantaloons?

5

The Physician

Hygiene is the corruption of medicine by morality. It is impossible to find a hygienist who does not debase his theory of the healthful with a theory of the virtuous. The whole hygienic art, indeed, resolves itself into an ethical exhortation, and, in the sub-department of sex, into a puerile and belated advocacy of asceticism. This brings it, at the end, into diametrical conflict with medicine proper. The aim of medicine is surely not to make men virtuous; it is to safeguard and rescue them from the consequences of their vices. The true physician does not preach repentance; he offers absolution.

6

The Scientist

The value the world sets upon motives is often grossly unjust and inaccurate. Consider, for example, two of them: mere insatiable curiosity and the desire to do good. The latter is put high above the former, and yet it is the former that moves some of the greatest men the human race has yet produced: the scientific investigators. What animates a great pathologist? Is it the desire to cure disease, to save life? Surely not, save perhaps as an afterthought. He is too intelligent, deep down in his soul, to see anything praiseworthy in such a desire. He knows by life-long observation that his discoveries will do quite as much harm as good, that a thousand scoundrels will profit to every honest man, that the folks who most deserve to be saved will probably be the last to be saved. No man of self-respect could devote himself to pathology on such terms. What actually moves him is his unquenchable curiosity—his boundless, almost pathological thirst to penetrate the unknown, to uncover the secret, to find out what has not been found out before. His prototype is not the liberator releasing slaves, the good Samaritan lifting up the fallen, but the dog sniffing tremendously at an infinite series of rat-holes. And yet he is one of the greatest and noblest of men. And yet he stands in the very front rank of the race.

7

The Business Man

It is, after all, a sound instinct which puts business below the professions, and burdens the business man with a social inferiority that he can never quite shake off, even in America. The business man, in fact, acquiesces in this assumption of his inferiority, even when he protests against it. He is the only man who is forever apologizing for his occupation. He is the only one who always seeks to make it appear, when he attains the object of his labors, *i. e.*, the making of a great deal of money, that it was not the object of his labors.

8

The King

Perhaps the most valuable asset that any man can have in this world is a naturally superior air, a talent for sniffishness and reserve. The generality of men are always greatly impressed by it, and accept it freely as a proof of genuine merit. One need but disdain them to gain their respect. Their congenital stupidity and timorousness make them turn to any leader who offers, and the sign of leadership that they recognize most readily is that which shows itself in external manner. This is the true explanation of the survival of monarchism, which invariably lives through its perennial deaths. It is the popular theory, at least in America, that monarchism is a curse fastened upon the common people from above—that the monarch saddles it upon them without their consent and against their will. The theory is without support in the facts. Kings are created, not by kings, but by the people. They visualize one of the ineradicable needs of all third-rate men, which means of nine men out of ten, and that is the need of something to venerate, to bow down to, to follow and obey.

The king business begins to grow precarious, not when kings reach out for greater powers, but when they begin to resign and renounce their powers. The czars of Russia were quite secure upon the throne so long as they ran Russia like a reformatory, but the moment they began to yield to liberal ideas, *i. e.*, by emancipating the serfs and setting up constitutionalism, their doom was sounded. The people saw this yielding as a sign of weakness; they began to suspect that the czars, after all, were not actually superior to other men. And so they turned to other and antagonistic leaders, all as cock-sure as the czars had once been, and in the course of time they were stimulated to rebellion. These leaders, or, at all events, the two or three most resolute and daring of them, then undertook to run the country in the precise way that it had been run in the palmy days of the monarchy. That is to say, they seized and exerted irresistible power and laid claim to infallible wisdom. History will date their downfall from the day they began to ease their pretensions. Once they confessed, even by implication, that they were merely human, the common people began to turn against them.

9

The Average Man

It is often urged against the so-called scientific Socialists, with their materialistic conception of history, that they overlook certain spiritual qualities that are independent of wage scales and metabolism. These qualities, it is argued, color the aspirations and activities of civilized man quite as much as they are colored by his material condition, and so make it impossible to consider him simply as an economic machine. As examples, the anti-Marxians cite patriotism, pity, the æsthetic sense and the yearning to know God. Unluckily, the examples are ill-chosen. Millions of men are quite devoid of patriotism, pity and the æsthetic sense, and have no very active desire to know God. Why don't the anti-Marxians cite a spiritual quality that is genuinely universal? There is one readily to hand. I allude to cowardice. It is, in one form or other, visible in every human being; it almost serves to mark off the human race from all the other higher animals. Cowardice, I believe, is at the bottom of the whole caste system, the foundation of every organized society, including the most democratic. In order to escape going to war himself, the peasant was willing to give the warrior certain privileges—and out of those privileges has grown the whole structure of civilization. Go back still further. Property arose out of the fact that a few relatively courageous men were able to accumulate more possessions than whole hordes of cowardly men, and, what is more, to retain them after accumulating them.

10

The Truth-Seeker

The man who boasts that he habitually tells the truth is simply a man with no respect for it. It is not a thing to be thrown about loosely, like small change; it is something to be cherished and hoarded, and disbursed only when absolutely necessary. The smallest atom of truth represents some man's bitter toil and agony; for every ponderable chunk of it there is a brave truth-seeker's grave upon some lonely ash-dump and a soul roasting in hell.

11

The Pacifist

Nietzsche, in altering Schopenhauer's will-to-live to will-to-power, probably fell into a capital error. The truth is that the thing the average man seeks in life is not primarily power, but peace; all his struggle is toward a state of tranquillity and equilibrium; what he always dreams of is a state in which he will have to do battle no longer. This dream plainly enters into his conception of Heaven; he thinks of himself, *post mortem*, browsing about the celestial meadows like a cow in a safe pasture. A few extraordinary men enjoy combat at all times, and all men are inclined toward it at orgiastic moments, but the race as a race craves peace, and man belongs among the more timorous, docile and unimaginative animals, along with the deer, the horse and the sheep. This craving for peace is vividly displayed in the ages-long conflict of the sexes. Every normal woman wants to be married, for the plain reason that marriage offers her security. And every normal man avoids marriage as long as possible, for the equally plain reason that marriage invades and threatens *his* security.

12

The Relative

The normal man's antipathy to his relatives, particularly of the second degree, is explained by psychologists in various tortured and improbable ways. The true explanation, I venture, is a good deal simpler. It lies in the plain fact that every man sees in his relatives, and especially in his cousins, a series of grotesque caricatures of himself. They exhibit his qualities in disconcerting augmentation or diminution; they fill him with a disquieting feeling that this, perhaps, is the way he appears to the world and so they wound his *amour propre* and give him intense discomfort. To admire his relatives whole-heartedly a man must be lacking in the finer sort of self-respect.

13

The Friend

One of the most mawkish of human delusions is the notion that friendship should be eternal, or, at all events, life-long, and that any act which puts a term to it is somehow discreditable. The fact is that a man of active and resilient mind outwears his friendships just as certainly as he outwears his love affairs, his politics and his epistemology. They become threadbare, shabby, pumped-up, irritating, depressing. They convert themselves from living realities into moribund artificialities, and stand in sinister opposition to freedom, self-respect and truth. It is as corrupting to preserve them after they have grown fly-blown and hollow as it is to keep up the forms of passion after passion itself is a corpse. Every act and attitude that they involve thus becomes an act of hypocrisy, an attitude of dishonesty. . . .

A prudent man, remembering that life is short, gives an hour or two, now and then, to a critical examination of his friendships. He weighs them, edits them, tests the metal of them. A few he retains, perhaps with radical changes in their terms. But the majority he expunges from his minutes and tries to forget, as he tries to forget the cold and clammy loves of year before last.

XV. THE DISMAL SCIENCE

EVERY man, as the Psalmist says, to his own poison, or poisons, as the case may be. One of mine, following hard after theology, is political economy. What! Political economy, that dismal science? Well, why not? Its dismalness is largely a delusion, due to the fact that its chief ornaments, at least in our own day, are university professors. The professor must be an obscurantist or he is nothing; he has a special and unmatchable talent for dullness; his central aim is not to expose the truth clearly, but to exhibit his profundity, his esotericity—in brief, to stagger sophomores and other professors. The notion that German is a gnarled and unintelligible language arises out of the circumstance that it is so much written by professors. It took a rebel member of the clan, swinging to the antipodes in his unearthly treason, to prove its explicitness, its resiliency, it downright beauty. But Nietzsches are few, and so German remains soggy, and political economy continues to be swathed in dullness. As I say, however, that dullness is only superficial. There is no more engrossing book in the English language than Adam Smith's "The Wealth of Nations"; surely the eighteenth century produced nothing that can be read with greater ease to-day. Nor is there any inherent reason why even the most technical divisions of its subject should have gathered cobwebs with the passing of the years. Taxation, for example, is eternally lively; it concerns nine-tenths of us more directly than either smallpox or golf, and has just as much drama in it; moreover, it has been mellowed and made gay by as many gaudy, preposterous theories. As for foreign exchange, it is almost as romantic as young love, and quite as resistent to formulæ. Do the professors make an autopsy of it? Then read the occasional treatises of some professor of it who is not a professor, say, Garet Garrett or John Moody.

Unluckily, Garretts and Moodys are almost as rare as Nietzsches, and so the amateur of such things must be content to wrestle with the professors, seeking the violet of human interest beneath the avalanche of their graceless parts of speech. A hard business, I daresay, to one not practiced, and to its hardness there is added the disquiet of a doubt. That doubt does not concern itself with the doctrine preached, at least not directly. There may be in it nothing intrinsically dubious; on the contrary, it may appear as sound as the binomial theorem, as well supported as the dogma of infant damnation. But all the time a troubling question keeps afloat in the air, and that is briefly this: What would happen to the learned professors if they took the other side? In other words, to what extent is political economy, as professors expound and practice it, a free science, in the sense that mathematics and physiology are free sciences? At what place, if any, is speculation pulled up by a rule that beyond lies treason, anarchy and disaster? These questions, I hope I need not add, are not inspired by any heterodoxy in my own black heart. I am, in many fields, a flouter of the accepted revelation and hence immoral, but the field of economics is not one of them. Here, indeed, I know of no man who is more orthodox than I am. I believe that the present organization of society, as bad as it is, is better than any other that has ever been proposed. I reject all the sure cures in current agitation, from government ownership to the single tax. I am in favor of free competition in all human enterprises, and to the utmost limit. I admire successful scoundrels, and shrink from Socialists as I shrink from Methodists. But all the same, the aforesaid doubt pursues me when I plow through the solemn disproofs and expositions of the learned professors of economics, and that doubt will not down. It is not logical or evidential, but purely psychological. And what it is grounded on is an unshakable belief that no man's opinion is worth a hoot, however well supported and maintained, so long as he is not absolutely free, if the spirit moves him, to support and maintain the exactly contrary opinion. In brief, human reason is a weak and paltry thing so long as it is not wholly free reason. The fact lies in its very nature, and is revealed by its entire history. A man may be perfectly honest in a contention, and he may be astute and persuasive in maintaining it, but the moment the slightest compulsion to maintain it is laid upon him, the moment the slightest external reward goes with his partisanship or the slightest penalty with its abandonment, then there appears a defect in his ratiocination that is more deep-seated than any error in fact and more destructive than any conscious and deliberate bias. He may seek the truth and the truth only, and bring up his highest talents and diligence to the business, but always there is a specter behind his chair, a warning in his ear. Always it is safer and more hygienic for him to think one way than to think another way, and in that bald fact there is excuse enough to hold his whole chain of syllogisms in suspicion. He may be earnest, he may be honest, but he is not free, and if he is not free, he is not anything.

Well, are the reverend professors of economics free? With the highest respect, I presume to question it. Their colleagues of archeology may be reasonably called free, and their colleagues of bacteriology, and those of Latin grammar and sidereal astronomy, and those of many another science and mystery, but when one comes to the faculty of political economy one finds that freedom as plainly conditioned, though perhaps not as openly, as in the faculty of theology. And for a plain reason. Political economy, so to speak, hits the employers of the professors where they live. It deals, not with ideas that affect those employers only occasionally or only indirectly or only as ideas, but with ideas that have an imminent and continuous influence upon their personal welfare and security, and that affect profoundly the very foundations of that social and economic structure upon which their whole existence is based. It is, in brief, the science of the ways and means whereby they have come to such estate, and maintain themselves in such estate, that they are able to hire and boss professors. It is the boat in which they sail down perilous waters—and they must needs yell, or be more or less than human, when it is rocked. Now and then that yell duly resounds in the groves of learning. One remembers, for example, the trial, condemnation and execution of Prof. Dr. Scott Nearing at the University of Pennsylvania, a seminary that is highly typical, both in its staff and in its control. Nearing, I have no doubt, was wrong in his notions—honestly, perhaps, but still wrong. In so far as I heard them stated at the time, they seemed to me to be hollow and of no validity. He has since discharged them from the chautauquan stump, and at the usual hinds. They have been chiefly accepted and celebrated by men I regard as asses. But Nearing was not thrown out of the University of Pennsylvania, angrily and ignominiously, because he was honestly wrong, or because his errors made him incompetent to prepare sophomores for their examinations; he was thrown out because his efforts to get at the truth disturbed the security and equanimity of the rich ignoranti who happened to control the university, and because the academic slaves and satellites of these shopmen were restive under his competition for the attention of the student-body. In three words, he was thrown out because he was not safe and sane and orthodox. Had his aberration gone in the other direction, had he defended child labor as ardently as he denounced it and denounced the minimum wage as ardently as he defended it, then he would have been quite as secure in his post, for all his cavorting in the newspapers, as Chancellor Day was at Syracuse.

Now consider the case of the professors of economics, near and far, who have *not* been thrown out. Who will say that the lesson of the Nearing *débâcle* has been lost upon them? Who will say that the potency of the wealthy men who command our universities—or most of them—has not stuck in their minds? And who will say that, with this sticking remembered, their arguments against Nearing's so-called ideas are as worthy of confidence and respect as they would be if they were quite free to go over to Nearing's side without damage? Who, indeed, will give them full credit, even when they are right, so long as they are hamstrung, nose-ringed and tied up in gilded pens? It seems to me that these considerations are enough to cast a glow of suspicion over the whole of American political economy, at least in so far as it comes from college economists. And, in the main, it has that source, for, barring a few brilliant journalists, all our economists of any repute are professors. Many of them are able men, and most of them are undoubtedly honest men, as honesty goes in the world, but over practically every one of them there stands a board of trustees with its legs in the stock-market and its eyes on the established order, and that board is ever alert for heresy in the science of its being, and has ready means of punishing it, and a hearty enthusiasm for the business. Not every professor, perhaps, may be sent straight to the block, as Nearing was, but there are plenty of pillories and guardhouses on the way, and every last pedagogue must be well aware of it.

Political economy, in so far as it is a science at all, was not pumped up and embellished by any such academic clients and ticket-of-leave men. It was put on its legs by inquirers who were not only safe from all dousing in the campus pump, but who were also free from the mental timorousness and conformity which go inevitably with school-teaching—in brief, by men of the world, accustomed to its free air, its hospitality to originality and plain speaking. Adam Smith, true enough, was once a professor, but he threw up his chair to go to Paris, and there he met, not more professors, but all the current enemies of professors—the Nearings and Henry Georges and Karl Marxes of the time. And the book that he wrote was not orthodox, but revolutionary. Consider the others of that bulk and beam: Bentham, Ricardo, Mill and their like. Bentham held no post at the mercy of bankers and tripesellers; he was a man of independent means, a lawyer and politician, and a heretic in general practice. It is impossible to imagine such a man occupying a chair at Harvard or Princeton. He had a hand in too many pies: he was too rebellious and contumacious: he had too little respect for authority, either academic or worldly. Moreover, his mind was too wide for a professor; he could never remain safely in a groove; the whole field of social organization invited his inquiries and experiments. Ricardo? Another man of easy means and great worldly experience—by academic standards, not even educated. To-day, I daresay, such meager diplomas as he could show would not suffice to get him an instructor's berth in a fresh-water seminary in Iowa. As for Mill, he was so well grounded by his father that he knew more, at eighteen, than any of the universities could teach him, and his life thereafter was the exact antithesis of that of a cloistered pedagogue. Moreover, he was a heretic in religion and probably violated the Mann act of those days—an offense almost as heinous, in a college professor of economics, as giving three cheers for Prince Kropotkin.

I might lengthen the list, but humanely refrain. The point is that these early English economists were all perfectly free men, with complete liberty to tell the truth as they saw it, regardless of its orthodoxy or lack of orthodoxy. I do not say that the typical American economist of to-day is not as honest, nor even that he is not as diligent and competent, but I do say that he is not as free—that penalties would come upon him for stating ideas that Smith or Ricardo or Bentham or Mill, had he so desired, would have been free to state without damage. And in that menace there is an ineradicable criticism of the ideas that he does state, and it lingers even when they are plausible and are accepted. In France and Germany, where the universities and colleges are controlled by the state, the practical effect of such pressure has been frequently demonstrated. In the former country the violent debate over social and economic problems during the quarter century before the war produced a long list of professors cashiered for heterodoxy, headed by the names of Jean Jaures and Gustave Herve. In Germany it needed no Nietzsche to point out the deadening produced by this state control. Germany, in fact, got out of it an entirely new species of economist—the state Socialist who flirted with radicalism with one eye and kept the other upon his chair, his salary and his pension.

The Nearing case and the rebellions of various pedagogues elsewhere show that we in America stand within the shadow of a somewhat similar danger. In economics, as in the other sciences, we are probably producing men who are as good as those on view in any other country. They are not to be surpassed for learning and originality, and there is no reason to believe that they lack honesty and courage. But honesty and courage, as men go in the world, are after all merely relative values. There comes a point at which even the most honest man considers consequences, and even the most courageous looks before he leaps. The difficulty lies in establishing the position of that point. So long as it is in doubt, there will remain, too, the other doubt that I have described. I rise in meeting, I repeat, not as a radical, but as one of the most hunkerous of the orthodox. I can imagine nothing more dubious in fact and wobbly in logic than some of the doctrines that amateur economists, chiefly Socialists, have set afloat in this country during the past dozen years. I have even gone to the trouble of writing a book against them; my convictions and instincts are all on the other side. But I should be a great deal more comfortable in those convictions and instincts if I were convinced that the learned professors were really in full and absolute possession of academic freedom—if I could imagine them taking the other tack now and then without damnation to their jobs, their lecture dates, their book sales and their hides.

XVI. MATTERS OF STATE

1

Le Contrat Social

ALL government, in its essence, is a conspiracy against the superior man: its one permanent object is to police him and cripple him. If it be aristocratio in organization, then it seeks to protect the man who is superior only in law against the man who is superior in fact; if it be democratic, then it seeks to protect the man who is inferior in every way against both. Thus one of its primary functions is to regiment men by force, to make them as much alike as possible and as dependent upon one another as possible, to search out and combat originality among them. All it can see in an original idea is potential change, and hence an invasion of its prerogatives. The most dangerous man, to any government, is the man who is able to think things out for himself, without regard to the prevailing superstitions and taboos. Almost inevitably he comes to the conclusion that the government he lives under is dishonest, insane and intolerable, and so, if he is romantic, he tries to change it. And even if he is not romantic personally he is very apt to spread discontent among those who are. Ludwig van Beethoven was certainly no politician. Nor was he a patriot. Nor had he any democratic illusions in him: he held the Viennese in even more contempt than he held the Hapsburgs. Nevertheless, I am convinced that the sharp criticism of the Hapsburg government that he used to loose in the cafés of Vienna had its effects—that some of his ideas of 1818, after a century of germination, got themselves translated into acts in 1918. Beethoven, like all other first-rate men, greatly disliked the government he lived under. I add the names of Goethe, Heine, Wagner and Nietzsche, to keep among Germans. That of Bismarck might follow: he admired the Hohenzollern idea, as Carlyle did, not the German people or the German administration. In his "Errinerungen," whenever he discusses the government that he was a part of, he has difficulty keeping his contempt within the bounds of decorum.

Nine times out of ten, it seems to me, the man who proposes a change in the government he lives under, no matter how defective it may be, is romantic to the verge of sentimentality. There is seldom, if ever, any evidence that the kind of government he is unlawfully inclined to would be any better than the government he proposes to supplant. Political revolutions, in truth, do not often accomplish anything of genuine value; their one undoubted effect is simply to throw out one gang of thieves and put in another. After a revolution, of course, the successful revolutionists always try to convince doubters that they have achieved great things, and usually they hang any man who denies it. But that surely doesn't prove their case. In Russia, for many years, the plain people were taught that getting rid of the Czar would make them all rich and happy, but now that they have got rid of him they are poorer and unhappier than ever before. The Germans, with the Kaiser in exile, have discovered that a shoemaker turned statesman is ten times as bad as a Hohenzollern. The Alsatians, having become Frenchmen again after 48 years anxious wait, have responded to the boon by becoming extravagant Germanomaniacs. The Tyrolese, though they hated the Austrians, now hate the Italians enormously more. The Irish, having rid themselves of the English after 700 years of struggle, instantly discovered that government by Englishmen, compared to government by Irishmen, was almost paradisiacal. Even the American colonies gained little by their revolt in 1776. For twenty-five years after the Revolution they were in far worse condition as free states than they would have been as colonies. Their government was more expensive, more inefficient, more dishonest, and more tyrannical. It was only the gradual material progress of the country that saved them from starvation and collapse, and that material progress was due, not to the virtues of their new government, but to the lavishness of nature. Under the British hoof they would have got on just as well, and probably a great deal better.

The ideal government of all reflective men, from Aristotle to Herbert Spencer, is one which lets the individual alone—one which barely escapes being no government at all. This ideal, I believe, will be realized in the world twenty or thirty centuries after I have passed from these scenes and taken up my home in Hell.

2

On Minorities

It is a commonplace of historical science that the forgotten worthies who framed the Constitution of the United States had no belief in democracy. Prof. Dr. Beard, in a slim, sad book, has laboriously proved that most obvious of obviousities. Two prime objects are visible in the Constitution, beautifully enshrouded in disarming words: to protect property and to safeguard minorities—in brief, to hold the superior few harmless against the inferior many. The first object is still carried out, despite the effort of democratic law to make capital an outlaw. The second, alas, has been defeated completely. What is worse, it has been defeated in the very holy of holies of those who sought to attain it, which is to say, in the funereal chamber of the Supreme Court of the United States. Bit by bit this great bench of master minds has gradually established the doctrine that a minority in the Republic has no rights whatever. If they still exist theoretically, as fossils surviving from better days, there is certainly no machinery left for protecting and enforcing them. The current majority, if it so desired to-morrow, could add an amendment to the Constitution prohibiting the ancient Confederate vice of chewing the compressed leaves of the tobacco plant (*Nicotiana tabacum*); the Supreme Court, which has long since forgotten the Bill of Rights, would promptly issue a writ of *nihil obstat*, with a series of moral reflections as *lagniappe*. More, the Supreme Court would as promptly uphold a law prohibiting the chewing of gum (*Achras sapota*)—on the ground that any unnecessary chewing, however harmless in itself, might tempt great hordes of morons to chew tobacco. This is not a mere torturing of sardonic theory: the thing has been actually done in the case of Prohibition. The Eighteenth Amendment prohibits the sale of intoxicating beverages; the Supreme Court has decided plainly that, in order to enforce it, Congress also has the right to prohibit the sale of beverages that are admittedly *not* intoxicating.

It could, indeed, specifically prohibit near-beer to-morrow, or any drink containing malt or hops, how-ever low in alcohol; the more extreme Prohibitionists actually demand that it do so forthwith.

Worse, a minority not only has no more inalienable rights in the United States; it is not even lawfully entitled to be heard. This was well established by the case of the Socialists elected to the New York Assembly. What the voters who elected these Socialists asked for was simply the privilege of choosing spokesmen to voice their doctrines in a perfectly lawful and peaceable manner,—nothing more. This privilege was denied them. In precisely the same way, the present national House of Representatives, which happens to be Republican in complexion, might expel all of its Democratic members. The voters who elected them would have no redress. If the same men were elected again, or other men of the same views, they might be expelled again. More, it would apparently be perfectly constitutional for the majority in Congress to pass a statute denying the use of the mails to the minority—that is, for the Republicans to bar all Democratic papers from the mails. I do not toy with mere theories. The thing has actually been done in the case of the Socialists. Under the present law, indeed—upheld by the Supreme Court—the Postmaster-General, without any further authority from Congress, might deny the mails to all Democrats. Or to all Catholics. Or to all single-taxers. Or to all violoncellists.

Yet more, a citizen who happens to belong to a minority is not even safe in his person: he may be put into prison, and for very long periods, for the simple offense of differing from the majority. This happened, it will be recalled, in the case of Debs. Debs by no means advised citizens subject to military duty, in time of war, to evade that duty, as the newspapers of the time alleged. On the contrary, he advised them to meet and discharge that duty. All he did was to say that, even in time of war, he was against war—that he regarded it as a barbarous method of settling disputes between nations. For thus differing from the majority on a question of mere theory he was sentenced to ten years in prison. The case of the three young Russians arrested in New York was even more curious. These poor idiots were jailed for the almost incredible crime of circulating purely academic protests against making war upon a country with which the United States was legally at peace, to wit, Russia. For this preposterous offense two of them were sent to prison for fifteen years, and one, a girl, for ten years, and the Supreme Court upheld their convictions. Here was a plain case of proscription and punishment for a mere opinion. There was absolutely no contention that the protest of the three prisoners could have any practical result

—that it might, for example, destroy the *morale* of American soldiers 6,000 miles away, and cut off from all communication with the United States. The three victims were ordered to be punished in that appalling manner simply because they ventured to criticise an executive usurpation which happened, at the moment, to have the support of public opinion, and particularly of the then President of the United States and of the holders of Russian government securities.

It must be obvious, viewing such leading cases critically—and hundreds like them might be cited—that the old rights of the free American, so carefully laid down by the Bill of Rights, are now worth nothing. Bit by bit, Congress and the State Legislatures have invaded and nullified them, and to-day they are so flimsy that no lawyer not insane would attempt to defend his client by bringing them up. Imagine trying to defend a man denied the use of the mails by the Postmaster-General, without hearing or even formal notice, on the ground that the Constitution guarantees the right of free speech! The very catchpolls in the courtroom would snicker. I say that the legislative arm is primarily responsible for this gradual enslavement of the Americano; the truth is, of course, that the executive and judicial arms are responsible to a scarcely less degree. Our law has not kept pace with the development of our bureaucracy;

there is no machinery provided for curbing its excesses. In Prussia, in the old days, there were special courts for the purpose, and a citizen oppressed by the police or by any other public official could get relief and redress. The guilty functionary could be fined, mulcted in damages, demoted, cashiered, or even jailed. But in the United States to-day there are no such tribunals. A citizen attacked by the Postmaster-General simply has no redress whatever; the courts have refused, over and over again, to interfere save in cases of obvious fraud. Nor is there, it would seem, any remedy for the unconstitutional acts of Prohibition agents. Some time ago, when Senator Stanley, of Kentucky, tried to have a law passed forbidding them to break into a citizen's house in violation of the Bill of Rights, the Prohibitionists mustered up their serfs in the Senate against him, and he was voted down.

The Supreme Court, had it been so disposed, might have put a stop to all this sinister buffoonery long ago. There was a time, indeed, when it was alert to do so. That was during the Civil War. But since then the court has gradually succumbed to the prevailing doctrine that the minority has no rights that the majority is bound to respect. As it is at present constituted, it shows little disposition to go to the rescue of the harassed freeman. When property is menaced it displays a laudable diligence, but when it comes to the mere rights of the citizen it seems hopelessly inclined to give the prosecution the benefit of every doubt. Two justices commonly dissent—two out of nine. They hold the last switch-trench of the old constitutional line. When they depart to realms of bliss the Bill of Rights will be buried with them.

XVII. REFLECTIONS ON THE DRAMA

THE drama is the most democratic of the art forms, and perhaps the only one that may legitimately bear the label. Painting, sculpture, music and literature, so far as they show any genuine æsthetic or intellectual content at all, are not for crowds, but for selected individuals, mostly with bad kidneys and worse morals, and three of the four are almost always enjoyed in actual solitude. Even architecture and religious ritual, though they are publicly displayed, make their chief appeal to man as individual, not to man as mass animal. One goes into a church as part of a crowd, true enough, but if it be a church that has risen above mere theological disputation to the beauty of ceremonial, one is, even in theory, alone with the Lord God Jehovah. And if, passing up Fifth Avenue in the 5 o'clock throng, one pauses before St. Thomas's to drink in the beauty of that archaic façade, one's drinking is almost sure to be done *a cappella;* of the other passers-by, not one in a thousand so much as glances at it.

But the drama, as representation, is inconceivable

save as a show for the mob, and so it has to take on protective coloration to survive. It must make its appeal, not to individuals as such, nor even to individuals as units in the mob, but to the mob as mob—a quite different thing, as Gustav Le Bon long ago demonstrated in his "Psychologie des Foules." Thus its intellectual content, like its æsthetic form, must be within the mental grasp of the mob, and what is more important, within the scope of its prejudices. *Per corollary*, anything even remotely approaching an original idea, or an unpopular idea, is foreign to it, and if it would make any impression at all, abhorrent to it. The best a dramatist can hope to do is to give poignant and arresting expression to an idea so simple that the average man will grasp it at once, and so banal that he will approve it in the next instant. The phrase "drama of ideas" thus becomes a mere phrase. What is actually meant by it is "drama of platitudes."

So much for the theory. An appeal to the facts quickly substantiates it. The more one looks into the so-called drama of ideas of the last age—that is, into the acting drama—the more one is astounded by the vacuity of its content. The younger Dumas' "La Dame aux Camélias," the first of all the propaganda plays (it raised a stupendous pother in 1852, the echoes of which yet roll), is based upon the sophomoric thesis that a prostitute is a human being like you and me, and suffers the slings and arrows of the same sorrows, and may be potentially quite as worthy of heaven. Augier's "La Mariage d'Olympe" (1854), another sensation-making pioneer, is even hollower; its four acts are devoted to rubbing in the revolutionary discovery that it is unwise for a young man of good family to marry an elderly cocotte. Proceed now to Ibsen. Here one finds the same tasteless platitudes—that it is unpleasant for a wife to be treated as a doll; that professional patriots and town boomers are frauds; that success in business is often grounded upon a mere willingness to do what a man of honor is incapable of; that a woman who continues to live with a debauched husband may expect to have unhealthy children; that a joint sorrow tends to bring husband and wife together; that a neurotic woman is apt to prefer death to maternity; that a man of 55 is an ass to fall in love with a flapper of 17. Do I burlesque? If you think so, turn to Ibsen's "Nachgelassene Schriften" and read his own statements of the ideas in his social dramas—read his own succinct summaries of their theses. You will imagine yourself, on more than one page, in the latest volume of mush by Orison Swett Marden. Such "ideas" are what one finds in newspaper editorials, speeches before Congress, sermons by evangelical divines—in brief, in the literature expressly addressed to those persons whose distinguishing mark is that ideas never enter their heads.

Ibsen himself, an excellent poet and a reflective man, was under no delusions about his "dramas of ideas." It astounded him greatly when the sentimental German middle-classes hailed "Ein Puppenheim" as a revolutionary document; he protested often and bitterly against being mistaken for a prophet of feminism. His own interest in this play and in those that followed it was chiefly technical; he was trying to displace the well-made play of Scribe and company with something simpler, more elastic and more hospitable to character. He wrote "Ghosts" to raise a laugh against the fools who had seen something novel and horrible in the idea of "A Doll's House"; he wanted to prove to them that that idea was no more than a platitude. Soon afterward he became thoroughly disgusted with the whole "drama of ideas." In "The Wild Duck" he cruelly burlesqued it, and made a low-comedy Ibsenist his chief butt. In "Hedda Gabler" he played a joke on the Ibsen fanatics by fashioning a first-rate drama out of the oldest, shoddiest materials of Sardou, Feuillet, and even Meilhac and Halévy. And beginning with "Little Eyolf" he threw the "drama of ideas" overboard forever, and took to mysticism. What could be more comical than the efforts of critical talmudists to read a thesis into "When We Dead Awaken"? I have put in many a gay hour perusing their commentaries. Ibsen, had he lived, would have roared over them—as he roared over the effort to inject portentous meanings into "The Master Builder," at bottom no more than a sentimental epitaph to a love affair that he himself had suffered at 60.

Gerhart Hauptmann, another dramatist of the first rank, has gone much the same road. As a very young man he succumbed to the "drama of ideas" gabble, and his first plays showed an effort to preach this or that in awful tones. But he soon discovered that the only ideas that would go down, so to speak, on the stage were ideas of such an austere platitudinousness that it was beneath his artistic dignity to merchant them, and so he gave over propaganda altogether. In other words, his genius burst through the narrow bounds of mob ratiocination, and he began appealing to the universal emotions—pity, religious sentiment, patriotism, amorousness. Even in his first play, "Vor Sonnenaufgang," his instinct got the better of his mistaken purpose, and reading it to-day one finds that the sheer horror of it is of vastly more effect than its nebulous and unimportant ideas. It really says nothing; it merely makes us dislike some very unpleasant people.

Turn now to Shaw. At once one finds that the only plays from his pen which contain actual ideas have failed dismally on the stage. These are the so-called "discussions"—*e. g.*, "Getting Married." The successful plays contain no ideas; they contain only platitudes, balderdash, buncombe that even a suffragette might think of. Of such sort are "Man and Superman," "Arms and the Man," "Candida," "Androcles and the Lion," and their like. Shaw has given all of these pieces a specious air of profundity by publishing them hooked to long and garrulous prefaces and by filling them with stage directions which describe and discuss the characters at great length. But as stage plays they are almost as empty as "Hedda Gabler." One searches them vainly for even the slightest novel contribution to the current theories of life, joy and crime. Shaw's prefaces, of course, have vastly more ideational force and respectability than his plays. If he fails to get any ideas of genuine savor into them it is not because the preface form bars them out but because he hasn't any to get in. By attaching them to his plays he converts the latter into colorable imitations of novels, and so opens the way for that superior reflectiveness which lifts the novel above the play, and makes it, as Arnold Bennett has convincingly shown, much harder to write. A stage play in the modern realistic manner—that is, without soliloquies and asides —can seldom rise above the mere representation of some infinitesimal episode, whereas even the worst novel may be, in some sense, an interpretation as well. Obviously, such episodes as may be exposed in 20,000 words—the extreme limit of the average play—are seldom significant, and not often clearly intelligible. The author has a hard enough job making his characters recognizable as human beings; he hasn't time to go behind their acts to their motives, or to deduce any conclusions worth hearing from their doings. One often leaves a "social drama," indeed, wondering what the deuce it is all about; the discussion of its meaning offers endless opportunities for theorists and fanatics. The Ibsen symbolists come to mind again. They read meanings into such plays as "Rosmersholm" and "The Wild Duck" that aroused Ibsen, a peaceful man, to positive fury. In the same way the suffragettes collared, "A Doll's House." Even "Peer Gynt" did not escape. There is actually an edition of it edited by a theosophist, in the preface to which it is hymned as a theosophical document. Luckily for Ibsen, he died before this edition was printed. But one may well imagine how it would have made him swear.

The notion that there are ideas in the "drama of ideas," in truth, is confined to a special class of illuminati, whose chief visible character is their capacity for ingesting nonsense—Maeterlinckians, uplifters, women's clubbers, believers in all the sure cures for all the sorrows of the world. To-day the

Drama League carries on the tradition. It is composed of the eternally young—unsuccessful dramatists who yet live in hope, young college professors, psychopathic old maids, middle-aged ladies of an incurable jejuneness, the innumerable caravan of the ingenuous and sentimental. Out of the same intellectual *Landsturm* comes the following of Bergson, the parlor metaphysician; and of the third-rate novelists praised by the newspapers; and of such composers as Wolf-Ferrari and Massenet. These are the fair ones, male and female, who were ecstatically shocked by the platitudes of "Damaged Goods," and who regard Augustus Thomas as a great dramatist, and what is more, as a great thinker. Their hero, during a season or two, was the Swedish John the Baptist, August Strindberg—a lunatic with a gift for turning the preposterous into the shocking. A glance at Strindberg's innumerable volumes of autobiography reveals the true horse-power of his so-called ideas. He believed in everything that was idiotic, from transcendentalism to witchcraft. He believed that his enemies were seeking to destroy him by magic; he spent a whole winter trying to find the philosopher's stone. Even among the clergy, it would be difficult to find a more astounding ass than Strindberg. But he had, for all his folly, a considerable native skill at devising effective stage-plays—a talent that some men seem to be born with—and under cover of it he acquired his reputation as a thinker. Here he was met half-way by the defective powers of observation and reflection of his followers, the half-wits aforesaid; they mistook their enjoyment of his adept technical trickery for an appreciation of ideas. Turn to the best of his plays, "The Father." Here the idea—that domestic nagging can cause insanity—is an almost perfect platitude, for on the one hand it is universally admitted and on the other hand it is not true. But as a stage play pure and simple, the piece is superb—a simple and yet enormously effective mechanism. So with "Countess Julie." The idea here is so vague and incomprehensible that no two commentators agree in stating it, and yet the play is so cleverly written, and appeals with such a sure touch to the universal human weakness for the obscene, that it never fails to enchant an audience. The case of "Hedda Gabler" is parallel. If the actresses playing Hedda in this country made up for the part in the scandalous way their sisters do in Germany (that is, by wearing bustles in front), it would be as great a success here as it is over there. Its general failure among us is due to the fact that it is not made indelicate enough. This also explains the comparative failure of the rest of the Ibsen plays. The crowd has been subtly made to believe that they are magnificently indecent—and is always dashed and displeased when it finds nothing to lift the diaphragm. I well remember the first production of "Ghosts" in America—a business in which I had a hand. So eager was the audience for the promised indecencies that it actually read them into the play, and there were protests against it on the ground that Mrs. Alving was represented as trying to seduce her own son! Here comstockery often helps the "drama of ideas." If no other idea is visible, it can always conjure up, out of its native swinishness, some idea that is offensively sexual, and hence pleasing to the mob.

That mob rules in the theater, and so the theater remains infantile and trivial—a scene, not of the exposure of ideas, nor even of the exhibition of beauty, but one merely of the parading of mental and physical prettiness and vulgarity. It is at its worst when its dramatists seek to corrupt this function by adding a moral or intellectual purpose. It is at its best when it confines itself to the unrealities that are its essence, and swings amiably from the romance that never was on land or sea to the buffoonery that is at the bottom of all we actually know of human life. Shakespeare was its greatest craftsman: he wasted no tortured ratiocination upon his plays. Instead, he filled them with the gaudy heroes that all of us see ourselves becoming on some bright to-morrow, and the lowly frauds and clowns we are to-day. No psychopathic problems engaged him; he took love and ambition and revenge and braggadocio as he found them. He held no clinics in dingy Norwegian apartment-houses: his field was Bohemia, glorious Rome, the Egypt of the scene-painter, Arcady. . . . But even Shakespeare, for all the vast potency of his incomparable, his stupefying poetry, could not long hold the talmudists out in front from their search for invisible significances. Think of all the tomes that have been written upon the profound and revolutionary "ideas" in the moony musings of the diabetic sophomore, Hamlet von Dänemark!

XVIII. ADVICE TO YOUNG MEN

1

To Him that Hath

THE most valuable of all human possessions, next to a superior and disdainful air, is the reputation of being well to do. Nothing else so neatly eases one's way through life, especially in democratic countries. There is in ninety-nine per cent. of all democrats an irresistible impulse to crook the knee to wealth, to defer humbly to the power that goes with it, to see all sorts of high merits in the man who has it, or is said to have it. True enough, envy goes with the pliant neck, but it is envy somehow purged of all menace: the inferior man is afraid to do evil to the man with money in eight banks; he is even afraid to *think* evil of him—that is, in any patent and offensive way. Against capital as an abstraction he rants incessantly, and all of the laws that he favors treat it as if it were criminal. But in the presence of the concrete capitalist he is singularly fawning. What makes him so is easy to discern. He yearns with a great yearning for a chance to tap the capitalist's purse, and he knows very well, deep down in his heart, that he is too craven and stupid to do it by force of arms. So he turns to politeness, and tries to cajole. Give out the news that one has just made a killing in the stock market, or robbed some confiding widow of her dower, or swindled the government in some patriotic enterprise, and at once one will discover that one's shabbiness is a charming eccentricity, and one's judgment of wines worth hearing, and one's politics worthy of attention and respect. The man who is thought to be poor never gets a fair chance. No one wants to listen to him. No one gives a damn what he thinks or knows or feels. No one has any active desire for his good opinion.

I discovered this principle early in life, and have put it to use ever since. I have got a great deal more out of men (and women) by having the name of being a well-heeled fellow than I have ever got by being decent to them, or by dazzling them with my sagacity, or by hard industry, or by a personal beauty that is singular and ineffable.

2

The Venerable Examined

The older I grow the more I distrust the familiar doctrine that age brings wisdom. It is my honest belief that I am no wiser to-day than I was five or ten years ago; in fact, I often suspect that I am appreciable *less* wise. Women can prevail over me to-day by devices that would have made me hoof them out of my studio when I was thirty-five. I am also an easier mark for male swindlers than I used to be; at fifty I'll probably be joining clubs and buying Mexican mine stock. The truth is that every man goes up-hill in sagacity to a certain point, and then begins sliding down again. Nearly all the old fellows that I know are more or less balmy. Theoretically, they should be much wiser than younger men, if only because of their greater experience, but actually they seem to take on folly faster than they take on wisdom. A man of thirty-five or thirty-eight is almost woman-proof. For a woman to marry him is a herculean feat. But by the time he is fifty he is quite as easy as a Yale sophomore. On other planes the same decay of the intelligence is visible. Certainly it would be difficult to imagine any committee of relatively young men, of thirty or thirty-five, showing the unbroken childishness, ignorance and lack of humor of the Supreme Court of the United States. The average age of the learned justices must be well beyond sixty, and all of them are supposed to be of finished and mellowed sagacity. Yet their knowledge of the most ordinary principles of justice often turns out to be extremely meager, and when they spread themselves grandly upon a great case their reasoning powers are usually found to be precisely equal to those of a respectable Pullman conductor.

3

Duty

Some of the loosest thinking in ethics has duty for its theme. Practically all writers on the subject agree that the individual owes certain unescapable duties to the race—for example, the duty of engaging in productive labor, and that of marrying and begetting offspring. In support of this position it is almost always argued that if *all* men neglected such duties the race would perish. The logic is hollow enough to be worthy of the college professors who are guilty of it. It simply confuses the conventionality, the pusillanimity, the lack of imagination of the majority of men with the duty of *all* men. There is not the slightest ground for assuming, even as a matter of mere argumentation, that *all* men will ever neglect these alleged duties. There will always remain a safe majority that is willing to do whatever is ordained—that accepts docilely the government it is born under, obeys its laws, and supports its theory. But that majority does not comprise the men who render the highest and most intelligent services to the race; it comprises those who render nothing save their obedience.

For the man who differs from this inert and well-regimented mass, however slightly, there are no duties *per se*. What he is spontaneously inclined to do is of vastly more value to all of us than what the majority is willing to do. There is, indeed, no such thing as duty-in-itself; it is a mere chimera of ethical theorists. Human progress is furthered, not by conformity, but by aberration. The very concept of duty is thus a function of inferiority; it belongs naturally only to timorous and incompetent men. Even on such levels it remains largely a self-delusion, a soothing apparition, a euphemism for necessity. When a man succumbs to duty he merely succumbs to the habit and inclination of other men. Their collective interests invariably pull against his individual interests. Some of us can resist a pretty strong pull—the pull, perhaps, of thousands. But it is only the miraculous man who can withstand the pull of a whole nation.

Martyrs

"History," says Henry Ford, "is bunk." I inscribe myself among those who dissent from this doctrine; nevertheless, I am often hauled up, in reading history, by a feeling that I am among unrealities. In particular, that feeling comes over me when I read about the religious wars of the past—wars in which thousands of men, women and children were butchered on account of puerile and unintelligible disputes over transubstantiation, the atonement, and other such metaphysical banshees. It does not surprise me that the majority murdered the minority; the majority, even to-day, does it whenever it is possible. What I can't understand is that the minority went voluntarily to the slaughter. Even in the worst persecutions known to history—say, for example, those of the Jews of Spain—it was always possible for a given member of the minority to save his hide by giving public assent to the religious notions of the majority. A Jew who was willing to be baptized, in the reign of Ferdinand and Isabella, was practically unmolested; his descendants today are 100% Spaniards. Well, then, why did so many Jews refuse? Why did so many prefer to be robbed, exiled, and sometimes murdered?

The answer given by philosophical historians is that they were a noble people, and preferred death to heresy. But this merely begs the question. Is it actually noble to cling to a religious idea so tenaciously? Certainly it doesn't seem so to me. After all, no human being really *knows* anything about the exalted matters with which all religions deal. The most he can do is to match his private guess against the guesses of his fellowmen. For any man to say absolutely, in such a field, that this or that is wholly and irrefragably true and this or that is utterly false is simply to talk nonsense. Personally, I have never encountered a religious idea—and I do not except even the idea of the existence of God—that was instantly and unchallengeably convincing, as, say, the Copernican astronomy is instantly and unchallengeably convincing. But neither have I ever encountered a religious idea that could be dismissed offhand as palpably and indubitably false. In even the worst nonsense of such theological mountebanks as the Rev. Dr. Billy Sunday, Brigham Young and Mrs. Eddy there is always enough lingering plausibility, or, at all events, possibility, to give the judicious pause. Whatever the weight of the probabilities against it, it nevertheless *may* be true that man, on his decease, turns into a gaseous vertebrate, and that this vertebrate, if its human larva has engaged in embezzlement, bootlegging, profanity or adultery on this earth, will be boiled for a million years in a cauldron of pitch. My private inclination, due to my defective upbringing, is to doubt it, and to set down any one who believes it as an ass, but it must be plain that I have no means of disproving it.

In view of this uncertainty it seems to me sheer vanity for any man to hold his religious views too firmly, or to submit to any inconvenience on account of them. It is far better, if they happen to offend, to conceal them discreetly, or to change them amiably as the delusions of the majority change. My own views in this department, being wholly skeptical and tolerant, are obnoxious to the subscribers to practically all other views; even atheists sometimes denounce me. At the moment, by an accident of American political history, these dissenters from my theology are forbidden to punish me for not agreeing with them. But at any succeeding moment some group or other among them may seize such power and proceed against me in the immemorial manner. If it ever happens, I give notice here and now that I shall get converted to their nonsense instantly, and so retire to safety with my right thumb laid against my nose and my fingers waving like wheat in the wind. I'd do it even to-day, if there were any practical advantage in it. Offer me a case of Rauenthaler 1903, and I engage to submit to baptism by any rite ever heard of, provided it does not expose my gothic nakedness. Make it ten cases, and I'll agree to be both baptized and confirmed. In such matters I am broad-minded. What, after all, is one more lie?

5

The Disabled Veteran

The science of psychological pathology is still in its infancy. In all its literature in three languages, I can't find a line about the permanent ill effects of acute emotional diseases—say, for example, love affairs. The common assumption of the world is that when a love affair is over it is over—that nothing remains behind. This is probably grossly untrue. It is my belief that every such experience leaves scars upon my psyche, and that they are quite as plain and quite as dangerous as the scars left on the neck by a carbuncle. A man who has passed through a love affair, even though he may eventually forget the lady's very name, is never quite the same thereafter. His scars may be small, but they are permanent. The sentimentalist, exposed incessantly, ends as a psychic cripple; he is as badly off as the man who has come home from the wars with shell-shock. The precise nature of the scars remains to be determined. My own notion is that they take the form of large yellow patches upon the self-esteem. Whenever a man thinks of one of his dead love affairs, and in particular whenever he allows his memory to dredge up an image of the woman he loved, he shivers like one taken in some unmanly and discreditable act.

Such shivers, repeated often enough, must inevitably shake his inner integrity off its base. No man can love, and yet remain truly proud. It is a disarming and humiliating experience.

6

Patriotism

Patriotism is conceivable to a civilized man in times of stress and storm, when his country is wobbling and sore beset. His country then appeals to him as any victim of misfortune appeals to him—say, a street-walker pursued by the police. But when it is safe, happy and prosperous it can only excite his loathing. The things that make countries safe, happy and prosperous—a secure peace, an active trade, political serenity at home—are all intrinsically corrupting and disgusting. It is as impossible for a civilized man to love his country in good times as it would be for him to respect a politician.

XIX. SUITE AMÉRICANE

1

Aspiration

POLICE sergeants praying humbly to God that Jews will start poker-rooms on their posts, and so enable them to educate their eldest sons for holy orders. . . . Newspaper reporters resolving firmly to work hard, keep sober and be polite to the city editor, and so be rewarded with jobs as copy-readers. . . . College professors in one-building universities on the prairie, still hoping, at the age of sixty, to get their whimsical essays into the *Atlantic Monthly*. . . . Car-conductors on lonely suburban lines, trying desperately to save up $500 and start a Ford garage. . . . Pastors of one-horse little churches in decadent villages, who, whenever they drink two cups of coffee at supper, dream all night that they have been elected bishops. . . . Movie actors who hope against hope that the next fan letter will be from Bar Harbor. . . . Delicatessen dealers who spend their whole lives searching for a cheap substitute for the embalmed veal used in chicken-salad. . . . Italians who wish that they were Irish. . . . Mulatto girls in Georgia and Alabama who send away greasy dollar bills for bottles of Mme. Celestine's Infallible Hair-Straightener. . . . Ash-men who pull wires to be appointed superintendents of city dumps. . . . Mothers who dream that the babies in their cradles will reach, in the mysterious after years, the highest chairs in the Red Men and the Maccabees. . . . Farmers who figure that, with good luck, they will be able to pay off their mortgages by 1943. . . . Contestants for the standing broad-jump championship of the Altoona, Pa., Y. M. C. A. . . . Editorial writers who essay to prove mathematically that a war between England and the United States is unthinkable. . . .

2

Virtue

Pale druggists in remote towns of the Epworth League and flannel nightgown belts, endlessly wrapping up bottles of Peruna. . . . Women hidden away in the damp kitchens of unpainted houses along the railroad tracks, frying tough beefsteaks. . . . Lime and cement dealers being initiated into the Knights of Pythias, the Red Men or the Woodmen of the World. . . . Watchmen at lonely railroad crossings in Iowa, hoping that they'll be able to get off to hear the United Brethren evangelist preach. . . . Ticket-choppers in the subway, breathing sweat in its gaseous form. . . . Family doctors in poor neighborhoods, faithfully relying upon the therapeutics taught in their Eclectic Medical College in 1884. . . . Farmers plowing sterile fields behind sad meditative horses, both suffering from the bites of insects. . . . Greeks tending all-night coffee-joints in the suburban wildernesses where the trolley-cars stop. . . . Grocery-clerks stealing prunes and ginger-snaps, and trying to make assignations with soapy servant-girls. . . . Women confined for the ninth or tenth time, wondering helplessly what it is all about. . . . Methodist preachers retired after forty years of service in the trenches of God, upon pensions of $600 a year. . . . Wives and daughters of Middle Western country bankers, marooned in Los Angeles, going tremblingly to swami séances in dark, smelly rooms. . . . Chauffeurs in huge fur coats waiting outside theaters filled with folks applauding Robert Edeson and Jane Cowl. . . . Decayed and hopeless men writing editorials at midnight for leading papers in Mississippi, Arkansas and Alabama. . . . Owners of the principal candy-stores in Green River, Neb., and Tyrone, Pa. . . . Presidents of one-building universities in the rural fastnesses of Kentucky and Tennessee. . . . Women with babies in their arms weeping over moving-pictures in the Elks' Hall at Schmidtsville, Mo. . . . Babies just born to the wives of milk-wagon drivers. . . . Judges on the benches of petty county courts in Virginia, Vermont and Idaho. . . . Conductors of accommodation trains running between Kokomo, Ind., and Logansport. . . .

3

Eminence

The leading Methodist layman of Pottawattamie county, Iowa. . . . The man who won the limerick contest conducted by the Toomsboro, Ga., *Banner*. . . . The secretary of the Little Rock, Ark., Kiwanis Club. . . . The president of the Johann Sebastian Bach *Bauverein* of Highlandtown, Md. . . . The girl who sold the most Liberty Bonds in Duquesne, Pa. . . . The captain of the champion basket-ball team at the Gary, Ind., Y. M. C. A. . . . The man who owns the best bull in Coosa county, Ala. . . . The tallest man in Covington, Ky. . . . The oldest subscriber to the Raleigh, N. C., *News and Observer*. . . . The most fashionable milliner in Bucyrus, O. . . . The business agent of the Plasterers' Union of Somerville, Mass. . . . The author of the ode read at the unveiling of the monument to General Robert E. Lee at Valdosta, Ga. . . . The original Henry Cabot Lodge man. . . . The owner of the champion Airedale of Buffalo, N. Y. . . . The first child named after the Hon. Warren Gamaliel Harding. . . . The old lady in Wahoo, Neb., who has read the Bible 38 times. . . . The boss who controls the Italian, Czecho-Slovak and Polish votes in Youngstown, O. . . . The professor of chemistry, Greek, rhetoric and piano at the Texas Christian University, Fort Worth, Tex. . . . The boy who sells 225 copies of the *Saturday Evening Post* every week in Cheyenne, Wyo. . . . The youngest murderer awaiting hanging in Chicago. . . . The leading dramatic critic of Pittsburgh. . . . The night watchman in Penn Yan, N. Y., who once shook hands with Chester A. Arthur. . . . The Lithuanian woman in Bluefield, W. Va., who has had five sets of triplets. . . . The actor who has played in "Lightning" 1,600 times. . . . The best horsedoctor in Oklahoma. . . . The highest-paid church-choir soprano in Knoxville, Tenn. . . . The most eligible bachelor in Cheyenne, Wyo. . . . The engineer of the locomotive which pulled the train which carried the Hon. A. Mitchell Palmer to the San Francisco Convention. . . . The girl who got the most votes in the popularity contest at Egg Harbor, N. J. . . .

INDEX